Sudden Future

Barbara G Tucker

Colorful Crow Publishing

Published by

Colorful Crow Publishing

Calhoun, Georgia

http://www.colorfulcrowpublishing.com

©2023 by Barbara G Tucker

All rights reserved

Published in the United States of America

First Edition

ISBN 979-8-9881845-0-8 (PB)

ISBN 979-8-9881845-1-5 (eB)

http://www.barbaragrahamtucker.com

Dedication
For Jihuan

Prologue

Kevin Elcott looked down at his mother's body. It lay, covered with a sheet, on a gurney in a back room of Babcock-Ziegler Funeral Home. In less than an hour, the corpse would be cremated. The funeral home required a close family member to identify the body before cremation or burial. Kevin qualified as Sabra Timothy's closest relative.

His mother was twenty-four hours dead. The form before him really bore little resemblance to his mother as he knew her, as he remembered her. Even since the day before, when he sat by her in her last hours and listened to her breathe and sometimes find a memory from years before to utter, her face had changed. The months of cells splitting according to a new, chaotic plan had ended. Disease seemed to be attacking her body still. But he knew better.

He wanted to catalog the emotions racing through his body at that moment, but he couldn't. The last two months had hinged on his mother's care, her decisions, her choices, even though for years now he had rarely thought about how her lifestyle affected him. That was the problem. He had seldom thought about her before her illness took over their lives. Before she placed an unforeseen burden on him, before she led to his ending the relationship with Felicity, before his career choices turned sideways.

He now had to set aside his anger that she had been taken so early and quickly so he could deal with his grief, and the grief melded with regret. Didn't it always? Not enough time, not enough holidays spent together, not enough "I love yous." But he knew there was more to what he was feeling than the usual "not enoughs." Before her death, Sabra had asked more of him than he had been ready for, more than he could accomplish. More than she had a right to ask. Yet she had asked it anyway.

Now that she was dead, she wouldn't know whether he fulfilled his promise or not. He could change his mind.

Chapter 1

During his morning commute on a Tuesday in mid-September, Kevin Elcott glanced at his chiming mobile phone. His mother's phone number lit up the screen.

What could she want now? He thought. He debated answering it; he could call her back, but Sabra Timothy called so rarely that something had to be wrong. His eyes left the busy street before him as he debated whether to pick up the call. When he looked up, he had to slam on his brakes to avoid ramming the back of the F10 truck in front of him.

Kevin cursed under his breath, unsure whether his anger stemmed from the unexpected phone call from his mother or the near accident. He strained to modulate his voice back into calmness. He did not consider an unexpected call from his mother on the way to work a welcome interruption.

"Hello, Mom. What's up?" Now he found himself dividing his attention between watching downtown Charlotte traffic, maneuvering his Acura sedan, and listening to Sabra.

"I really need you to come see me."

He felt the internal sigh, followed by the accelerated heartbeat. She only calls when she wants something, he thought. No, that's not fair. Well, maybe it is. "I'm really busy right now. What's so important?" They hadn't spoken in several months, it seemed.

"Are you dating anyone?"

"Yes, a woman named Felicity."

"Is it serious?"

"Not sure how to take that, Mom. She's the only woman I'm seeing now if that's what you mean."

"No, it's not what I mean."

"Then what do you mean?"

"Do you think you'll marry her?"

He slowed his car down for the stop light two blocks from the gallery. "Marriage and me, that's something I don't know about."

"Kevin, you shouldn't say that."

"Mom, I can't talk about this now. I haven't seen you in over fourteen months. Why the hurry?"

"And I'm only 130 miles away."

"Yeah. Well."

"I need you to come here."

"Why?"

"I can't tell you over the phone. Just come."

"All right, let me think about my schedule." This really would be easier if I were at my desk, he thought. He was silent for several seconds as he visualized the days before him.

"I can come next weekend, but not this—I'm flying to New York to oversee the transfer of a couple of Picasso sketches here to the gallery, and it's a super big deal. I can't miss it or change it."

"Yes, it sounds like a big thing." She paused. "But you can come on the fifteenth?"

"Uh, yeah, I can drive down on Friday night. Can you tell me what the problem is?"

"No, not yet. It will be better for us to talk face to face."

"If you say so, Mom."

"Can you bring, uh, Felicia?"

"Felicity, Mom. I'll see. She's in finance. She works sixty hours a week sometimes."

"That's cruel. No one should work like that. Those corporations are monsters."

"Yeah, well, I gotta go. I promise, Friday the fifteenth, I'll come."

"Um, call me before you leave. I may need you to meet me somewhere else."

"Like where?"

"Just call me."

"All right, bye, love ya. Mean it."

"I love you, Kevin. Very much. Always remember that."

Mom, he thought. What was up with the "Very Much"? He had no idea and no time to figure it out.

That was his mother. Some people would call her unpredictable, a free spirit, empathetic. He had known his mother for thirty-one years and still didn't have a clue what made her tick, why she made the choices she did.

Not that his mother was a needy person. In fact, it might have been better if she had been needy—maybe she would have stayed with Kevin's father instead of divorcing him for another man, a work colleague, when Kevin was fourteen. Sabra Timothy—she reverted to her birth name a few years after the divorce—had been a licensed social worker in Charlotte's public hospital for twenty years, and after the divorce returned to graduate school and became an academic, teaching social sciences courses at a private college near Fayetteville.

But that biography did not define her. Sabra was open-hearted to a fault, to a vice. She fell in love with a man who ended her marriage and then dropped her. She let strangers into her life who scammed her—on two occasions. She let students stay at her house freely until the college administration forbade it, threatening to block her tenure. Kevin figured some funky things went down when Sabra wasn't watching her student friends, but he didn't ask. She traveled in the summers to exotic but not really safe places in South America and Africa; Ethiopia was one of her favorite retreats. Maybe it was like the line from Shakespeare. "She loved not wisely, but too well." He couldn't fault her motives, only her lack of street smarts.

Kevin muddled over the facts of his mother's devoted and bohemian existence, but didn't let himself wonder about the reason for her urgent request to see him. They loved each other at a distance but tolerated each other in person, really. He couldn't stay with her too long—she had no Internet service, for one thing, or hadn't any the last time he visited. Due to her past victimizations by those she befriended, she lived on a shoestring to pay for her mortgage and her trips—or so she said.

No, he admitted to himself. I don't want to think about this now. Her lack of Wi-Fi has nothing to do with it. That's just one of her quirks. She saves money for her adventures by not paying for technology.

His contentious relationship with his mother ran deeper than her frugalities, and now was not the time to revisit therapy sessions from high school. Later. This afternoon, as the Managing Director of Charlotte's Fordyce Gallery, he had to meet with the Governing Board for their monthly meeting and justify the costs of funding the Picasso sketches against the reality of lean donations.

Chapter 2

Kevin Elcott was not an artist. He had no pretensions to talents in painting, sculpture, or photography. He did not major in art history. When he began at Fordyce Gallery, he didn't know a Perugino from a Verrocchio or a Pollock from a Krasner. He still didn't, without some homework. Outside of a drawing class as an elective in college, he had little experience in the visual arts. His expertise was budgeting, finance, marketing, development, and his hometown, Charlotte—and he knew them all well. Since graduating from Chapel Hill, he had worked for Bank of America and Citibank, and at 30 decided to step into something different. It was a lateral move money-wise, but he liked the atmosphere of Charlotte's Premier Gallery of Fine Arts. Even more, he liked the breadth of the connections he made, and he really liked the wealth those connections possessed and the opportunity to enjoy them socially.

Despite what he told his mother, his trip to New York was not entirely about the Picassos. Those were two small charcoal sketches the Museum of Modern Art agreed to let go to raise money for something bigger. He also planned to meet with the Vice President of Operations at the Gunther Museum of American Art to discuss his moving there as Director of Development. He hadn't revealed this interview to anyone but Felicity. The competition was not just stiff; it was impenetrable. But the opportunity made throwing himself against the gates of the New York art world worth a try.

The morning's demands pushed Sabra's call out of his mind. Several hours of correspondence, short meetings to address staff concerns, interviews with new interns from a local university, and an online training session on fundraising occupied him. The Board meeting focused him from 1:00-4:30. He presented evidence the Picasso sketches were inexpensive compared to going prices for comparable works. Other museums, he argued, saw significant upticks in visitors and donations after obtaining Picassos. The collection's curator presented the provenance of the sketches and how they would be displayed.

Kevin chose not to remind the nervous board members they had approved the purchase months before. For some reason, a couple of the more influential ones had developed second thoughts and begun spreading anxiety, so the board needed reassurance. From 4:00 to the end of the workday, he answered emails. The next day, his flight left for New York at 9, and he wouldn't return to the office until Monday.

He had arranged a dinner date with Felicity at a bistro with live music two blocks from the gallery. He asked for an early reservation since he still had to pack for the trip to New York. He arrived first, but he knew he would not wait long. He slipped into the seat to which the hostess directed him with two minutes to spare. Felicity had proven her punctuality multiple times. At exactly 6:30 she entered: all confidence, navy blue suit with a hint of red shell peeking out from beneath the jacket, three-inch heels on which she traversed the dining room flawlessly. Her long, dark but slightly auburn hair, held back with a turquoise clasp, swung just enough to indicate she didn't want to be late.

Yes, appearance-wise, she was perfect, slender, composed, and everything corporate America wants to put on their marketing. She had modeled for a few months during college, but hated how counterfeit it made her feel. When she said that on their first date, her words sealed it for him, at least in the sense he would call her again, and maybe again. He'd kept calling for four months, but their dates tended to be once-per-week dinner engagements or attendance at Fordyce gatherings.

Besides the ability to turn heads on an entrance, Felicity had "depth," a pretentious and condescending word to describe a woman, but the best he could do. She had an MBA from Duke, but her roots were firmly planted in Louisville, Kentucky. She played golf with a much better handicap than he did. She came from a big family and knew the difference between entitlement and normalcy. She had a sense of humor and liked a good basketball game, although she pulled for the wrong side, of course.

And New York was getting in the way.

They greeted each other with a discreet kiss, chatted about their days, ordered wine and dinner, and settled in for more human talk beneath the veneer.

"I heard from my mom today."

"Oh?" she took a sip of her Pinot Grigio.

"Yes. I'm going to need to go see her next weekend."

"And you said she lives . . .. Where did you say she lives again?"

"I never actually did. She lives in Fayetteville. That's about two hours away, or a little more." It occurred to Kevin he had not really talked about his mother much with Felicity. He had told stories about himself and his dad enjoying sports and hunting, but in the few months he'd known Felicity, he'd only said his parents were divorced and his mom worked as a college professor. Somewhere. Felicity, on the other hand, spoke freely and lovingly of her brothers, sisters, nieces, nephews, and parents.

"Oh, that's not so far. What's up?"

"I don't know. She was adamant though, and she never is super concerned about my coming to see her, even at Christmas."

"No idea why?"

"No. But I can't really say no."

"Of course not. She's your mom. Mommas get what they want. Don't you know that? You *were* raised in the South, weren't you?"

He smiled; this remark meant Felicity had dropped the corporate veneer and let her real, open self peek out. He could see himself falling in love with this woman, hard. But.

"My upbringing was a little different. Mom, well, she's, I don't know, not a bad person. She's actually a wonderful person, in a lot of ways. But when she was younger, she wasn't the most, what's the nicer way to say it, focused or prudent person ever. She liked adventure, she liked to help people, she liked to try new things . . . new relationships . . . if you get my drift."

"Oh." That was Felicity's go-to response. It was safe. She said it as if she understood everything, which she couldn't.

"That led to the divorce, and I was able to choose who to live with, so it wasn't her. Dad finished raising me until I went to college, then he moved to Memphis for work, remarried a younger woman with two children, and restarted his life. So, not very traditional."

"No, not really."

The response was a slight improvement from "Oh."

"Don't worry, I'm not psycho," he said. "Just not really close to my mom. Much closer to Dad, all things considered."

"Do you ever talk with her about what she . . . chose?"

"No. And she never asked for forgiveness."

"Should she?"

"I think she should. Yes." The conversation was not going like he wanted. "Well, enough of that."

"Do you want some company when you go see her?" Felicity said.

This offer surprised him. "Are you available next weekend?"

"Believe it or not, I am. My company has finally realized health and life-balance mean something. So they are restricting us on our hours over the month. And I need to get out of town for a bit. I'm sure Fayetteville has some nice small-town sites to see, and maybe I just want to get away from Charlotte and see farmland." She paused. "Unless you don't want company."

Kevin recognized this deal-breaker moment. If he said "no" to her company, she might take that as a "no" to the next step in their relationship. If he said yes, he might be stuck with a companion who would muddy the waters with Sabra. And Felicity seemed to sense it.

"Don't worry. I'll stay out of your way. I don't even have to meet your mom if you think it's bad timing. I'll just be a traveling buddy."

He wondered if "buddy" carried more than a casual meaning.

"I don't plan to stay at her house," he said.

"Sure. Can you get us hotel rooms?"

The plural spoke volumes. He figured, all things considered, she just wanted to get a break from work and, maybe, see where their relationship went next. Meeting a parent meant a step forward. "Absolutely," he said.

The server arrived with their entrees, her salmon and his steak. He welcomed the intermission from talk about Sabra and her insistence on a visit. The subject exhausted him.

Chapter 3

T he New York trip, five days with a return on Sunday night, proved fun but inconclusive: a good interview, the sketches obtained and shipment finalized, a Broadway musical that set him back $500, some great food. But no promise of a job at the Gunther, not yet. Monday through Thursday of the next workweek meant meeting after meeting, closing a small exhibit of lesser-known French Impressionists, and dinner with the Chamber of Commerce. Felicity did not change her mind about the trip, and affirmed during their dinner date on Tuesday that she looked forward to getting away.

He pushed back the dread of seeing his mother. He didn't want to be a snowflake and relive his past as if he were a victim. Actually, his younger childhood had been a lot of fun, with a mother who played kickball with him and the neighborhood kids when they needed an extra player. Sabra was never shocked by anything he tried even when she had to dissuade him of its merits and apply some boundaries—like the six-pack of beer she found hidden in his room when he was twelve. He benefited from a mother who "advocated" for him, in her activist way, when he didn't get into the honors program in middle school despite acing the test.

But he'd wished for brothers; he'd wished his parents didn't fight so much over Sabra's spending and forgetfulness about household responsibilities. He wished his mother hadn't found love, temporarily, in the arms of an orthopedic surgeon. She'd met him while advocating for a low-income child who needed complicated knee surgery. Kevin wished he hadn't had to spend hours with a therapist who listened but had no answers for his family falling apart in his teenage years. He wished his dad had shown some emotions, some indication the end of his sixteen-year marriage bothered him. Some sign there had been love between his parents, even lost love, would have mattered at the time.

He picked Felicity up at her apartment at 5:00 on Friday. They would stop for dinner somewhere out of town; she said Cracker Barrel sounded good, and travelers were never at a loss for one in North Carolina.

"Oh, I forgot," he brought up. "I was supposed to call my mom before now. Something about her maybe not being at home."

He ordered his phone to call "Sabra" and he switched it to speaker.

"Yes."

"Mom, it's me, Kevin. We're on our way to your house."

"Oh, Kevin." She sounded tired, confused. "I'm not there."

"Well, where are you?"

"Come to Fayetteville General Hospital. I'm in Room 307."

"You're in the hospital? What happened? Why didn't you tell me?"

"I—didn't know. Just come here, Kevin. I'll explain face to face." She abruptly hung up.

He cursed under his breath, hardly a whisper.

Great, he mused. I bring Felicity along, she's a sport, all good, and then Mom just happens to tell me, last minute, she's in the hospital. Did she know about this before? Is this why she insisted, no, why she demanded I come?

"I'm sorry, Felicity. If I'd known this was going to happen, I wouldn't have invited you."

"I asked, remember," she said. "I more or less invited myself. So no need to apologize. Maybe you'll need a backup, if it's something serious about her health."

"I have no idea what's wrong, why she's there, if she's even the one in the hospital. She could be visiting someone and just wants me to come by there. It's hard to tell with my mother."

"We'll see. By the way, my family calls me CeeCee. It was too hard for all of the kids, when we were younger, to say a four-syllable name. For me, too."

He wasn't ready for family nicknames. "Thanks. We can turn around, though, and I'll go alone."

"Of course not. Anyway, I'm sleeping in tomorrow and getting room service in the hotel, so a long night won't hurt me."

She was too accommodating, too giving, which scared him. What did she want? Well, she didn't want sex, apparently, or didn't assume it. That was, oddly, a relief now, especially if he had to deal with his mom in the hospital with some mysterious illness she chose not to reveal to him before this.

Kevin spent the rest of the trip with his teeth clenched and his hands grappling the steering wheel, expecting the worst, expecting little, not knowing what to expect.

Chapter 4

F elicity and Kevin pulled into the hospital parking lot at 8:30. He hoped the hospital didn't enforce strict visitors' hours. He'd have to pull the "I drove two hours to get here" ploy and hope it worked. It would be true, though. He paused at the receptionist's desk, his eyes searching for directions and signposts, with Felicity patiently in tow.

"Can I help you?"

"I'm supposed to see Sabra Timothy in 307."

"Oh. Yes. She told us you would be coming."

"It's not past visiting hours, is it? I drove two hours to get here. She just told me this evening she was here. She's my mom."

"No, we have lenient visiting hours . . . in some cases," the receptionist hesitated and bit her lip after glancing at the screen. "Take elevator B, over there, sir" she pointed, "and up one floor. This entrance is on the second floor."

"Great, thanks."

They managed to get to the elevator before its doors closed, its only other occupant a stocky man in scrubs and a hospital ID pinned to his chest. One flight up, the doors slid open to signs for rooms 300-320 pointing them to the left. Kevin noticed the huge sign over the nurses' station: Oncology. His heart jumped.

In ten seconds, he knocked on the door of 307. "Come in." He recognized his mother's voice, but it lacked her usual exuberance and sense of command.

He spoke as he slowly pushed the door open and entered. "Hi, Mom. We're here."

"Kevin," she struggled to sit up, forgetting to use the button to raise the bed. Sabra Timothy looked different from any way Kevin had ever seen her. For one, she resembled a woman in her 70s, not 56. Her skin was gray and her cheekbones prominent. She had lost twenty pounds, at least, and her expression bore defeat. For all her faults of judgment and infuriating choices, Sabra made up for it as an extravert, and a physical one—she could be expected to hug, touch, kiss and beam with happiness. No broad smile from her tonight, simply an acknowledgment of their presence with a slight upturn of her lips.

"Mom, this is Felicity Thomas." That was all—not girlfriend, not friend, not coworker, not neighbor. Explaining his relationship with Felicity was the least of his worries right now.

"Hello, Felicity," Sabra offered her hand weakly, and Felicity shook it gently. "Nice to meet you, Dr. Timothy—."

"None of that. Call me Sabra."

"I've never heard that name before."

"I know. I've spent my life explaining it to people. My parents thought it . . . exotic, but they didn't realize it would become a brand of hummus. They were from Carolina sharecropper stock and wouldn't have even known what hummus is."

"Mom, I hate to be rude, but let's cut to the chase. What are you doing here? What's wrong?"

"Well, that's direct, Kevin. But I guess I deserve it. I should have been honest with you last week when I called. Actually, I should have been honest with you well over a month ago and called you then."

"We're both sorry and have a lot to apologize for. But this is the cancer ward, right? What's wrong? Why are you here?"

"I have pancreatic cancer, plain and simple."

He stopped himself from any kind of immediate verbal response because he feared saying the worst possible thing. Her own pronouncement was as matter of fact as if she had only stubbed her toe. He wondered if he had heard correctly. He knew one thing about pancreatic cancer. It was one of the very worst and most aggressive forms. Felicity stepped in.

"I'm so sorry to hear that, Sabra. This is devastating for you."

"So what's being done?" Kevin said. "How long have you been in the hospital? Have you started chemotherapy?" He surveyed the IV bags to which she was tethered, squinting to read labels but unable to decipher the chemical names in the dim room.

"I was admitted today. I waited as long as I could. And . . . I'm still undecided about . . . treatments. It's probably advanced too far. I was already in Stage Four when I got the diagnosis. The doctors and I talked about some experimental treatments, but they couldn't give me much hope other than I'd be miserable, beyond anything I could imagine. And I'm a coward."

"No, you're not a coward, Mom."

"In this I am. I'm scared, to be honest. I'm going to die, not long from now. Maybe a month is what I have. Treatments would probably only lengthen my life by a few months, at most."

Kevin could only stare. Felicity reached for his hand and squeezed it. He hadn't realized what a caring human she could be. Her responses were far more compassionate and composed than his.

"What—why didn't you tell me?" his voice barely reached a whisper.

"I—don't know. It doesn't matter now. I'm sorry. We have a lot to talk about, to figure out."

"Yes, of course. I can take a leave of absence to be here, to do some legal work, and—and oversee your care."

"Actually, Kevin, that's not really the main thing we need to figure out. I've got my will taken care of, and there's good life insurance from the college. It's something else, something more important than all of that."

"What, Mom? What could be more important than your having terminal cancer?"

"We need to talk about Mei."

"Who is May? A friend of yours?"

Sabra sighed, peering out the window. The late summer sun had set, leaving its wisps behind with deep hues of indigo, purple, and gold. She turned back to gaze at Kevin, sadly, searching for understanding in the eyes and face of her son, so much like her ex-husband's. She took in his brown eyes and close-cropped sandy hair, finding it hard to say the words she had practiced.

"She's your little sister."

Chapter 5

"My little sister?"

"Yes."

"Since when do I have a sister?" His mind flew to his stepbrothers, the two children of his father's second wife, college-aged guys—were they even in college now? He only really saw them on Christmas visits. Was his mother hallucinating? "What are you talking about?"

"She's over there. Asleep." She pointed to a pullout sofa behind the large hospital room door. In their rush to see Sabra, they had ignored everything but her and the equipment to which she was connected.

There, under a colorful flannel blanket, lay a small child, who appeared to be of Asian descent, sleeping soundly but in an awkward position. She wore her clothes rather than pajamas and clasped a stuffed animal. Kevin walked over to the sofa and gazed down at her, mystified and entranced until he realized he had stared too long and became uncomfortable. The child was pretty, delicate, and vulnerable. He tried to do the math in his head.

He hadn't seen his mother in fourteen months—how had she managed to become the guardian, or parent, or whatever, of this child in the last year? And why hadn't she said a word about it to him?

"Mom, when did you—where-" he couldn't go on. Thirty-one was a little old to find out you have siblings. This would take some processing.

"Sit down, Kevin, Felicity. We have some things to talk about."

"No, you and I do. Felicity is my friend, my guest, but not part of this," he could hear the tension in his voice. Felicity didn't sign on to referee, and he wasn't going to put her through it.

"I tell you what," said Felicity. "Let me go check into the hotel. When you're ready, just give me a call, Kevin, and I'll come pick you . . ." she glanced over at the bundle on the sofa . . . "two up." She bent down and gave him a kiss on the cheek. "It will be okay," she whispered.

She's better than I deserve. What a mess, he thought.

Felicity left after touching Mei's hair and pulling the blanket over her. She had nieces and nephews; children held no fears for her.

"Okay, Mom. Spill it. Where did you get her?"

"Her name is Mei. Mei Louise Timothy."

"All right, Mei. How old is she?"

"Five."

"She's little."

"Yes."

"What is she?"

"She's a child, Kevin."

"I know that. Is she Chinese? Korean? Cambodian?"

"Chinese. I adopted her seven months ago from an orphanage in the Hunan Province. The college has connections with it through its church affiliations, and I worked with a local international adoption agency."

"Church? You don't do church."

"Maybe I do, now. It doesn't matter. I started the proceedings two years ago. It took a long time and a lot of money. I went there in the early spring and adopted her."

"And didn't tell me? You adopted a child from China and didn't tell me? Did you tell anyone? Dad?"

"No. You know I don't really speak to your father. What I do is hardly any of his business, anyway. I was going to tell you, eventually. Soon. You and I don't exactly talk that much."

"No kidding. And is that entirely my doing?" he said.

"No, it's not."

He rubbed his eyes. This was too much revelation for ten minutes. "Mom, why did you adopt a child? At your age?"

"I wanted a child. A little girl."

"I can't believe an agency let you have a child."

"Am I such a train wreck?"

"No, that's not what I mean. Never mind. But, you're unmarried. I thought they only wanted to adopt out children to married couples. And it's not like you're at a typical child-raising age."

"I was willing to take an older child. I'm not exactly ancient. And, well, I had connections."

He did not want to pursue the question of what those connections might be. "And now you have terminal pancreatic cancer."

"Yes."

He sat there in silence. He wanted to comfort her; he really did. He wanted her to explain her disease. He wanted her to get a second and third and fourth opinion. To fight the cancer. To take all the chemotherapy or radiation or infusions or whatever medical science offered, no matter the cost or if she had to travel or if he had to take leave to help. He wasn't ready to lose a parent. And yet he wanted to let her know how irresponsible of her it was to take on raising a child under her circumstances.

And then it hit him. "Who is going to take care of her?"

"Mei. Her name is Mei."

"Yes, Mei. Who is going to take care of her? You can't send her back to China. What happens to her if you die?"

"Not if, Kevin. When I die. I'm sorry. It's going to happen."

"All right." They were talking so frankly, he did not realize his emotional numbness. "So what happens to Mei?"

"She has family to take care of her," Sabra said.

"Who?"

"You."

Chapter 6

Later he wondered why her one-word answer struck him as surprising or unusual. Of course. Who else was she going to call on in her darkest hour? Sabra had two much older sisters, his Aunts Linda and Marjorie, but they lived in Colorado and Arizona. She couldn't ask either of them to take on a child in their sixties.

In the moment, all he could think—or not think—to say was, "Are you crazy?" He regretted it as soon as he heard the words emerge from his mouth and betray him, but they revealed his true thoughts.

"No, I'm not crazy. I've thought about it a lot."

"I can't take on and raise a little girl I've never met." He wanted to add, "Just because you thought it was a great idea to adopt an orphan from China in your 50s, doesn't make it my responsibility." But he checked himself. If she really was dying of incurable pancreatic cancer, this was no time for accusations or theatrics.

"You'll meet her. Once you get to know her, you'll fall in love with her. Everyone does."

"I'm sure she's sweet, Mom. I'm sure she's wonderful. But seriously, I can't believe we're having this conversation. There is no way I'm capable of raising a child. I'm not married. I'm not sure the courts would give me custody of a child."

"It's in my will."

"You put me as her guardian in your will without asking?"

"Yes."

Kevin wondered, for a brief moment, if this was some kind of prank or joke, or if it was even legal. The thought was tasteless and sick, but he couldn't make sense of what was happening. Then he started to feel the anger. No one had a right to expect anyone to take on a child without being consulted.

"Mom, I—I don't know what to say. This is too much. Be realistic."

"I'm sorry to hit you with two big things at once, Kevin, but the situation wouldn't be any better if I did it in stages. I'm dying. Even if I were to decide, against my judgment, to try chemotherapy, I couldn't take care of Mei. When I get out of the hospital, we'll have to have caregivers and hospice nurses come in. I won't be able even to get her to school, or anything else. I am the one being realistic. You are a responsible young man with a good job. I trust you. My life insurance and the sale of my house will go to you to take care of Mei. It should be enough for many years."

"It's not the money, Mom."

"Then what is it?"

"It's . . ." he looked at her, this time really observing, and he wondered if anyone could seem more tired, drained, or empty. The conversation, and his pushing back, had exhausted her. She fought to keep her eyes open and her head erect. She really is dying, he thought. In a month or so, if she's right, she'll be gone. Has she given up? Has she been told to give up?

His mother was always a fighter. She fought for causes and the homeless and her clients and . . . well, she hadn't fought for her marriage or fought to have Kevin stay with her after the divorce. Had she decided she doesn't have that strength any longer? This would be easier if their past were less complicated, he thought. But if that were so, she wouldn't be telling him in the last few weeks of her life about an adopted sister he now had to take responsibility for.

"Kevin." She struggled to get the name out. She spoke slightly above a whisper, fighting against the fatigue to produce a breathy sentence. Her lips seemed to lack energy to move. "Let's talk about it tomorrow. I'm too tired." She closed her eyes and her body went slack.

"All right," he said, more to himself. But he wasn't ready to leave. What was he going to do? He needed another person, another mind, clearer than his own.

He found Felicity's number in Contacts and punched the call button.

"Yes?" she answered.
"Have you checked into the hotel?"
"No, I haven't arrived there yet."
"Can you come pick me up now?"
"Sure. Let me come up to room 307 again," she offered.
"All right, if you don't mind."
"I'll be there soon."

Chapter 7

Kevin sat in the padded, generic chair by Sabra's bed, waiting for Felicity to return, listening to Sabra's labored and irregular breathing. He wondered if she was getting anything for pain, or if pain was even a concern yet. The disease probably leeched everything from her.

He wanted to make plans, be in control, but he couldn't. All that power had been taken from him. "Damn," he thought. "Damn it." He wanted to blame, to shout re-criminations. He wondered if the adoption agency took children back and placed them in better homes, solid families with two normal parents and other children. It was irresponsible for anyone to give Sabra Timothy a child to raise. She hadn't done such a hot job the first time.

That was the core of it. He wasn't upset his mother had cancer, or even that she had unwisely brought a dependent child into her life. He was angry for something seventeen years before: her sitting him down at the dinner table one night after Dad had already left because he wouldn't stay with a woman who cheated on him. Her explaining to him she "loved his father, but sometimes married people stop wanting to be married and want to be with someone else." Like he at fourteen would understand her pseudo-defense of her actions.

So why should he be the victim, or really, the corrector, of her bad decisions again?

He heard a murmur from behind him. It was Mei, waking up. A hospital sofa at almost 10:00 at night was no place for a child.

He rose to talk to her. "Hello, Mei."

"Who you?" Her words were slow. He wondered how good her English was at this point, seven months in the U.S.

"I'm Kevin."

"Are you doctor?"

"No."

"Ke-vin."

"Yes."

"Momma sick."

"Yes, she is."

"I no like here."

"I know. I don't like it either."

"I want go home. With Momma." She sat up, pushing her hair out of her eyes, focusing on Sabra in the bed. Her defenseless beauty was more evident now she was awake.

"I know."

"My bed." She pointed to herself.

"Yes."

She took off the blanket, determined to leave.

"No, not yet. We have to wait."

At that moment, a rap at the door was followed by Felicity's entrance.

"What's going on?"

"Oh, more than you can imagine. Mei is awake," he motioned his head toward the bed.

"Oh, hello, Mei.

Mei seemed to brighten at the greeting of this pretty young woman. "Hello. Who you?"

"I'm Felicity. You can call me CeeCee."

"Cee--Cee?"

"Yes, that's right."

"I want go home."

Felicity's eyes shot to Kevin. She pulled him aside, closer to the door and lowered her voice. "This child needs to be in bed, not here."

"What do you suggest?"

"We can't take her anywhere without your mother's consent."

"Oh, I think we can. She's my inheritance."

"What?"

"Mom wants me to take care of her. To have custody. Raise her, I guess. It's in her will, without my consent or knowledge, of course."

"Oh, my."

"Listen, if you want out of this crazy dysfunctional situation, we can see about renting you a car and you can drive back in the morning . . .."

"Uh, just let me get this straight first." She sat down. "Mei, your pony is pretty."

Mei hugged the pink stuffed unicorn to her, with a frown, as if she thought Felicity would take it. Seven or more months under Sabra's protection had probably not wiped away all the deprivation she suffered for her first five years.

"Mei, can Mr. Kevin and I walk outside, and you be a good girl? Not very long?"

Mei frowned again.

"We'll be right back."

"I stay here."

"Good, honey. Come outside, Mr. Kevin," Felicity said.

They closed the hospital room door. Felicity led the way confidently to the waiting area near Sabra's room.

"Felicity, what are you doing?"

"Listen, Kevin, I don't know how to say this nicely, but you look shell-shocked or something. And you probably should. You found out your mother is dying, you found out you're a brother, and you found out you're, well, a sort of daddy, in a few minutes. I could be wrong, but you looked like you needed help. And you do. I think I have more experience with family stuff and with kids than you do. Let's either take Mei back to the hotel and she can stay in my room, if that would make you more comfortable, or we can take her to your mother's house and she can sleep in her own bed, which given the circumstances, would be better for her."

"I—don't know. This is asking an awful lot of you. You didn't sign up for this."

"Well, bad stuff happens. I'm not the one dying of cancer or the one who just became a parent. You need help. I'm here, so I might as well give it."

"I don't know what to say."

"Just say thank you." She rubbed his shoulder in a comforting way. "But I'm still sleeping in tomorrow. We'll figure this out."

"You're incredible." Her competence and control in his distraught situation almost frightened him.

"Yeah, I know. Now, let's talk to the nurse on duty."

Felicity approached the nurses' station as if she were totally in charge. She spoke directly to get the nurse's attention. "Excuse me. This is the son of Sabra Timothy, the patient in 307." She gestured to Kevin, who couldn't help but feel like a ventriloquist's dummy. "He'd like to talk to someone, her nurse, about her care."

"Is something wrong? And who are you?"

"I'm a friend of her son, here. This is Kevin Elcott." She motioned to Kevin to speak.

"Uh, yes, I wanted to know about my mother's condition."

"How do we know you are her son?" the nurse seemed unusually confrontational.

"I—you'd have to get her to confirm it, I guess. I don't know why I'd be here otherwise. I drove from Charlotte." He paused. "I have a picture of her on my phone," he said, thinking that might be some form of proof. He pulled it out and began scrolling.

The nurse softened. "Okay. I can't tell you much. Regulations, HIPPA, you know. But I can say she's not well. At all. I'm sure you can see that. Her doctor will be in early, around 8:00, so you can talk to him then, with her there."

"What medications are in the bags?" Kevin asked.

The nurse examined a chart. "I can't really say specifically. She is receiving meds to build up her system and prepare her for chemotherapy if she begins it. And something non-narcotic for the pain. That's helping her sleep."

Felicity jumped in. "We are concerned about the little girl in there with her. She can't stay there. Do you have some kind of family center where she could stay?"

"Not unsupervised. This isn't a day care. Ms. Timothy said the little girl would have to stay in her room until someone from the family came."

"I'm the only family she has east of the Mississippi."

"Then you either need to stay here in the hospital with the little girl or take her somewhere."

"Are you telling me I can just walk out of here with the child?"

"Let me back up. When Ms. Timothy was admitted this morning, she brought her will and a lot of other papers. She wanted us to know that. She said her son would be taking the little girl and would have custody of her. So, the short answer is yes, although I'm not sure it's the best. The child can't stay here in her room all night. The only other option is . . ." she paused, "for us to call Child Protective Services."

"Oh, no, she's with us," Felicity interjected.

"Felicity, are you--" said Kevin.

"Very well, Mr. Timothy is free to take the little girl or stay the night."

"It's Kevin Elcott," he corrected, from long habit.

"Thank you," Felicity said. "Mr. Elcott will be back early in the morning to speak to the doctor."

Chapter 8

They re-entered Sabra's room. Mei had lain down again, clutching her blanket and unicorn, but her wide-open eyes held an expression Kevin couldn't decipher. What could she be thinking? he wondered.

"Mei, CeeCee and I are going to take you home, okay?"

She nodded but did not move.

"Let me talk to your momma."

Kevin touched his mother's shoulder; Sabra gave no response, so he shook her gently. "Mom. Sabra."

"Hmm? Kevin?"

"We are going to take Mei to your home to sleep. I will be back early in the morning to speak to your doctor."

"All right," she whispered. "Thank you."

"Do you hurt, Mom?"

"Not when I sleep," she replied. "Oh." She roused herself. "Take my keys—they are in my coat pocket, in the cabinet there." She pointed across the room. "Mei will need to be in a car seat. Drive my car." She fell back, spent.

"I'll see you in the morning. Don't worry about Mei." He reached over and kissed her cheek, although he wasn't sure why. It seemed like the thing to do.

For the first time in his life, he helped a child into the elevated seat in the back of Sabra's car, and he led the way as Felicity followed him in his car. Two minutes into the ride to the hotel Mei fell back asleep, despite the strangers in the front seat and the uncomfortable car seat into which she'd been strapped. They drove to Sabra's modest home near the college.

"I really can't thank you enough, Felicity. This is turning out a nightmare."

"Please stop saying that, Kevin. I'm perfectly fine. Really. We'll get her to bed and pack it in ourselves. I am tired. But you know, it's actually a little bit refreshing to deal with something other than actuarial tables, spreadsheets, and computer screens."

"Still, this wasn't the plan. I feel like I owe you a story, an explanation, but I don't want to bore you with my life story."

"Maybe later. Let's just deal with one crisis at a time."

Kevin rose early and showered, leaving Felicity asleep in Sabra's room and Mei safely in her own bed.

By 7:30 Kevin entered his mother's hospital room. She was awake, with a tray table in front of her. She stared at the food, blankly, as if confused about what to do with the contents on the plate before her.

"Mom, I'm here."

"Thank you, Kevin."

"I want to see the doctor. I haven't missed him, have I?"

"No," she said. She pushed the table away.

"Have you eaten anything?"

"Some sips, a few bites. I'm not really hungry."

"We need to talk. Last night was . . ."

"Yes, I know." She turned her head toward the window. "It's a mess. But I don't know what to do." Her tears began to well in her eyes. Kevin wanted to comfort Sabra but found it easier to change the subject.

"Maybe you can go back and tell me about the cancer. That's a place to start."

"You're so like your father. Logical. Methodical." Her voice did not sound as if she meant it as a compliment.

"That's not a crime."

"No," she admitted. "I suppose not." After a sigh, she started. "All right. I've had Mei for seven months. After I brought her home, I noticed how tired I was. I thought it was due to taking care of a young child. Actually, thinking back, I was tired and had back pain before I left for China, but I ignored it. I was so excited, there was so much to do to get her room ready . . ."

"Mom, I do want to talk about Mei later. Now let's talk about your . . . illness."

"All right," Sabra said, with that tone he knew so well as if she thought she was giving in to his unreasonable whims. "In late spring I noticed I was losing weight and overly thirsty, so I had myself checked out for Type II diabetes. You know it runs in the family. My mother had it. I did test positive for it, and began to do the lifestyle changes to address it, but . . . that didn't help the back pain. I went to a chiropractor . . . not really thinking it would help, and it didn't. I just lived with it, figuring it was old age or I needed a new mattress I couldn't afford at the moment."

She's not getting to the point, Kevin thought. "And?"

"Three weeks ago my, well, bowel movements were not right, nor the urine. Really not right in color or . . . and my skin was not right either."

"So you went to the doctor then?"

"It took a few days to get in. The family practice doctor did some tests, and the next day I was sent to a urologist, and then an oncologist—last week. That's when I called you. I knew something was wrong."

"You should have told me sooner."

"You had your trip to New York."

"Well, yes, but . . ." It would have been inconvenient to cancel that trip, but not impossible, he thought. It didn't matter now.

At that moment there was a knock and the door opened. A short, bearded, graying man entered. "Good morning, Ms. Timothy." He did not look up from his charts until he was fully by her bedside and aware of Kevin's presence.

"Call me Sabra, Dr. Tedeschi. This is my son, Kevin Elcott."

They shook hands. "I'm glad you're here. She needs a family member to discuss her care options."

"Dr. Tedeschi, my mother was just getting to what's been going on in the last week. Can you explain to me the big picture?"

"Yes. Your mother has, and she knows, Stage Four pancreatic cancer. To be honest, that means it's advanced, and it has metastasized to her liver and kidneys and some other organs."

Kevin knew enough to understand the extent and severity. "And?"

"Your mother should take extensive, intensive chemotherapy. She would be taking a combination of strong medications."

"Will that arrest the cancer—at all?"

"We can't know. I don't believe she is a candidate for a clinical trial, since the cancer has spread. However, I recommend the most aggressive conventional treatment at this point."

Kevin sat down for the first time. Sabra had not spoken.

"I've been thinking about it a lot, Dr. Tedeschi. Under other circumstances, I would opt not to take treatment and let the disease . . . just happen, take its course. But I have a responsibility now. Kevin did not know about the child I adopted, and he's still trying to deal with the news about the cancer."

"So you plan to take the treatments? I would need to arrange for those to start immediately."

"I didn't say that. I'm still not sure."

"We shouldn't delay any longer, Sabra. At this stage, there is no time to waste on beginning them. You should start the treatments tomorrow or Monday, at the latest."

"Thank you, Dr. Tedeschi. I'll consider that and let you know."

"I don't think you understand, Sabra. Your cancer is extremely advanced. The only hope is to start treatments now."

"Mom," Kevin interrupted. "It seems pretty clear."

"Not to me."

"Excuse me, Dr.," Kevin turned to the doctor. "Is there anything else you need to say to my mother? I think we need to speak about this privately, now that I know what's going on."

"Very well. Here's my card. Call me as soon as you make a decision so we can move forward immediately." The doctor abruptly handed them his card and just as abruptly left the room, without a goodbye. While Kevin did not find this professional, he understood Dr. Tedeschi's frustration with Sabra's response to common sense and the lifeline he offered.

"So, Mom, explain why you aren't jumping on the treatment wagon right this minute. If there's a hope being held out to you, why don't you take it?"

"It's not that simple, Kevin. I don't know how I can take care of Mei and go through chemo."

"But, Mom, your other option, and I'm sorry to be so crass, is to die and leave her alone in the world. If the treatments are successful at any level and give you months or even years more life, you will still be around for Mei."

"So, Kevin, look at my options. I spend however long it takes to get these treatments to the point where I'm in remission, if that happens. Have you ever known someone going through chemo?"

"No," he admitted. He didn't really know anyone who had dealt with terminal illness. How had he gotten to thirty-one without that knowledge? "I know the chemo is rough, but it works . . . most of the time."

"Maybe. Maybe not. The second option is just that, to have the treatments and still die in a month or so. The third is to do nothing, enjoy—if you can call it enjoying—the time I have left, and then die."

He was uncomfortable with how directly and coldly she spoke. "Mom, be realistic. You sound like you're talking about someone you don't even know, rather than yourself."

"What do you think I've been doing the last week, other than being realistic? I know you think I'm a flake, Kevin. Maybe I've deserved that description in the past. But I'm not stupid or deluded. I'm intelligent. I worked in a hospital with dying cancer patients for years. I know what I'm in for, either way."

"So, let me argue, then. You have a child. I don't know why you decided in your fifties to bring a child from Asia to this country and raise her, keeping it a secret from me, no less, thanks a lot. But you did it. I don't and can't know what the kid's life was like before she came here, but it couldn't have been too great. You owe it to her not to make it any harder than she's already had it. If you can live, live. Do what you can. Fight, Mom. For Pete's sake."

"Mei is the only thing that keeps me from calling hospice right now and going home."

"If that's what it takes, then I'm going to play that card."

Sabra slid down into the bed. "I'm exhausted. Can you let me rest a bit? Let me just close my eyes and think. Go get some coffee. Come back in twenty minutes."

Her sudden dismissal took him off-guard, but he decided to grant her wish. "All right." Some coffee sounded good, if there was a decent coffee shop in the hospital complex. He could stand a bagel or something, too. He wandered to the nurses' station and asked about a Starbucks. He was directed to a differently branded coffee shop across the street from the hospital. He walked there, barely noticing his surroundings, numb.

His mother would probably be dead in the near future. Maybe not, but . . . very likely. He didn't know if he'd ever have the time or wisdom to sort that out.

Chapter 9

At the coffee shop he bought a bagel and large coffee, pouring too much sugar and milk into it because he wasn't paying attention. He sat down in the most remote corner of the restaurant, which was relatively vacant that early Saturday morning. He'd bought the bread out of obedience to an earlier impulse, but now taking a couple of bites seemed like a chore. All of a sudden the truth of Sabra's condition hit him, and he hung his head and buried his eyes in his hand. He didn't want to cry in a public place, but there were so few people around he didn't care.

He hated it when people said relationships were "complicated," because it sounded like an excuse, but that was the only word he could think of when he thought about his mother. It took him years, well into college, to forgive her. He always thought he was too old to have abandonment issues, but something kept him from trusting his mother; something kept them both at arm's length. They saw each other about once a year, talked on the phone maybe once a month, but neither the visits nor calls were regular or scheduled. Sabra didn't do schedules in relationships. She might call two or three times in one month and then not again for four. She'd been particularly absent from his life for the last year. Or had he been from hers?

It wasn't an issue of love, or lack of it. It was a matter of trust. And comfort.

Maybe she would change her mind, now that he was there, advocating for treatment, advocating for Mei. Sabra had probably been so overwhelmed by the fact of the diagnosis she couldn't think straight, couldn't see beyond the suffering she now faced. She hadn't even arranged for a sitter for Mei, which seemed odd. Why had she kept the child in the hospital with her last night? Was it all for his sake, to surprise him and put him in an impossible situation such that he had to say, "yes" to her plans? Or was she just not thinking straight and making bad decisions?

He tossed the half-eaten bagel and started to walk, a bit aimlessly, to kill time. His mind turned over and over while his emotions sat like a stone, unable to fathom his mother was that ill. The prospect he would have to become Mei's guardian did not fit into his own future, his own life, even his own ability to imagine it. Sabra must be mistaken about whether he could legally be "willed" custody of a human being. Perhaps there was some way the adoption agency could place Mei in another home.

Yes, it would be disruptive for her, but better she have a real family than a dying woman old enough to be her grandmother. Or even worse, in the custody of a guy who had no clue what children even ate or wore or slept, especially a little girl. Well, it wasn't like Mei was a baby, or a toddler. It's not like she had to be toilet-trained or couldn't talk. She seemed to understand English pretty well. She also seemed to be vaguely suspicious of him, but less so of Felicity . . .

No. This was unacceptable. All of it.

As soon as Sabra made a decision about her treatment, he would press the matter of Mei. They could hire a nanny to take care of Mei in Sabra's home while she took treatments. His taking Mei home with him was out of the question.

Having fulfilled his mother's request to leave her alone for a while, Kevin returned to Sabra's room in about half an hour.

"Did you get some rest?"

"Yes. I feel clearer."

"You need anything? Should I call the nurse for you?"

"No. I don't have much appetite. That's one of the symptoms."

"Oh."

"So."

"You do seem a lot thinner," he said.

"I've lost thirty pounds. I started to lose when I found out about the diabetes. Under other circumstances, I'd be glad. Now, not so much."

"Did you make a decision?"

"Yes. I'll think seriously about getting the treatments . . . if."

"If?"

"You take full custody of Mei. Take her back to Charlotte with you."

"What?" He had a vague sense of what blackmail must be like.

"Kevin, you were an only child. You're unmarried. You have never had to take care of anyone but yourself. That's over. Legally, she is your sister. Legally, it's in my will for you to take care of her at my death."

"You can't put that on me. You can't ask a person to adopt, or take over, or whatever, a child without asking them."

"Who else?"

"Okay, let's go back." He sat down and tried to slow his breathing. "Why did you adopt a child at your age in the first place?"

"I didn't plan on dying."

"I didn't ask that. Why did you adopt her?"

"Why does anyone adopt a child?"

"I don't know. I guess I can understand why some married couples would, but I don't understand why someone like you—why you period—would. It makes no sense to me."

"I wanted a child in my life."

"Is that supposed to be some 'you didn't give me grand-children so it's your fault, Kevin' thing? I don't remember signing a paper somewhere saying it was my responsi-bility to get married and have kids for you." I didn't sign a paper about taking over one for you, either, he thought.

"No, Kevin. Believe it or not, this isn't about you. I wanted to raise a little girl. It was what I wanted."

"But did you think of the consequences? Was it really the best for the child?"

"In Mei's case, I would say a loving home in the U.S. is a lot better than an orphanage. I went through all the tests and visits and interviews anyone else would. The agency deemed me fit. I had a right to adopt a child. I have a right to love someone if I want to."

This last sentence was more than he could bear. He stood up. "I'll be back in a minute," he said, rushing from the room to keep himself from saying what he really wanted to say: "You have a right to love someone. That is your brand, Mom. Your slogan. But do you have enough responsibility to love?"

Chapter 10

He paced in the waiting area, seething. A voice in him said, "She didn't love you enough to save her marriage when you were a kid. But she went out of her way to find another kid to love, now." Is this sibling rivalry? He thought. Well, I never had it as a kid. Am I seriously jealous about an Asian orphan twenty-six years younger than me? Good grief. This is what his mom could do to him, sometimes. Drive him to emotions he didn't think possible. Shit. He was too old to be fighting this battle in himself.

"Man up," he told himself, in a low voice to make it seem more real. "There's no way I can take on the raising of a five-year-old. I'm trying to move to New York. My job is too demanding. She's got to understand. She's got to get help from social services. She's got to—"

He stopped himself. "What? She's got to what? She might be dead in a month."

So this was what being trapped felt like.

Exhausted, Kevin re-entered his mother's room. Her eyes were closed, but she responded to the quiet swishing of the heavy, wide hospital door. "So?"

"I think it would be best for you to ask the agency to take her back, find another home for her."

"You can't return a child, Kevin. She's not a piece of furniture."

"But you can ask if they will place her with another family. One with other kids, maybe. I thought people were trying to adopt kids from overseas all the time."

"I don't want to do that."

"But you could ask."

"I could do a lot of things."

"Mom, you're blackmailing me. You'll take chemo if I take Mei. But if you don't take chemo, I end up with her all the same. I'm damned either way."

"She's not a curse, Kevin."

"I am not saying that. I just don't think this is best for her."

"No, you're saying it's not best for you. It's not convenient for you."

"Convenient? You act like it's the difference between washing my car by myself and taking it to a car wash. I don't know anything about how to raise a child."

"A few people have done it before. I think you're smart enough." He could hear the sarcasm in her voice, even in her fatigue.

"It's not about smarts. I'm not even married. A kid needs two parents."

"About that . . . "

"Felicity and I are not remotely talking about marriage. She came along to get a trip out of town. She's a good sport. She had no idea what she was getting into and she'd be a nanny. She'll probably never talk to me after this weekend. So, thanks for that."

"I think she's a better person than how you are portraying her."

"I'm sure she is. She's great. That's hardly the point here."

"How did you meet Felicity?" his mother seemed interested and her face displayed a sudden brightness as if she wanted a happy story. She had diverted the subject, but he chose not to fight her.

"On a dating app."

"That's not very romantic, Kevin."

"Maybe not, but it's what most guys my age do now. Us millennials have to work all the time, so we outsource our social lives."

"She's nice-looking. And she takes charge."

"Yeah."

"You could use someone like her in your life."

"I'm doing okay." His discomfort rose; anyway, Felicity would probably dump him by Sunday night. "Let's change the subject off of Felicity. She's not obligated to go along with this crazy scheme of yours."

"It's not a crazy scheme, Kevin."

"I think it is. Why expect your child to be raised by an unmarried guy who's never even held a baby?"

She sighed. "Kevin, this is wearing me out. But let me get this out, and then you can leave. I need some more rest." She paused. He recognized her angry voice; it hadn't changed much from his childhood. Now it was only more tense and weak.

"You are her brother. She is your sister. Whether you like it or not. We don't get to choose our families. You know that, don't you? We don't get to choose cancer, or when we die, or whether chemo will work. I know you have a lot of bitterness toward me. I deserve some of it. I don't deserve all of it. You have lived a charmed life, except for the divorce. You are one of the most privileged and entitled people I know. Don't you think it's time, considering the situation I'm in, to think less like an entitled, privileged prick and see you're needed, for once, to be a man?"

At least that was out in the open. He didn't like being called to task by her. He wasn't sure she had the right. He felt the muscles through his neck and hands tighten and words of accusation from so many years ago boiling up. Who was she to talk to him like that?

His mother. She was his mother. And at some level, moms got to talk that way. He didn't like it. But they did.

He didn't speak for several seconds. He stared out the window, not seeing. The seconds stretched into minutes.

"I'll have to take her to Charlotte," he said quietly. "I have to be there for work. I can get some time off through Family Medical Leave to get her settled in my place. There's an extra bedroom in the apartment. I use it as an office, but we'll manage. For now. I'll have to see about a school. I don't know about the school system there. She might have to go to a private school. She'll need a nanny, part-time. That's going to cost something. I can make sure her physical needs are taken care of. I don't know about her emotional needs. I can't promise to be a good father. That's not what I am. I'm just her guardian, some sort of brother or caretaker. A brother is not a daddy. You have to know that."

"For now, if it's the best we can do in this impossible situation, it will work."

"But what about your treatments?"

"I'll keep thinking about it. I really will. That's all I can say. I have no faith in them."

He sighed. Was she already changing her mind and taking back her promise?

"I can get some type of home health care if I take chemo," she continued. "Our insurance at the college is overpriced but good about these kinds of things. I'll cross that bridge."

"Then you are going to call the doctor?"

"Yes, I will."

He paused, considered his words, but ultimately said what he felt. "You got your way."

"No, Kevin. Excuse me, but what an incredibly stupid thing for you to say. You of all people would think that way, Kevin. My way would be no cancer, to be as healthy as a 56-year-old woman with Type II diabetes can be. To raise Mei. To have a better relationship with my son. To feed the hungry and see world peace." She paused and closed her eyes. "My life is likely to be very short. That's not *my way*, Kevin. Now I only want to make sure Mei is cared for."

Chapter 11

By 10:30 a.m. he entered the front door of his mother's home. "Anyone home?"

"We're back here," Felicity's voice came from the kitchen. "We're eating pancakes."

Sabra's modest rancher, a definite throwback to the '60s, needed some updates badly but was in generally good repair. Her style was eclectic, part homey and kitschy, part intercultural museum, decorated with many physical memories of her travels to non-Western parts of the world. African masks adorned one wall of the living room. Figures made by Ethiopian craftsmen sat on various surfaces, as did multiple Southeast Asian baskets. A large photographic print of Machu Picchu hung over the fireplace with fake logs. Sabra hadn't hiked up to it, but she had visited Peru.

All this juxtaposed with her kitchen decked with blue gingham and a turtle motif. Kevin found Felicity and his new sister there. Mei sat at the table, still in her pajamas, spearing pancakes awkwardly with a determined look on her face. Felicity drank coffee, her own plate of mostly-eaten pancakes pushed away.

"She told me she's never had pancakes before," Felicity provided. "That's too bad. What does your mom feed her?"

"No telling. I'm sure it's healthy, though."

"I made these from scratch. Not bad if I do say so myself," she said. He could tell she was trying to be upbeat.

Kevin sat down and ran his fingers through his hair.

"You look beat."

"I am."

"Where Momma?" Mei asked him, sternly.

"Momma is still at the hospital."

"I not like it there." She pinched her nose and made a face. "Smelly."

"Yes, it is," he grinned at her. Might as well be agreeable, he thought. I'm in for the long haul.

"Do you like the pancakes, Mei?" Felicity asked.

Mei smiled at Felicity, fully approving of this new lady in her life. "Yes. Like cake."

"Yes, I guess they are," Felicity said.

"My mom was always strict on me about sugar and Cokes and stuff. Being health-conscious didn't seem to pay off for her."

"That's kind of harsh, Kevin."

"Well, I'm in a harsh mood." He turned to his new little sister. "Mei, CeeCee and I are going to talk in the other room. When you finish your pancakes, can you then go play in your room?"

As if she were still not sure what to think of this strange creature called Kevin, she nodded, without smiling, but didn't speak.

Maybe she's not been around a lot of men, he thought. She's lived in a Chinese orphanage and with a middle-aged woman who has a bunch of middle-aged female friends. She would have to get used to a man, and quick.

Felicity followed him to the living room and sat down. "So, what's going on?"

"I'm a dad, in essence. I'm raising a kid."

"You're kidding."

"I wish I were. Sabra told me she wouldn't even think about the chemo unless I took custody of Mei. But no matter what she says, I think she's waffling on that point still. I don't know what she'll do."

"I'm so sorry."

"I know what you're thinking, and I agree," he said. "It's a crappy thing for her to do. In her mind, she has no options. I guess she's right. She's damned if she does and damned if she doesn't. "

"Still . . ."

"Yep. I know." He paused, and sighed deeply, trying to use his diplomacy skills. "So, listen, you've been great. You didn't know what you were getting into and rolled with it. Mei obviously likes you a lot more than she likes me. She looks at me like she doesn't know what I am. I figure she hasn't been around men much. Who knows what she's been through? You hear stories about those places . . .. Anyway, if you'd like me to rent a car for you so you can drive home, we'll call it a day. I really appreciate what you've done."

"Whoa. You're not getting rid of me that fast. I wanted to poke around some of the antique stores here, get a feel for the place. It reminds me of the town my grandparents lived in, in Western Kentucky. I'm not ready to go back to Charlotte yet. It's my work-life-balance weekend, remember?"

"Okay. You can use my car today; I'll use Moms. I've got a lot to do if I'm taking Mei home with me tomorrow."

"You're serious about this?" He couldn't tell if her words and look displayed concern or disbelief.

"Yes. I have to be. As weird as it is, she's my sister and I'm responsible for her now. I don't think I'll ever get used to it, but somehow I have to make at least some sense of it. For now."

A part of him wanted Felicity to offer her help with the little girl clothes and hair things and furnishings he would have to pack before the next day. If nothing else, Felicity could run interference for him by entertaining his taciturn little sister. The other part of him knew she'd done enough and he was on his own.

"Wow. Honestly, I don't know what to say. This is huge for you," Felicity said. She paused, as if she wanted to say more, offer more, but something held her back. Instead, she stood up. "If it's all right, I'm going to get ready and take a ride around, spend some time to myself."

"Sure. Be my guest. I'm grateful for what you've done."

After Felicity left, taking his car, he felt vulnerable. He was alone in the house with a five-year-old. He wondered how he would explain if a neighbor, or worse, a cop were to come to the door. Taking a deep breath, he knocked on Mei's door, even though it was open.

"Mei, can I come in?"

"You come in."

He entered. She was sitting at her child-sized desk, working on some kind of coloring book with stickers.

"I want to see Momma."

"Yes, we'll go see Momma in a little bit. She wants to see you."

"Is she still sick?"

"Yes. Momma is very sick. Very bad sick."

Mei turned back to her stickers and did not speak. He had served his purpose for now.

"Do you know who I am?"

"You are man who come with CeeCee."

"That's true. Do you remember my name?"

She thought for a second and formed the unusual word. "Ke-Vun."

"Right. Do you know why I am here?"

"Momma want to see you."

"Yes. Listen, Mei, can you look at me for a second?"

She pasted the sticker on her finger into place and turned to him. Was that a scowl?

"Your momma is my momma too."

She shook her head emphatically. "No. You big man."

"I know. But I used to be little like you, a long time ago. Your momma is my momma. I just don't live with her now, since I'm a big man."

"How old you?

"Thirty-one. Do you know your numbers?"

"Yes. That is lot of numbers."

"Yes, that's true. I am older than you. But Momma is still my momma."

"Okay."

"Do you know what that means?"

"No."

"It means I am your brother."

Mei pondered this for a few seconds. Kevin didn't know if she understood the concept of "brother," having lived in an orphanage. "You not Chinese like me."

"I know. But I am still your brother because your momma is my momma too."

Mei had to think about this. She tilted her head to examine this new person, this new relationship. Finally, she spoke, "I want to go see Momma."

"Yes, I know. Listen, Mei. Momma is very sick and has to stay in the hospital and get lots of medicine. She wants me to take you to my house and you stay with me."

"No. I don't like that."

"I know, but you have to come with me. You can't stay here by yourself. Momma wants me to take care of you."

"Do you live with CeeCee?"

"No. She is my friend. She is not my wife."

"I not know that word."

"I know. CeeCee and I are not married. We are not in a family together. She is my friend."

"I want to see Momma. We go in the car to see Momma at the ho-pi-tal."

"Okay." He figured that was enough for a five-year-old brain with limited English and an even more limited understanding of family connections.

Chapter 12

He drove his mother's ten-year-old Subaru, equipped with a seat for Mei that would soon be in the back seat of his own car, back to the hospital after a meager lunch of what he could find in the house. He texted Felicity about their location; he'd been sure to give her the back door key before she left to explore the town and check out antique shops.

Kevin really did not know how to take care of a child or how to converse with one. He decided, all things considered for now, to let Mei lead the way for now.

"When Momma come home from ho-pi-tal?"

"I don't know."

"Then who take care of me?"

"I am going to take care of you."

"Why?"

"Your momma—our momma—is very sick."

I thought I just explained this to her, he thought. Does she have a learning disability? Maybe it's the English language thing. She doesn't seem to understand. On the other hand, maybe it was just a five-year-old kid thing.

"She get better?"

"No, I don't think so."

Mei did not speak for a few blocks. Maybe he had said too much.

"Momma not get better, ever?"

"I don't know, Mei. She's very sick. She's . . . going to try, I think, to get better. The doctor will try to help her."

"She die?"

"I don't know. "

"She go to Heaven?"

He paused. Children's questions were so insistent. "Only if she dies. We hope she doesn't die, Mei."

They arrived at the hospital before she asked any more unanswerable questions. He released her from the seat and let her out of the car. Children have a lot of stuff, he thought. They need special furniture just to ride in a car. She insisted on bringing one of her dolls and grasped it tightly, but upside down. In the parking lot he became aware of all the dangers to a small, fragile child, even though on a Saturday there were few cars and little traffic. She reached up to hold his hand. Kevin felt a new—was it an emotion? Or simply a sensation? The best description he could give it was protectiveness.

Without asking or being asked, Mei quietly climbed up into the hospital bed with Sabra. Kevin could see his mother wince as Mei settled herself in, inadvertently kicked Sabra, and tugged at an IV.

"Mom, are you sure she should be up there with you?'

"It's fine. She needs good physical touch. It's hard to know what is going through her mind."

Kevin had an inkling of Mei's thoughts. Clearly Mei was tired of this man who had driven her in the car and taken her away from the pretty lady who made pancakes. Sabra let Mei cuddle beside her. Soon Mei was asleep.

"She still takes naps," Sabra explained. "I don't guess she slept very well last night, with all this change."

"She didn't complain."

"That's not her style. Sometimes she just gets out of bed early in the morning, turns her lights on, and plays in her room. It's like she never got over the jet lag from the trip here."

Sabra brushed Mei's hair off her forehead and otherwise caressed her gently, off and on.

"She seems to have taken to Felicity. More than to me."

"She hasn't had much experience with men. All the workers in the children's center where she lived were women. Her preschool teachers here are women. Her pediatrician is a woman."

"I'm sort of like an alien, then."

"Only because you are a man. She'll get used to you. She's very adaptable."

Kevin kept his doubts to himself. "What do you know about her?"

"Her mother gave birth and skipped the abortion the government wanted her to have. I guess she was able to hide the pregnancy. Her parents lived in a part of China where the one-child policy was strict. Some families can get away with more than one child, especially if they have money or party connections, but her parents already had a boy and they were poor and unconnected. They had to put her in the orphanage when she was a toddler."

"I thought the Chinese government was cracking down on these adoptions. Didn't I hear that on the news?"

"They are now. I got in under the radar before the regulations got stiffer."

So, he thought, this child has a family. A perfectly good one, disadvantaged, of course, oppressed, but two parents and a brother. Would she have been better off in China? Clearly not. Circumstances beyond her family's control meant permanent separation. Oppressive laws about family size in a Communist country combined with thousands of years of preference for boys. What a string of events.

They sat silently for a while. Sabra closed her eyes. He saw her body go slack; she dozed. The mixture of drugs in the IV probably included a mild—or maybe not so mild—sedative, and they worked so well he couldn't have a complete conversation with her. Kevin wanted her to answer questions, to know what was going through her mind about treatments and her future. He realized he might sit there a long time before an answer came. He took out his phone to check emails and messages.

Felicity checked in through a text, saying she was browsing little shops in the downtown area and planning to get a late lunch. "Is everything okay?" she asked.

He texted back, "Sure. Enjoy yourself. Mei is happy to see--" he paused, "her mom," he finished. "Both resting."

After twenty minutes of Kevin's fiddling with his phone, texts, and social media feeds, Sabra roused. "Could you get me a washcloth and wet it? I want to wipe my face."

Kevin complied. Sabra dabbed her face and placed the folded rag on her forehead. "So, I guess we need to talk."

"Yeah."

"Kevin, I know you will argue with me about it, and you'll be angry after my promise this morning. But I've thought a lot about it, and I've changed my mind. I've definitely chosen not to take the treatments."

He felt as if he were in a time loop, having the same conversation, making the same arguments over and over.

"What? How can you say that? Getting chemo is your only hope."

"I don't see it that way. I don't believe treatments will work."

"It's not about believing, Mom. You have to try them."

"No, I don't."

"Then . . ."

"I know. I'll die."

"I can't believe you are saying this. Surely you'll change your mind tomorrow."

"No. You heard the doctor. I have to start now."

"Wait a minute. You said you'd take the treatments if I take Mei. You lied."

"No, that wasn't a lie. I said I would think about it."

"That's not how I remember it."

"Well, then, I changed my mind."

"Maybe it was a lie. So what if I say, no deal? I don't take her. I'm not up to this. I don't know what to do with a kid, especially a little girl that young. It's too much to ask."

"You don't mean it."

"Yeah, I do." He paused. He did mean his frustration with her, with her decision, but he didn't mean his threat of abandoning Mei. Not right now.

"I know you're angry, Kevin. I guess I just can't explain it, about the treatments." She closed her eyes and removed the damp cloth; he noticed how her hands moved slowly, trembling. "I'm so tired, Kevin. You know I've always been high energy. Maybe too high. I can barely move now. I know the cancer is just too far advanced."

"Mom, despite our differences, you've always been a fighter. You were the person concerned about the little guy. Why can't you fight for yourself now?"

"I don't know. Maybe it's depression. Maybe it's despair. Maybe I've been healthy and lived pretty healthy all my life and now I think it was all for nothing because I still got desperately sick. Maybe I'm really a coward, now I have to face real illness."

He wanted to argue. He had a lot of debate material.

"I want you to call your aunts, Linda and Marjorie," Sabra said. "One or both of them need to come out and see me, help me through this, along with the home health and hospice. You'll have your hands full with Mei. You have to work and can't take off an infinite amount of time, and she needs to be in school and settled in Charlotte. I can't expect you or professionals to do everything. Can you do that, call Marjorie and Linda? Today?"

She had changed the subject. Once she made up her mind, no matter how unstable the grounds upon which she made her decisions, she would not change.

"All right," he acquiesced. They sat quietly again for a timeless moment. He knew for the next month or so of his life, or whatever was the remainder of Sabra's, he would spend more time with her than he had since his teenage years. Most of it would be like this, long stretches of silence, her speaking at intervals, usually asking for something he would try to provide. He would try and he would fail and end up feeling helpless and ineffectual.

Chapter 13

He realized Sabra had fallen asleep again. With Mei still napping soundly, he decided this was as good a time as any to call his aunts, Linda in Denver and Marjorie in Flagstaff. It was his job to bear the bad news and ask for the next few weeks of their lives. He slipped out of the room and walked out on a patio for some air.

His aunts took his calls almost suspiciously at first. He probably deserved it. How long ago since he had last spoken to them? Why was his family so dysfunctional, so distant? But after he explained Sabra's condition, they both softened.

"What about that little Chinese girl she got in the spring?" Linda asked directly.

"Well, um, I guess she's my . . . inheritance?"

"Your inheritance? She's leaving you a child to raise?"

"Yes. But, uh, what I, and she, really want to know is, if you and Marjorie, or either of you, or maybe both, could come spend some time with her? I mean, before she . . . uh, goes. She'll have hospice and visiting care, but she really needs someone here with her all the time. I mean, she wants her sisters with her."

Linda, always the most confrontational but loyal of the three sisters, said, "Of course. My husband can take care of himself for a while. I'll see what I can arrange and get back to you later today."

"Thank you, Aunt Linda."

Marjorie balked at the request. She didn't like to fly, which always struck Kevin as odd—why move so far away from her family then? Marjorie had been married and divorced early in life, never had kids, and worked as the office manager for a real estate firm until she retired. "This is a hard time to get away."

Kevin rolled his eyes. How could any time be hard to get away when you're retired, have no family in town, and your sister is dying?

"Linda is coming, or she's working on it." Kevin thought this might serve as bait.

"Well, I'll see." That was the extent of Marjorie's commitment. No wonder Sabra searched for relationships in the wrong places, Kevin thought, with that kind of older sister. Sheesh. This was Marjorie's last chance to see her sister and yet she hesitated to get on a plane. It's not like there weren't trains or cars, too.

That task at least attempted, Kevin re-entered Sabra's room.

"Did you call them?" she asked.

Kevin did not want to recount the conversations. "Linda is working on getting here. Marjorie's thinking about it."

"That sounds about right," Sabra sighed. "Don't expect much from Marjorie, but we gave her a chance. Linda's a sweetheart when it comes down to really helping."

"I got that impression."

"Thanks for calling them. I couldn't do it."

"Sure."

"Can you move Mei and lay her down over there on the pullout sofa? My arm's gone to sleep from the pressure of her lying on it."

He complied. Complying had, in the last eighteen hours or so, become a fact of life.

Kevin lifted the body of his new sister, limp and oblivious, and laid her down. She murmured in sounds he didn't understand. He found a blanket and covered her. The room was cold, the air conditioning on even though fall had begun.

He sat down by Sabra again. "Mom, if you feel like it, we have to talk. I can't just take Mei home with me. There must be papers, her birth certificate, adoption documents, that kind of thing."

"Some of the papers you need are over there," she pointed to a shelf in the open closet. "I brought them to the hospital so they wouldn't question your taking her."

He moved over to the closet to retrieve the black expanding portfolio. After sitting down, he unbound it and checked for legal documents. He found Sabra's will and skimmed it. Yes, there it was. Kevin Timothy Elcott named as guardian of her minor child, Mei Louise Timothy. In black and white, notarized, with the right letterheads and stamps.

"The rest of what you need is in my home office. On the right corner of the desk. Everything. Her documents from China, the orphanage, her citizenship, Social Security card, and medical records. It's all there. No one will question you."

"My neighbors might. They might think I kidnapped her or something."

"Tell them the truth before they get any ideas. I made sure it's all legal, Kevin. You don't need to worry on that score."

"I don't even know what grade she's in, or should be."

"She's in pre-kindergarten. She should be in kindergarten, but she's behind in the language. She's not behind otherwise. She's ahead of most kids, just not in English."

"But I—I mean, what does she like to eat? Play with?"

"Kevin, she'll tell you. She's not shy about that. She's rather bold, actually. She doesn't like white potatoes but she does like yams. She likes pasta; macaroni and cheese suits her fine. She has no allergies that I know of. She's had all the shots she's supposed to. She knows her alphabet and her numbers up to fifty. I started her with piano lessons."

"Piano? At five?"

"Of course."

"You're a tiger mom."

"None of that. It's racist. And one thing I won't tolerate is her feeling different because of her background. She must feel like she belongs."

Kevin wondered how his mother could be so idealistic after all these years. Mei would face a lifetime of assumptions and stereotypes because of her "background." And now she had to put up with a clueless guardian and a dying mother.

"I didn't mean it that way. I just meant you were getting her started early. You didn't make me take music lessons until I was eight, and you let me drop them when I was eleven."

"I'm 25 years older and wiser now. I let you get away with things."

"Ha!"

"I made mistakes, too. I know I did. I know I hurt you deeply, Kevin. Getting Mei was not because I was trying to make up for the past." She looked away from him, out the window.

This confession made him uncomfortable. He viewed her profile. Everything about her appearance said severe illness. Her face had always been round and a little chubby, not unlike an apple. Now he could see her facial bones, and the eyes appeared sunken, surrounded by pale skin with a slight yellow-gray cast.

"I still don't know what I'm going to do with her," he confessed.

"Kevin," she turned back and looked at him squarely. "I have no doubt you will come to love her. I know you don't now. You couldn't. I also have no doubt you'll figure it out."

Chapter 14

Once Mei woke up from her nap on Saturday afternoon, Sabra managed with effort and a great deal of adjusting tubes and furniture, to move herself into a chair. As Mei sat on her lap, Sabra explained Mei was going to go on a long ride with Kevin and CeeCee and stay with Kevin for a while. In a few days, they would come back to see Momma. Mei listened quietly, processing as if coming to a decision.

"I not want to go with that man," Mei concluded.

"I know, baby," said Sabra. "But Momma is very sick. Momma can't take care of you right now. So Kevin is going to take care of you for . . . a while."

"How long?" Mei asked directly.

"Right now, a school week. Five days. He'll bring you back after five days."

"I not like that."

Sabra held her close. "I know. I don't like it either. I will miss you, Mei honey. But you'll be very safe with Kevin. He is your brother."

Kevin listened to this, feeling like a mental patient who was being talked about in his presence. "He is your brother," Sabra had said. Well, legally, he guessed. Brothers and sisters weren't supposed to be twenty-five or twenty-six years apart, of different races, and total strangers to each other. Siblings weren't supposed to be surprises, not like this, anyway. Every minute would be a new step. If this was some kind of surrogate parenting, he had a lot to learn. At least he didn't have to potty train.

Sabra played with Mei, read to her, and sang some children's songs with her. She clearly wanted this last day before their separation to be pleasant for Mei. After three hours of the visit, Sabra reached her limit of strength. It was time for the meager dinner she would be able to eat, time for Kevin and Mei to leave.

"Give me a hug and kiss goodbye, Mei darling," Sabra asked. Mei obeyed, unwillingly; she was getting hungry, cranky, and uninterested in anything to do with Kevin. "goodbye, Mei. Please do what Kevin and CeeCee ask you to."

Kevin wondered how it was going to work—a five-year-old being requested to go along, happily, with the demands of two strangers. Sabra had a lot of faith in her ability to request the best of people and get it. Four decades of disappointment in that arena had not changed her mind.

Sabra did not seem to communicate, perhaps did not want to tell him, very much of who Mei really was. In fact, her vagueness, even about Mei's daily habits, started to gnaw at him. Questions swirled in Kevin's mind, questions he would never have thought about forty-eight hours prior. What was life in the orphanage like? How long did Mei live there? Did Mei ever have contact with her real parents before Sabra took over her life? What memories did she have, shrouded in her first language? What had happened in the early days of her life in the U.S., with Sabra? Mei was a blank slate to him. Well, they were equals in that regard. He was a blank slate to parenting—and that's what he was, a parent, no matter how Sabra tried to color it.

Felicity texted she would be back at Sabra's home by 6:00 and bring take-out of any variety Kevin desired; he asked for a pizza and salads. Their dinner together was subdued. Kevin didn't have much to say. Mei pointed out she didn't like meat on her pizza and Felicity gently pulled off the sausage pieces to suit her. Felicity mentioned she enjoyed a day to herself, browsing antique stores and gift shops, picking up some Christmas gifts for her family, and spending some time in a coffee shop just reading a magazine. Kevin knew she worked harder and longer hours than he did. He didn't push her for details. She presented Mei with a child-sized, inexpensive necklace she had found in one of the gift shops. She hooked it behind Mei's neck and guided her to a mirror to see how pretty it looked. For the first time in hours, Mei smiled, something she had yet to do for her new big brother. Best of all, Felicity offered to help Mei with her bath. Bathing a child had not occurred to Kevin.

He received a call from his Aunt Linda at 10:00 p.m. She'd arranged a flight for Monday morning. She assured him she'd talked to Sabra for a half hour earlier that evening. Linda always seemed to forget the two-hours' time difference between Denver and the East Coast. Linda committed to helping transition Sabra to hospice care in her home, but before that she would use every argument she could to convince Sabra to take treatments. "I'll be there with her a while," she promised. "As long as it . . . might take."

"Thank you, Aunt Linda," he said. "I'll be back on Friday evening. You are saving my life and sanity."

He never heard from Marjorie.

Chapter 15

On Sunday morning Kevin faced the task, with Felicity's help, of negotiating with Mei on what she could take to Charlotte and what would need to be left. Mei had acclimated from the orphanage, where she probably had very little, to the U.S., where Sabra had managed to ensure Mei was surrounded with the common cultural items of American capitalism and five-year-old-ness. Pink clothes with happy figures, tennis shoes with flashing lights in the soles, multi-colored ribbons and bows for her silky hair. Sabra clearly had fun buying for and accessorizing the petite, accepting Mei. What were those early days here like for her? Strange, in every way, but also probably paradise to her young mind.

Mei insisted on dressing herself on Sunday morning. She wanted to surprise Felicity with her choices. When she emerged from her room Mei had truly picked her own clothes. A striped blue and white skirt and a green, short-sleeved pullover top with pink flowers, little purple socks—everything about her was tiny and delicate—and untied sneakers whose lighted soles bounced around the room. She looked, well, cute and silly, and the adults stifled a laugh, especially when they realized her top was on backwards.

The amount of stuff related to a child had overwhelmed him, but Felicity seemed unsurprised and undaunted. Still, she left it to him to make the decisions and do the packing; she contented herself with asking Mei about her favorite items, sounding like an interviewer on a daytime talk show. After the fact, Kevin realized she was distracting the child from getting in his way. At the same time, he wondered if Felicity was sending an unspoken message for him to hear loudly and clearly: "I'll help you navigate this mess, and I know it's overwhelming you, but don't assume I'm a permanent babysitter or even thinking about co-parenting."

After four hours of the packing, Kevin was exhausted, and puzzled about why; it wasn't exactly physical work. They ate grilled cheese sandwiches for lunch, since Mei chose that and since there was really little in the house to eat other than multigrain bread and organic vegetarian cheese slices. Apparently Sabra's sudden diagnosis diminished her ability to manage the household well, and the full kitchen trash can bore the signs of several nights of take-out. The dirty clothes hamper was full, but only with Sabra's clothes and household linens. Kevin realized at that moment whatever strength Sabra had in the last few weeks had gone to caring for Mei, getting her to school and keeping her fed and clean. All of Mei's clothes hung neatly in the closet or lay folded in the drawers. Before leaving, Kevin made sure the garbage was ready for pickup so it would not greet Linda with smells and flies.

After lunch Kevin loaded four boxes of Mei's clothes and items she insisted on taking—a lamp with a Disney princess figure on it, some books, her electronics, her bedspread—and still managed to get his and Felicity's luggage in the trunk of his Acura. Installing the car seat was more complicated than he would have thought. He knew eventually he would be bringing every item in Mei's bedroom back with them. But she accepted that for this trip they would have to leave some things at home. He satisfied himself Mei would have enough of her belongings to feel comforted in the absence of her momma.

Kevin packed Mei's documents into his professional satchel he kept in the car. He made a mental note he would need to sit down soon and go through them meticulously, but later. Forty-eight hours before his life had taken a sharp left turn. Right now he couldn't think much about it. There was too much to do.

After Mei crawled into her car seat and snapped herself in, he took one last glance at his mother's house and sighed. He entered his car.

"Are you ready?" he asked Felicity.

"Sure. Let's do this," she answered, as if they were getting ready to zipline. He remembered she had played volleyball in college on scholarship, and sometimes that enthusiastic athlete persona exuded from her. Of all the women he'd dated or been involved with, Felicity came closest to that delicate balance of intelligent, fun loving, warm, and level headed he thought he wanted in a long-term partner. For most women he'd known, he could check off one or two of those boxes. Felicity had four checkmarks by her name. Too bad checkmarks didn't really mean anything.

Chapter 16

After they had driven for ten minutes, Kevin checked to see that Mei had drifted off to sleep in her car seat. Assured their conversation would not register with Mei, he began the script he had been planning for the last 24 hours.

"I can't thank you enough. This was not what I expected when we planned the trip. Needless to say."

"I got that impression really fast," Felicity responded slowly. She seemed to want to step around the land mines in their relationship as much as he did.

"We have two elephants in the car to talk about."

"Maybe three or four." Her voice sounded firm, as if she were ready to tackle what lay between them, and to do it before they reached Charlotte.

So he began. "I need to say this, even if it sounds totally self-absorbed. Before we came, when we decided to come together, I really had absolutely no idea about–all this. About Mei, or Sabra's cancer. Or her plan to make me the guardian. It's important for me that you know that and believe me. I'm walking through this like a zombie. I don't have a clue. So, every minute, everything you did, well, I owe you. Big time, for years and years."

"I did what any friend would do. It's bad enough your mom is dying. I don't know what to think about her decision not to get treatment. I'm not in a position to comment on that—"

"I know. It's sad, strange, frustrating, all those words. I can't figure it out. I would think with Mei to take care of, she would fight this. Maybe Linda will help Mom change her mind and it won't be too late. The cancer is, apparently, really aggressive. I don't pretend to understand that."

"I do, a little bit," she said. "I come from a big family, both sides, so we've faced it. Cancer treatment isn't pretty, but it works. At least for a while, most of the time. There's usually hope."

"Yes. All I can figure is Sabra is in a pretty bad depression and doesn't even realize it. She always fixed other people's problems, or thought she did. I don't believe she sees her own mental state."

"Can I ask you a question?" she twisted her body in the seat so she could look at him.

He glanced at her. Felicity was attractive. Not beautiful, but a real, healthy, strong-featured woman. "Uh, sure."

"Why do you call your mother by her name?"

"I—don't know. Don't a lot of people call their parents by their first names when they get to be in their twenties?"

"Not really. Nobody I know, except you."

"Okay. I can stop."

"That's not really the point, Kevin. I think—it means something."

"Probably. Like I said before, it has always been complicated with my mother. Now it's much more complicated. Obviously." He paused in his speech to take an exit that would lead them to Charlotte. "Maybe I don't think she's been much of a mother in several years. No, that's harsh. We've just grown apart and I see her as another adult."

"You wouldn't agree to take over the raising the child of just any other adult."

"True." He looked back at Mei, who managed to sleep with her head in an awkward, uncomfortable position, puppet-like. Their silence grew too long. "Anyway, thanks a lot for this weekend and helping. I would have been lost without you."

"Sure." She readjusted herself in her seat and stared forward. "I think I need to tell you something before this ride is over."

He could feel his stomach tighten. This was the "I don't want to see you again" speech, although Felicity could be trusted to do it with some class. "Okay."

"First, I was married before."

This was not at all what he expected. "Oh." He tried to make it sound neutral but interested, accepting but not nosy, and most of all, not shocked. Although he was shocked, and a little perturbed for a few seconds. Why had she never brought it up before in their months of casual dating?

"Yes. Right out of college, at 23, I married. College sweetheart, sort of. We had a big wedding. It all seemed great. I worked for a couple of years, and Todd had a decent job in investments, like I did in financial services, but with different firms. We were going to buy a house."

Kevin listened. He didn't want to say, "So what happened?" He wasn't going to say anything because nothing would come out right.

"Anyway. I got pregnant. It was all perfect." Clearly, whatever perfection Felicity and Todd had lived in disappeared. "Until I had a miscarriage at four months."

"I'm so-sorry."

"Yes. I know. It's hard for anyone to understand the miscarriage 'thing'—I don't know what to call it. One book I read called it a journey. That doesn't work because you don't go anywhere. You are stuck. In grief and confusion and . . . anger."

She paused. He knew she tried to stifle tears, but they were coming out. "So Todd and I went through all that. I waited. In seven months I was pregnant again. I wasn't ready. But it didn't matter. I miscarried that baby at three months."

"Felicity. If I had known what would happen this weekend, and about your—struggle, I never would have asked you--"

"No. No, Kevin. I'm not—this isn't about your mom, or Mei, or this weekend. I should have told you sooner, but we haven't been dating that long, and it's not the kind of thing—I don't talk about it much. Ever. Even with close friends from back then. I had a couple of years of therapy; I was distraught, clinically depressed for a long time. Especially after Todd just couldn't—he couldn't handle my grief any more, and I wasn't able to help him with his, and he asked for a divorce. What was I going to do? I was twenty-seven, I didn't know anything. I could barely function. Somehow I got out of bed and went to the office and put on a face for eight hours and then came home and lay on the couch staring at the TV or the walls for hours until I feel asleep."

So that was the elephant in the car she spoke of. An inadequate metaphor for Felicity's truth. He couldn't guess, not fully, why she chose now to tell him, but would there ever be a better time?

"It took me a year after the divorce to get back on my feet. Then decided to get my MBA. I poured myself into schooling and getting a job that would pay me as much as possible. I didn't care about the long hours, since childbirth seemed to be out of the question for me and I certainly wasn't interested in men after that. So here I am. Thirty-one. Well-paid. Well-educated. Childless and divorced. I'm not a mess any more. I got through it. But I don't want to go through it again. Ever. Whatever it means, losing two children is my limit. I don't believe I can ever put myself in that situation again."

Those words were final. This weekend—the trip, Sabra, Mei, packing, cancer—had acted like a catalyst on their relationship. The natural processes of self-disclosure and revelations had sped up and she was telling him now her deepest pain. She wasn't saying it, not loudly or bluntly, but undoubtedly. If he somehow thought Mei would bind her to him, that she would be more drawn to marriage with Kevin because of a ready-made family and an adorable Chinese child, if some motherly instinct would be ignited in Felicity to make her want to consider Kevin as a husband--then, no, that "if" had no basis. Yes, she was breaking up with him, but she had at least given him good reasons, reasons that had nothing to do with him. It was not because she was horrified by the idea of her boyfriend now having custody of a child he'd never met before. It was because she could not bear motherhood; it was because she would see her lost children in five-year-old Mei, who was about the age her older miscarried baby would be now.

He realized he had not spoken in a while. She had emptied her heart and pain and he was driving, yes, like a zombie. "Felicity. I don't know what to say. I'm so sorry. I really wish now I hadn't put you through this. It was not my plan. That's all I can say. I'm really sorry."

"No, Kevin. No blame. And I know what you're thinking, this is the kiss-off, that I'm dumping you. That's not it. I just want to be friends, if that's possible. For one thing, Mei has—well, she likes me. More than you, I think."

"No doubt about that. She doesn't like men, and I don't think she can figure out this white guy can be her brother."

"And I like her. I've connected with her, maybe a little. It would just be wrong for me to disappear from her life right now. She needs some stability, and you need help. I'm part of this. I just can't be--"

"I understand. I appreciate it. Whatever, however you feel like you want to be part of this new arrangement, this brother-parent-guardian-I don't know what thing I'm expected to do, you're welcome in."

"Thank you."

He drove for a few minutes. Mei roused. Her eyes tried to focus and figure out where she was and with whom. "I'm thirsty."

"We can stop and get some iced tea or something. I'm thirsty too," said Kevin.

"That would be nice," Felicity answered.

He pulled over into a fast-food restaurant. It didn't matter they were within twenty miles of Felicity's apartment. Mei wanted something, and for now, he would do whatever he could to satisfy her needs and wants. Even more, the air was clear between Felicity and Kevin. They could move on with real boundaries. He had lost a regular Tuesday evening date, a girlfriend, a possible fiancée and wife. But maybe he had gained something else.

Chapter 17

At 2:45, Kevin dropped Felicity at her apartment building. She lived in a renovated building in the downtown area. After decades of decline, her area was gentrifying and now qualified out as one of *the* places to live. Her address testified to the fact she made more money than he, as would be expected—a financial services consultant's salary for the second largest firm in the country compared to the pay of an executive director of a gallery, even the oldest and most storied in the city. She gave him a hug goodbye. "Call me in a day or so. Or I'll call you. I can eat dinner with you two sometime later in the week. I mean it."

He knew she did. He decided his texts from now on would be informational and friendly, rather than persuasive and bordering on intimate.

It took twenty minutes to pull up to his apartment complex in the residential area near the gallery. After unpacking the boxes, he planned to take Mei to IKEA for a bed and a dresser. His basically bare second bedroom currently housed only an office desk, swivel chair, and computer. Eventually, those would have to be moved elsewhere. For now, Mei needed a place to sleep and a way to keep her clothes organized.

He congratulated himself on having held on to the pickup truck he drove in college. He kept a cover over it and paid an extra fee each month for the parking space, but it came in handy for outdoor events and hauling. Today its service was needed—somehow he had to get two child-sized pieces of furniture home.

The IKEA trip on late Sunday afternoon taxed his patience, between the crowds and Mei's stating adamantly she wanted a bed with Elsa's picture on it.

"Who is Elsa? I don't know Elsa," answered Kevin.

"She in movie. *Frozen*. She pretty."

Kevin still didn't know who Elsa was. An actress? A cartoon character?

"Your bed at home didn't have a picture on it."

"Momma say she get me one for Christmas."

"Christmas? It's not time for Christmas yet."

"I want Elsa on my bed."

Kevin wondered how Mei had learned so quickly to expect and demand pop culture references to surround her. He got down on one knee to talk to her face-to-face.

"This store doesn't sell beds with anybody's picture on them. I tell you what, let's buy this bed here," he pointed to a basic twin frame fitted with a simple mattress—"it's the right size for you. We'll get a picture of Ella--"

"Elsa!"

"Okay, Elsa, we'll get her picture somewhere, and put it at the top and the bottom, and you can pick out the picture yourself. How's that?"

"When?"

"Soon. Let's just buy this furniture and get out of here."

Mei decided to comply this time, although he wasn't sure why. The furniture purchased and loaded, he drove home, stopping on the way at a big box hardware store to pick up a screwdriver and hammer to assemble Mei's new possessions. He also drove through a Wendy's to pick up sandwiches for dinner. Eventually, he'd have to learn to cook—or something—to ensure more nourishment for Mei than restaurant food.

For her part, Mei liked sitting in the front seat of the truck's high cab, since there was no back seat, the place children were always relegated. "It's a good thing she's small and can barely see over the window," he mused. "Maybe I won't get pulled over for having a child without a legal seat. I don't even really know the laws about these things." If he were pulled over, the cop might question why he had an Asian five-year-old with him and why he didn't restrain her correctly. He carried her documents with him in case there was a question, but he hoped he wouldn't have to explain. Yet. There would be enough of that in the next few days.

Assembling the bed was as frustrating as he'd heard people claim, and he decided the dresser could wait a while. Mei fell asleep by 8:00, satisfied when he printed out two pictures of the blonde Disney character from his computer and taped them to the headboard and footboard of the child-sized bed. Kevin pointed the remote at the TV and watched ten minutes of a football game before succumbing to sleep himself.

He awoke thirty minutes later, startled. Something felt wrong—he remembered he was not alone in the apartment. Then he remembered his mother. Yes, it was late, but he'd promised to call. Her hospital room phone rang seven times before she answered. "Hello."

"Mom. It's me."

"Oh, Kevin."

"Yeah. Listen, it's all good. Mei's asleep. I got her a kid's bed and dresser at IKEA."

"Is she happy?"

"No, but she's not complaining. As long as I obey her every command."

"Don't talk like that, Kevin."

"Don't worry. I'm kidding. Sort of. She doesn't talk to me except to ask for things, all of which she gets. I think she's got me figured out."

"What about tomorrow?"

"I'll have to spend some time at the office dealing with paperwork to take some leave time. Then I'll see about school for her. That's enough for one day." And he thought, I'll look into hiring a nanny, but he didn't say so to his mother. She would have an opinion about it.

Anyway, he could tell the phone call itself was a burden for her.

"All right."

"Are you—okay? How are you feeling?"

"Not good. Very tired. Nauseated."

"Nauseated?"

"I don't want to eat."

"Isn't there a pill for that? Or a form of marijuana?"

"Probably." He heard her sigh. "Linda is coming. Not Marjorie. Of course. How selfish can a person be? Oh, well."

"Mom--"

"Yes?"

He wanted to say many things. He was doing the best he could, but he knew it wasn't enough, and he wished he could be there for her. He wished the last ten or so years had been different. He wanted her to take every treatment they could throw at her and beat the cancer, and he didn't understand her decision, and he didn't have a clue what to do with Mei and why she put him in his situation. He wanted to rant, and he wanted to plead. His pause went on too long.

"Kevin?"

"I, uh, I love you. I'll call tomorrow."

"All right. Thank you, Kevin. Good night." Her voice trailed off, and he heard the receiver drop onto the base of the phone.

Chapter 18

At 6:30 his alarm sounded and woke him from a deep sleep that had taken a while to sink into the night before. He got his bearings—oh, no—what about the little girl in his apartment—Mei—where was she?

He pulled on sweatpants and hurried to her room. She sat there looking at one of her picture books, telling herself a story in a language he didn't understand. He didn't even know if she spoke Mandarin or Cantonese or some other dialect.

"Mei—you're up! Are you okay?"

She looked up at him from her book. Was that judgment? "You sleep long time. Momma not sleep long time. She always up when I up."

"I know, Mei. I won't let this happen again." He guessed he'd have to set his alarm for 5:30.

"We have to get dressed and eat breakfast and go this morning," he said.

"I go to my school."

"Not today. We're going to find a new school for you."
He tried to make it sound like an adventure.

"Why new school? I like my school. My teacher pretty and nice."

"We'll find you another nice and pretty teacher here. You're going to live with me now."

"I don't like."

"I know, but we've talked about this. Remember?"

She eyed him disapprovingly. While her English was rudimentary, she seemed to understand—when she wanted to. "I don't like."

"Well, me neither," he said. "Can you dress yourself?"

"What clothes?"

"You can pick. Like a big girl. I'll put some breakfast on the table for you and you can eat while I get ready."

She gave him one of those suspicious looks again. His annoyance started to grow, but he checked himself—something he was getting used to doing. Why shouldn't she be suspicious of him, of this situation? Who wouldn't be?

Kevin dreaded this Monday morning. First, because he always dreaded Mondays. Second, he couldn't shake the uneasiness of having a miniature person in his apartment, especially a female one. Third, he had three mammoth goals, so this morning felt like the starting line of a marathon. He had to explain to his supervisor, the chairman of the gallery's board, what was going on. Then enroll Mei in school, and third, start to find some sort of part-time nanny or childcare worker.

He rushed to the bathroom and hurried through a shower, shave, and dressing. Holding a conversation with himself in the mirror, he thought out loud about how he was going to explain his needed absences over the next month or more. He rehearsed his explanation to the board chairman a few times while getting ready. A mother with cancer was enough for Family Medical Leave Act time off. Custody of a new child, too. Both at once would be hard to explain, and he hoped to dodge any too-invasive questions.

Of course, being the only male on staff at the Gallery, other than custodians, meant clucking, concerned women surrounded him. He knew he would get plenty of sympathy after the initial shock. The women would bombard him with advice and probably want to bombard him with help. He'd seen their generosity at showers for female coworkers about to deliver babies—showers for which he bought gift cards and where he had stuck his head in the door to say hello, where he had grabbed some food, and which he had otherwise avoided. He promised himself he would not take advantage of the motherly types who worked in accounting and human resources. Although it would be tempting . . .

He would say to the Chairman of the Board his mother had been diagnosed with terminal cancer. He now had custody of his mother's adopted child (the concept of Mei as his sister didn't fit any categories in his brain yet), and he would have to take time off, not constantly, but when needed. He estimated it would result in part-time hours for as long as it took, and he would have to spend time on weekends in Fayetteville, if not during the week. That meant he would have to miss any events or openings on the weekends for now.

So he had a spiel. He'd been at the Gallery long enough to have accumulated the time off. It was just going to be difficult to balance making everyone in his world happy, a responsibility he had never considered before.

He couldn't help thinking about Felicity. Although he didn't let her know, he found himself deeply disappointed with her "define the relationship talk" on the ride home and not a little depressed. Even so, he had no time to reflect on it.

Like the day before, Mei's fashion choices made him stifle a laugh. She liked stripes with flowered prints, olive greens combined with lilacs and bright orange. She showed individuality, he decided, even if she'd bought into the Disney Princess mythos. As always, her sneakers' soles glittered with every step. At least the Velcro closures meant they could postpone learning to tie laces. However, he'd have to teach her this morning how to tell the front of a shirt from the back. Kevin's sense of style wanted to turn the top around, but his fear of physical contact with Mei held him back.

"Mei, honey," he said, echoing his grandma Timothy, the most Southern of Southern grandmas. "I'm glad you can dress yourself. But you need to turn your top around. The tag goes in the back, on your neck, you know, below your hair."

Instead of complying, she said, "I like this way."

"We are going to visit your new school. Don't you want it to look like it's supposed to?"

She made a face, but his argument worked. "I change." She stomped into her room. She emerged with a different top, one even busier and more clashing, but with the tag in the back.

He breathed a sigh of relief. He won a little skirmish and so far, he had not touched her. He did not plan to. He did not plan to help her bathe, to see her dress, to help her with the bathroom. All that was off-limits. He did not want her to say or imply, by mistake or innocently, to anyone at her school, or elsewhere, "Kevin saw me naked." Suspicion of possible child abuse was the one contingency Sabra had not thought through when she willed Mei to him. On Saturday evening, Felicity, sensing his discomfort, had volunteered to help Mei with her evening bath—another thing he owed her for. But she would not be around now.

The entire existence of a five-year-old female child in his apartment was fraught with problems; in fact, he wondered when he would have to answer to someone for Mei's presence in his home, despite the ample paperwork in his briefcase. For now, each step was careful. At some point, he knew he'd have to pick her up and carry her to bed when she fell asleep in the car, but that would be the limit of physical contact. She would want to sit close to him on the couch and watch television. But he couldn't. And that lack of touch would be bad for Mei; she would crave touch from someone, and it couldn't be from him.

All these thoughts made him angry. Anger made him tired and added to his depression over Felicity's setting of boundaries. And anger wheeled back around to Sabra, and then distorted into guilt that his first concern was not his dying mother.

Chapter 19

By 8:00, his usual time to leave his apartment and begin to fight Charlotte's traffic to reach the Gallery by 8:30, he was on the road with Mei in the back seat. Moms in the U.S. must feel like chauffeurs, he thought. He'd never driven with just one other companion occupying the back seat. Mei needed only to command, "Home, James," to make the feeling complete. Instead, she said, "Where we go?"

"To my work," Kevin answered.

"I want to go to school."

"We will after I go to work, Mei. First things first."

"No. School first."

"Mei," he glanced at her in the rear-view mirror. "Sometimes you will have to do what I say, all right?"

She looked at him passively. He wondered if she was thinking, "Maybe for now, until I get you trained," and he had to smile at the thought.

"What is this place?" She said when they parked at the Gallery. "This my school?"

"No, this is my job. My work. We have to go in here. I will show you the pretty pictures here."

"Can I draw?"

"Yes, there is a place you can draw." That might work, he thought. Put her in the children's section, a small room doubling as studio and classroom, with a generous variety of art supplies. Beyond serving as a community education space, it entertained kids who got bored while their parents toured the gallery. Kids could try to copy some of the famous but more simple works, or they could express themselves, whatever that meant.

They entered by the main door with his key card and passcode. The Gallery opened to the public at 9:00 a.m., although visitors were rare at that time. To the immediate right was the reception desk to the 33,000-foot facility. To the left, a thirty-foot glass panel separated the administrative offices from the rest of space. Kevin, despite Mei's presence, felt the familiar surge of contentment and authority as he passed down the hall to his office. The Fordyce's spacious, clean lines stood as a symbol of the modernist art in its third floor collection. The light colors throughout, mostly in the robin's egg blue to soft maroon range, led the eye to its French and American Impressionists on the second floor. The first floor housed its visiting collections and new acquisitions he, as the Director, in collaboration with the board and the curator, wanted to spotlight. The Picasso sketches would soon be among them. The design made it a beautiful and serene place to work and helped a little with allaying the stress of running the Gallery's staff, development, and acquisitions.

His staff consisted of a full-time curator and one part-time assistant, one educational liaison, one marketing director, and five office administrators and clerical workers. After depositing his briefcase on his desk, he called the educational liaison, Amelia, an energetic recent art graduate from NC State who was willing to work at a pitiful salary to get a start.

"Amelia, I have a big favor to ask you this morning. Are you super busy?"

"No," she laughed. "This is the slow day. Tomorrow I've got a first grade class coming in. It's good you're asking today."

"Great. If you could come on down, I'll explain what I need."

He thumbed through the messages and work placed on his desk by his own administrative assistant, Naomi Sutton. In two minutes, Amelia was at the door. Amelia was the kind of young woman he would want to date if she weren't an employee and weren't eight years younger than he. In the back of his mind he thought of Felicity, feeling guilty over thinking of another woman and then remembering Felicity had sort of, in a very nice way, called it quits.

"Good morning, Amelia. I'd like you to meet Mei. Mei, this is Amelia. She works here and helps children learn about pretty pictures."

Mei took in the attractive young woman. "Hello." Was that a smile? He thought. It was Mei's first in a morning of scowls and complaints.

"Shake hands with Amelia, Mei."

Amelia didn't attempt to hide her surprised expression. "Oh, hello, Mei." She reached out to shake Mei's delicate, stretched out hand. At least she understood that etiquette, thought Kevin.

"Mei is staying with me for . . . a while." He didn't want to get into explanations the first day with an employee. "Could you let her have access to the educational room and draw for the next, oh, hour or so, while I deal with some business here? Then I'm leaving for the rest of the day to take care of personal matters."

Amelia recognized this as a non-negotiable assignment couched in polite language. "Absolutely," she nodded vigorously. She turned to her new charge. "Mei, I have some really fun things for you to look at and do in my classroom."

"Are you a teacher? Is this school?"

"No, Mei," said Kevin, "but we can pretend like it is for now. Please go with Amelia."

At work, Kevin had to speak in formal, controlled, and distant ways to Mei; he knew within five minutes the staff would be texting each other about him, the little

Asian girl he'd brought to work, what was going on, and whether it was appropriate to have a child with him when it really violated policy.

With Mei taken care of temporarily, he called the Human Resources manager, Faith Kowalski, and asked for a meeting as soon as possible. She could see him immediately, and he said he would come to her space.

"Faith," he said. "Good morning. I'm glad you can see me so quickly."

"You're the boss."

"That's true, but I'm sort of in a situation here and need to deal with some things fast. I need to do the paperwork for FMLA leave for, well, let's say two months for now. Then I'll talk to the chairman of the board and explain what's going on. I'll work part-time hours for now. I know it might affect my salary at some point, but I'll cross that bridge if I have to."

"Sure, Kevin," Faith, a middle-aged woman whose knowledge of employment law was greater than her pay indicated. "May I ask, what's . . .."

He explained, unemotionally, what his last 72 hours had involved. Faith's mouth dropped open slightly as he revealed more details.

"I'm so sorry about your mother, Kevin," she said. "That's just, my goodness, terrible for you. What a tragic thing to go through."

"Thank you, Faith. I'm in a bind right now. I've got to find a school and some kind of backup care for the little girl and a bunch of other things."

"I'll fill out the paperwork right now," she said. "Do you have an hour before you need to leave? You'll need to sign it."

"Yes, that'll be great. Give me a call when it's ready. I appreciate it."

He left, wondering what the flying texts said now.

An hour later, before 10 a.m., he signed the forms and promised to get any needed documentation from Sabra's healthcare providers sent by fax or email as soon as possible. He called the Chairman of the Board and explained his position, giving several promises and assurances he would be in Charlotte most of the time. Relieved to hang up the phone, he prepared to fetch Mei from the educational room.

Amelia had done her magic. "See?" Mei showed him her artwork, far more than a coloring sheet. Sparkling paint, stickers, stamped images, and her childish signature adorned a once-crisp 17X17 card stock. Kevin wasn't sure what she had tried to create, but Amelia helped.

"I showed her this landscape," Amelia pointed to an oil painting from, Kevin guessed, the 1800s, "and told her to imagine a story there," she explained. "Mei, can you tell us about your story?"

"A little girl found horse near the water and rided it. It is pretty horse, and strong. The horse and girl went to her momma's house. The momma was better and not sick no more."

"Thank you, Mei," said Amelia. "Thank you for sharing your story and picture."

Kevin noticed Amelia refrained from judgments on Mei's work, but decided Mei needed a little more from him. "Me, too, Mei. I like it. Very much. You did a good job."

She glared at him. "I draw it for *Momma.*" The emphasis on the last word was not a childish mistake. Kevin had no part in her inspiration.

"Of course you did. We'll take it to her soon."

"Your momma will like it, Mei," added Amelia.

"Say goodbye to Miss Amelia. We have to go now."

"Goodbye, Mizz Ameya." She waved and seemed content to leave without a fuss or even a scowl. Kevin whispered a thank you to Amelia as he left. He then breathed a thank you for small favors to whoever else was listening.

Mei followed him and consented without being asked to hold his hand in the parking lot.

"Where we go now?"

"To find you a school," he said as if they would shop for tennis shoes. Inside, he realized he didn't have a clue what he was doing.

Chapter 20

Cornerstone Primary School was located two miles from his apartment complex and was, according to its website, the school zoned for his address. Granted, he would have preferred a private school, but that was out of the question right now. One, the expense, and two, the access—the good ones had waitlists, and the school year had already started. A quick Internet search told him Cornerstone was rated highly by a couple of state and national associations purporting to rate public schools. It claimed healthy teacher/student ratios, and the city provided school bus service to his apartment complex. Not that he would entrust the tiny and confused Mei to a public school bus any time soon; he'd have to drive her and pick her up for now.

The visit to the school to enroll Mei meant another long explanation, this time with an official-looking, no-nonsense, middle-aged woman. Selma Martinez, the Vice Principal, or so her name badge said, emerged from her office after he asked the receptionist in the large, bustling office about how to enroll a child in school.

"Yes. I'm the Vice Principal. How can I help you?"

"I need to enroll this child in Pre-Kindergarten." He gestured to Mei. "Her name is Mei Timothy." This was a new world for him. Talking to his HR manager was one thing. The manner and official badge of Selma Martinez made him feel like a child in, well, the vice-principal's office again.

"Very good. Can you come into my office to discuss the matter?"

"Sure." In order to maneuver the counters and furniture of the sprawling office, he had to be buzzed through a waist-high door, with Mei following behind. She clutched a small stuffed bear to her chest. For the first time, he saw real fear on her face. She appeared terrified by her surroundings. Perhaps she realized she was in the principal's office and had already learned that was the last place in school a child wanted to find herself.

"Please have a seat," she pointed, and Mei wiggled into a chair beside him as he sat. "First, Mr.--"

"My name is Kevin Elcott, Ms. Martinez. So, the first question is, I know, what is my relationship to this little girl? That's complicated, but it's all legal and I'll explain. Here are her papers and the documents giving me custody of Mei." He reached into his briefcase and passed over the already worn-looking folder.

He let her examine them for as long as it took.

"So, you are—"

"Mei's legal guardian. In my mother's eyes, I'm her older brother, but that's not my particular view. I'm her guardian. I'm the only adult—the only healthy adult—in her life. To make a long story short, my mother was recently, very recently, diagnosed with terminal cancer, and she's asked me to take care of Mei. It's like I say, complicated, and odd, I know, but legal, and the child is in no danger. All this is totally new to me, and unusual, I understand. I'd like her to be in school as soon as possible, for a number of reasons."

"I see," Ms. Martinez. She appeared to be only ten years older than he but exuded an old-school manner. She turned to Mei. "Mei, how old are you?"

"Five," she managed to say. She'd been still and polite for the past few minutes. All her self-confidence and power over the adults in her life had disappeared once they walked into Cornerstone Primary School.

"She's been in pre-kindergarten, you say? She's old enough for kindergarten, according to her birth certificate."

"Her English is, well, kind of basic. She's been speaking it only about seven or eight months now. And she's small. My mother wants her in Pre-K. I agree."

"That won't be a problem. You understand we will have to look into this." She gestured to the papers to indicate her *this*.

"Why? I have identification. I'm gainfully employed, and all the papers are there. She's not kidnapped or anything."

"I understand, but we will have to make some calls. To her former school in Fayetteville, for one."

"When can she start school?"

"Do you think she's ready for that, considering the trauma in her life now?" Ms. Martinez asked, arching her left eyebrow. He felt himself bristle.

"Yes. She needs stability, and she doesn't need to be following me around all day. Doesn't she have to be in school?"

"Pre-K is not mandatory in this district."

"Either way, it's best for her to be in school."

"Very well," Ms. Martinez said, showing no signs of approval about his arguments. "She can start tomorrow." She turned to her computer and typed. "She'll be in Mr. Benson's class."

"Mr. Benson? The teacher is a guy, I mean, male?"

"Mr. Benson is one of our best. He's young. The children find him energetic, creative, and firm." Kevin truly doubted the five-year-olds articulated these views of their pre-K teacher.

"Mei does better with women, I think. Until me, I think she only dealt with women."

"Obviously, that's going to have to change, Mr. Elcott. Mr. Benson is not a threatening person. We are happy to have him on our faculty."

Kevin had never met a man who taught early elementary schoolchildren, but realized he would need to lay aside his stereotypes. He would prefer a female teacher. "Are there no female teachers available?"

"No," said Ms. Martinez, without explanation.

"Okay, then," he consented, feeling he had no choice. That feeling was becoming familiar.

"Here is a list of supplies she'll need to bring tomorrow," the Vice Principal stated, handing him a photocopied list. "We start the day at 8:00. Pick-up is at 2:00. The Pre-K children get out earlier than the other students. Their lunch is at 11, followed by a rest-time from 11:40-1:00, and then an hour of less focused learning activities. Here is our parent information packet." This time she passed to him a slim bound copy with the school's logo. "It has all the numbers, schedules, holidays, rules, and policies you need to know. Dress code, all that." She turned to observe for the first time Mei's multi-colored and multi-design outfit, and Kevin detected a slight smile, finally. "Do you like lots of colors in your clothes, Mei?"

Mei nodded carefully a few times.

Ms. Martinez looked at her watch, then at the computer screen. "Mr. Benson's class is having their game time in the gym right now. Perhaps we can go meet him briefly."

"That would be great."

"Very well." Without further instructions, she rose from her desk and escorted Kevin and Mei, who insisted on holding his hand and walking close beside him, down the decorated halls Kevin described to himself as "up-beat." He could hear the sound of children shouting and playing as they approached the gym.

A young woman was engaging the five-year-olds in a game that looked like a version of soccer. A burly, bearded young man in his late twenties stood by watching and calling encouragement to selected children. The three of them approached him, and Kevin could read the name "Chad Benson" on his name badge.

"Mr. Benson," Ms. Martinez began. "Tomorrow you will have a new student. This is Mei, Mei Timothy."

"Well, hey there, Mei Timothy," Chad squatted to Mei's level. His exuberant voice, which probably worked for most of his charges, had the opposite effect on Mei. For the first time in four days, she appealed to Kevin for protection. Grasping her stuffed puppy, she leaned into him and seemed ready to hide behind his legs. Her head did not reach Kevin's waist.

"Mei," Kevin gently moved her from her position glued to his right leg. "This is Mr. Benson. He's your new teacher at this school."

"This is school? This my new school?"

"Yes."

"My teacher at other school was a lady. She was pretty," Mei offered as a reminder that he had promised a pretty teacher.

"Oh, I'm not a pretty lady," Chad Benson said. "I'm sorry about that. I'm a man with a beard! But I think you'll have fun in our class just the same. We have a great class. See how much fun the other students are having?" He pointed to the melee on the gym floor. Mei gazed at the soccer players. Six children gathered around the ball trying to pound it with their feet, less concerned with where the ball landed than with the prospect of making contact more frequently than their classmates. The twelve or so others waited for their chance, although a few looked as if they had given up on that possibility.

Mei returned her eyes to him. "Why you have hair on face?"

"Oh, my beard!" He rubbed it. "You know, my wife likes it. Now my wife, she's a pretty lady. Let me show you." He pulled his mobile phone from his back pocket and swiped a few times. "See? Isn't she pretty?"

Mei considered the young redhead's photo. "Yes."

"If you can stop by at the end of the day, we'll talk about Mei," Ms. Martinez said to Chad. "I'll work on getting her records from the school in Fayetteville."

"That'll be great. And you are--" Chad turned to Kevin and offered to shake hands.

"Kevin Elcott. I'm Mei's, uh, guardian. I think Ms. Martinez will explain it. I'm glad to get her into a good school like this so fast."

"Yep, we're a great school. Great parents, too," Chad said, again with exuberance. "I've been here four years since graduating. I love it here."

"I'm glad to hear it," said Kevin. If he had assumed any-thing about a male elementary school teacher, and he had envisioned a cross between Mr. Rogers and Justin Bieber, Chad Benson burst his assumptions. Mr. Benson probably appealed to the little boys, some of whom lacked dads at home, and to little girls who could brag they had a man teacher instead of a plain old lady teacher. And the guy did emanate a type of charisma all his own.

They said their goodbyes and walked back to the main office. Children of various sizes lined up to move, some-where, cajoled by teachers to stay in line and use quiet voices in the hallway. In the office, Ms. Martinez turned him over to a clerical staffer with whom he filled out paperwork. The staffer made copies of all his documents.

Their business at Cornerstone School concluded at almost noon. He found himself exhausted, hungry, and in charge of an even hungrier and now cranky Mei.

"Let's go home now, Mei. It's time for you to have a rest, I think. I need one also."

"I am hungry."

"Me, too."

"I want McDonald's."

"Not today. We had fast food last night, remember?"

"I want McDonald's."

"I know, but not today."

"You mean."

"Maybe. But no McDonald's today."

"When?"

"Later."

"When later?"

What did he expect? Up to this point, her demands had worked. "Listen, Mei. I know you don't understand this, but McDonald's is a corporation that doesn't care about nutrition or your health. They say they do, but it's not true. It's also more expensive to eat out than to eat at home. McDonald's is not for every day. It's for maybe once a week. And not now, later."

Then it hit him. Beyond milk and breakfast cereal, his staple, he had no food in the house. No bread or lunch-meat for sandwiches, no fruit, no meal preparation ingredients.

"When later?" she repeated.

"Now later," he conceded, and started exploring for a McDonald's.

Chapter 21

After Mei got what she wanted, he drove her home and sent her to her room for a nap. She was groggy after the meal and nodded off in the car, so she accepted her fate. He needed to make phone calls to find a nanny.

He remembered an old movie he'd seen once and wasn't sure why—maybe watching it with an old girlfriend sometime in his past--where a career woman had to take custody of a child unexpectedly and found herself interviewing nannies. It was one of those typical "let's laugh at all the weird encounters with even weirder nannies." Who but a slightly desperate woman with no real marketable skills would want to be a nanny anyway? One of Hollywood's hidden messages: only a loser who couldn't get another job would want to take care of someone else's children for a living.

And that would have been his view until some friends had children. He wised up to the need for young professionals who became parents to have reliable childcare. "Nanny" was probably an outdated term for what he wanted: a responsible young woman, probably a part-time college student, with flexible hours to pick up Mei from school and watch her until he could come home, which at times might be later in the evening. He also recognized he needed someone willing to work for something slightly higher than minimum wage while fulfilling the important job of caring for a young life.

How hard could it be to find someone like that?

Who was he kidding?

Like anyone his age, Kevin started on the Internet to find a caregiver for Mei, who by 1:00 was fast asleep after a morning that stressed Kevin but probably confused, exhausted, and terrified her. He learned a great deal in the first five minutes. There were national organizations that accredited caregiving services companies; there were national brands of child caregiving services that licensed franchisees; there were lots of levels of caregiving services (both in quality and price), and there were services specializing in types of children or types of caregivers. There was even one called College Students Who Nanny. He wondered if that was supposed to be clever, rather than a lame play on words. Its ratings were high, so he started with it.

He learned he could apply to receive their services online or at their office in the suburbs of Charlotte, but since he would have to provide all sorts of documentation, it would make more sense to come to the location. He asked how long it would take to hire someone. The receptionists answered vaguely. "We have to do background checks on the parent. That takes a week or more. During that time, you will have to come in and let us get to know your child so we can assign the best fit for him or her."

"So, you interview us?"

"Well, not exactly, but--"

"It sounds like an interview to me. I thought I was hiring the nanny. When do I get to interview the prospective caregiver?"

"You get to meet the one assigned to you. If you have any real objections, we will work with you."

"So, let me get this straight. You decide on the caregiver, not me?"

"Ah, I suppose you could put it that way."

"Is this standard operating procedure?"

"It is for College Students Who Nanny. I am not aware of how other companies would handle the process."

"I'll get back to you, then, thanks," he said and hung up.

Hoping for something better, where he called some of the shots, he moved on to the next company, Nanny Services, Inc. Its Internet ratings were essentially the same. He knew those ratings could be manipulated, so he dug deeper and found satisfactory information. He punched in their number.

"Nanny Services. How may I help you?"

"I'd like to know about your procedures for hiring a nanny."

"Sir, let me direct your call to our client services coordinator."

So far, so good. After a few clicks, another female voice spoke.

"Client services."

"Yes, I need to hire a part-time, on-site caregiver for my, um, child." That didn't sound right, but they didn't need to know his life story.

"If you would like to hire a nanny, we suggest you come in to fill out the application, have a meeting with the coordinator, and then after the paperwork and background checks are completed, we will ask you to meet with three possibilities best suited to your need."

"That's more like it. How long does it usually take?"

"If you can come in this afternoon, we can begin the process. I can't promise a specific date, but it's usually five to seven business days."

"Thank you. I'll probably call back in a few minutes for an appointment."

Kevin called Charlotte Child Caregivers, even though their fees were double what he expected to pay. The website implied their clientele were highly paid, double-income professional couples, and it smacked a little too much of elitism. He could take elitism when he had to for work, but . . . he'd pass for now. Nanny Services, Inc., made the cut, at least this Monday. He called back and set a 3:00 appointment.

While Mei finished her nap, he ordered $200 worth of groceries online from Publix and scheduled a delivery for 6:00, when he hoped he'd be on his way to hiring help with parenting.

Mei wandered into his living room, holding her blanket, while he finished his grocery order.

"I'm thirsty."

"I'll get you a glass of water."

"I want orange juice."

"All right." Her wish is my command, he thought. But, she's been a trooper today. I have to remember this is a trauma for her and she's doing the best she can.

He poured her a small cup of juice. "If you want more, let me know." She sipped it slowly, observing him quietly over the cup rim as he moved around the kitchen and living room.

Finally she announced, "I want to talk to Momma." That was an improvement. She didn't say, "See Momma." "I talk to her on the phone."

He checked his watch. Linda wouldn't be there until later that evening, flying into Charlotte from Denver, and then renting a car for the drive to Fayetteville. Linda, an independent traveler, could handle it. He could have offered to meet her at the airport, but that would have meant one more thing to squeeze into an already impossible day.

"Okay." He punched in the right numbers to Sabra's cell phone, hoping she had it on, and turned on the speakerphone. It rang until the voicemail came on.

Mei looked at him quizzically, as if wondering why her mother's voice was speaking to her but not using Mei's name. "That's not her, Mei. Let me try another number." This time he punched in the hospital room and after six rings, Sabra's diminished voice, unusually low-pitched, answered.

"Mom, it's Kevin. Mei wanted to talk to you."

"Is she all right? Is something wrong?"

"No, she just wants to talk. Go ahead, Mei." He punched the speaker button on the phone.

"Momma. Where are you?"

"Hello, Mei, darling. I'm in the hospital."

"When you come get me?"

"I can't, Mei. Don't you remember? Kevin is going to take care of you."

"You come get me. I sad."

"What did you do today, Mei?" Sabra tried to change the subject.

"We go to big building. I drawed picture for you. I want to show you."

Kevin interjected. "I took her by the gallery and the educational liaison let her play with the art supplies. She did make a . . . uh, creative expression."

"I want to show you my picture. It is horse in the woods."

"That sounds beautiful. What else did you do?"

"I took her to enroll in a school," Kevin answered.

"Already?"

"Why not? It's a good public school. She's already signed up and met her teacher."

"He is man. He has hairy face."

"Her teacher is a man with a beard, is that what she's saying?"

"Yes, I tried to get a woman teacher, but he was the next in line, I guess. No women Pre-K teachers available, they said. I met him. Seems like a nice guy, young, married, been teaching a few years."

"She's not used to men."

"I know, Mom, I figured that out early on. But, hey, if I'm her guardian, she'll have to get used to men pretty soon." He could hear the sarcasm in his voice. Sabra wanted to it both ways: to depend on Kevin to take over Mei's upbringing and to tell him how to do it. She might as well know that could not happen. She would either have to trust him or find other arrangements for Mei.

"I'd prefer she had a female teacher."

"Yes, I know." He didn't want to take the "my way or the highway" bit too far right now.

"Will you and Mei see Felicity today?"

"Felicity and I are just friends now, Mom."

"What happened?"

"I don't want to get into it. It's complicated. She's a good person. She's been through a lot in her life and I don't think she's in a place where she can take our relationship any further. She promised to keep in touch, though. She knows I'll need help."

"Oh." Sabra sounded truly disappointed, but Kevin could not be sure why. He decided to change the subject, too.

"Tell Momma where we had lunch."

"McDonald's," Mei complied. "I like chicken nuts."

"Nuggets, Mei," he corrected, stifling a laugh.

"She shouldn't eat fast food every day."

"I know. I just ordered a boatload of healthy food from a supermarket, fruit and vegetables, and all that stuff. It's not like I've had time to shop, by the way." He checked himself; something about his mother's natural tone could push him to annoyance so easily. "And by the way, when do you expect Aunt Linda?"

"Around six, maybe later. It will be a long day for her, coming from Denver."

"Sure will. Any day you have to fly is a long day. Call me or text when she gets in, okay?"

"Yes. Can I talk to Mei, privately?"

He made a face, but turned off the speakerphone. "Here, Mei, you can talk to your momma."

Mei held the phone to her ear and listened. "Yes. Yes. No. Yes. No. Goodbye, Momma. I love you."

"She not talk anymore." Mei handed the phone back to Kevin. Sabra must have fallen into deep fatigue all of a sudden. He imagined this would be the case for the duration.

Chapter 22

"Let's go, Mei. We need to visit one more place today."

"I stay here."

"I don't think so." Her response caused him to laugh and get short with Mei at the same time. She really did have a mind of her own. "There's no way I'm leaving you by yourself. Let's take your tablet for you to play with. I have to talk to some ladies."

The drive to Nanny Services, Inc., took ten minutes. It was housed in an office park alongside insurance agencies, offices for logistics companies, a few nonprofits, and some tech businesses. The appearance of the place satisfied him—no empty storefronts, no litter on the sidewalk, clean windows, lots of parking, and the cars in the lot were higher-end and late model. He entered with Mei and her gear in tow. She carried a backpack with a stuffed toy, coloring book, crayons, and her tablet. The office contained ten seats for waiting and in the corner stood neatly arranged toys to amuse the children who might be visiting: colorful books, large blocks, and a non-electrical train set and track Kevin recognized from his childhood.

An attractive young woman greeted him. Her name badge said Saia, and her exotic looks matched the name. "Welcome to Nanny Services, Inc. How may I help you?"

"I have an appointment for 3:00. I would like to hire a part-time caregiver."

"Please have a seat. Could you please fill out this application form?"

"Sure. Come on, Mei."

He took a seat, and Mei climbed up next to him on the adjoining padded chair. He began to peruse what he was expected to tell them on the application. He answered what he could. Some of the questions concerned the child's likes, dislikes, habits, allergies, and fears. After less than four days of knowing about his adopted sister's existence, he couldn't give good responses to many of those. She liked fast food. Not exactly unusual for a five-year-old, he figured. Sabra said she had no allergies. He hoped that was right. Fears? After what this kid had been through, she seemed pretty fearless to him. Dislikes: men with beards, but she'd get over it. She obviously hadn't been exposed to Santa Claus yet.

He had to agree to a background check for himself. He had nothing to hide, other than some speeding tickets from years before, but he was more interested in the background check of anyone who would take care of Mei. He knew the background check was as much about his finances and credit as any criminal activity. Those were in order.

In filling out the papers he realized he had not really thought about what he expected the nanny to do. He could take Mei to school. The nanny would have to pick her up from school, which meant a safe driving record and car ownership; would have to stay with her from 2:00 until he came home; would perhaps need to stay late some nights when he had events at the gallery or needed a night out. All of a sudden he recognized he was asking a lot. The caregiver would have to work at least fifteen to twenty, sometimes even a flexible twenty-five, hours a week. And, oh yes, by the way, the child had only been living in the U.S. since the early spring, had lived in an orphanage in China for who knows how long, knew English at a basic level only, had recently been moved to a new home, and might be traumatized by the death of her adopted mother in the near future.

What was he thinking?

Too late. The receptionist called his name for his appointment. "Mr. Elcott, you can go through those doors right there."

"Come on, Mei."

She had played a game with some sort of Disney character while he completed, or tried to complete, the application. "Where we go?"

"To talk to someone. Gather your stuff."

Mei gave an audible sigh. Well, she deserved to sigh. She grasped her book bag and tablet and scrambled down from the seat. He held her hand. He didn't know why, but he thought he was supposed to make a good impression.

Isabella Greene, according to her badge, stuck out her hand as soon as they closed the door behind them. "Welcome to Nanny Services, Inc. Mr. Elcott. I'm Isabella. I'm in charge of interviewing clients to understand their needs for a caregiver and discussing with our staff who would be best for the job. She turned to Mei. "And what is your name?"

"Mei Louise Timothy." This time she spoke up. Mei liked pretty young ladies and felt immediately safe around them. Isabella fit that category. At least to Kevin. A head shorter than Kevin, her long, deeply brunette hair was pulled back in a neat, thick braid but still swung freely. She seemed athletic and outdoorsy.

"Mei, my name is Isabella. Let's all come into my office and get comfortable. This will take a while." They entered a small space decorated with photographs of the Appalachian Mountains and the coast but little else. "If you don't mind, let me read what you have here and then we'll talk."

She read over the application while Kevin asked Mei to explain her game. He had pretty much given up on video gaming after college. This one was simple but the graphics on the tablet looked much more realistic than those on the Xbox he used in high school.

"So, Mr. Elcott, I think I need to start with understanding your, um, relationship to Mei."

"I'm her guardian. As of, well, three, four days ago. Technically, I guess, she's my stepsister, or no, my adopted sister. That I didn't know about until Friday." He found himself embarrassed. "It's hard to explain. My mother adopted her earlier this year. She didn't bother to tell me, but that's not unusual."

"And, I'm sorry, this is a difficult question, but I have to ask it. We have to know your needs for a caregiver and understand the situation. Why is she now in your custody?"

"My mother is, uh," he glanced at Mei, whose tablet, thankfully, mesmerized her at the moment. "Very ill. Metastasized pancreatic cancer. That's another story, and she's in Fayetteville. I have all the paperwork. It's perfectly legal, at least, she says it is and it appears so to me." He handed over the thick folder, making a mental note he needed to make the time to read through all the documents carefully. "I know this is unusual. I didn't expect this a week ago, but here we are. I need help in the afternoons with someone to pick Mei up from school—she starts Cornerstone Primary, Pre-K, tomorrow—and watch over her until I get home from where I work, at the Gallery."

"Oh, yes, I see that. You are the director of Fordyce Gallery? I love that place."

"Yes. I'm glad to hear it. You're an art lover, then?"

"Photography, mostly. I took a class in college and fell in love with it. Just an elective. I'm not good enough to do it for money. But it fascinates me. You all had a great exhibit of Steinmetz two years ago."

"Yes, that was something." He had to think a minute about what she referred to.

"I have to be honest with you, Mr. Elcott."

"You can call me Kevin."

She made one of those faces meant to signify confidentiality and lowered her voice. "Company policy. Sorry. Mr. Elcott, most of our clients are, well, the parents, a mom, and a dad. So, your situation is somewhat out of the ordinary. However, some of the caregivers might be able to meet your hours. We have a few college and grad school students who schedule their classes in the morning or online so they can do exactly what you are asking for, afternoon, after school hours with the children."

"That's great. It's what I hoped for."

"Yes, but . . . like I say, most of our clients are couples, a mom and dad. Before we have you meet the candidates, we'll have to explain to them no mother is involved, and the situation is atypical. In other words, the nanny will have to be comfortable with being in the apartment, even for a short time, with a man."

"I see. Maybe we could just meet in the hall and never be in the same room together?" After he said it, he knew it sounded sarcastic. He didn't intend it; at this point he realized he should be nervous about finding anyone who met his specifications.

"I don't think that will be necessary, but we will have to be careful." Kevin knew this meant he would have to be the cautious one to avoid any implication of impropriety.

Isabella asked some more questions; he did his best to answer. Finally, she said, "We will complete your background check. Can you come back on Thursday to meet the two or three candidates for the job? If anything is a problem with the background check, and I'm sure there won't be, we will not complete the process until it's all satisfactory."

"Of course." He felt as if he had passed all his final exams.

"And, oh, yes, I'll need to copy some of these legal documents, your driver's license, and get a $100 deposit."

Somewhat relieved, he handed over everything she requested without questions. Man, he was tired. He felt a slight weight on his upper arm. Mei was resting her head on his shoulder.

Chapter 23

Three tasks marked off the list. A full day of paper-work. Hard conversations that sometimes felt like interrogations. Rush hour traffic. The grocery delivery. And only a couple of times did he think about his mother's illness and impending death.

After putting up the groceries, he created a meal based on Mei's wants about entrees and preferences on vegetables. "I like peas."

"Uh, what kind?"

"Peas. They green, like little balls." She made a circle with her fingers.

"Okay," he said, thankful frozen English peas had been on the list.

"I want pizza."

"Not tonight. We've got some fish sticks, some macaroni and cheese, and peas." That at least was not too monochromatic. "And fruit. You like cherries?"

"What cherries?"

"Like these." He showed her the clear pint container of dark red cherries.

"What they taste like?"

"Here," he gave her one. "Be careful. Take a little bite. There's a big seed in it."

Mei bit into it slowly and chewed. "Okay, I like."

"That's settled, then. We have a menu for dinner," Kevin thought. The dependence on fast food was conquered for one night.

He called his Aunt Linda after dinner. Mei seemed happy to retreat to her new room and toys. He was happy to let her. Space. They would need to give each other space sometimes, although a five-year-old would not understand the concept, only that she wanted to play by herself and get away from the big, bossy man.

"Hello. Is this Kevin?"

"Yes, Aunt Linda. Where are you right now?"

"I've just arrived at the hospital, well, ten minutes ago."

"So you're in Mom's room?"

"I was. I've stepped out into the hall."

"And . . . "

"She looks bad, Kevin honey. Real bad."

"You need to talk to her doctor. You need to be with her when he comes. Maybe you can talk some sense—I mean, convince her to get the treatments."

"I know, I know. I've tried so far. She is deeply depressed. At least, I think so. She can barely stay awake for any length of time, and she's not eating. She pushes it away."

"That's how she was when I was there, although, to be honest, I was too much in shock to notice everything I should have. I really hoped she would listen to you, Aunt Linda. Maybe when the doctor comes in tomorrow, you and he can talk."

"Sure." She paused. "How is the little girl?"

"She's holding her own. Not really friendly with me, but I'm a stranger to her. She at least listens to me most of the time, usually does what I ask. I'm big and male, and she seems to like women better. I got her enrolled in school today, and she'll start tomorrow. I'm going to hire a nanny for after school. That's harder than the school thing."

His aunt sighed. "It's bad enough you are facing your momma's . . . this illness. Are you really going to try to raise a child by yourself?"

He paused. "I don't know, Aunt Linda. She doesn't fit into my plans as of last Friday. I was looking for a move up north . . . I don't think I would be the best parent for her. She needs two parents. That's only fair for her. She needs siblings her age and a house and a dog and yard and stuff. I guess her being with me is better than being in an orphanage in China, but still not great."

"You're too hard on yourself, Kevin. But I understand. Right now, it's just--"

"One day at a time. One step at a time. All that kind of stuff people say. I know. I've gotten Family Medical Leave for when I have to be out. Hopefully, I can keep my board of directors happy enough I don't lose my job."

"When do you think you can come back?" He detected a request for support.

"Friday night, when Mei gets out of school. I want her to have as much normalcy as possible, and she needs to be around someone who can help her learn English. She's behind on that, but hey, I don't speak Chinese or whatever it is she does speak. I don't even know what her first language is."

"All right. I'll look for you Friday evening. We'll talk again. If I can't convince your mother into treatments as a last-ditch effort, we may go home with hospice soon. But I'll keep my fingers crossed and try to argue with her."

"Mom's . . . well . . ."

"She's a hardhead. She always does her own thing. I think that goes without saying. And sometimes she doesn't care about the consequences."

"That's . . . honest, Aunt Linda."

"I've known her longer than you have, Kevin."

After ending his call with his aunt, Kevin looked in on Mei, who turned pages in a book and made sounds he couldn't decipher. Sabra probably read to her and Mei was mimicking her momma, but Mei slipped back into her first language. At least he assumed so. He would have to, at some point, find out what she actually spoke—maybe it was in the paperwork—and find someone who could help her keep that language. For now, he'd let her alone.

Tomorrow she would be submerged in a busy American school with hundreds of other children.

School! He slapped his head. She needed those supplies! That meant a trip to Target or Walmart or one of those kinds of stores he avoided. They gave him a list. Where was the list? He rifled through his briefcase and found the green photocopy. Whatever he thought was not this; he only remembered high school, when his dad expected him to figure it out and buy his own supplies. This was more like a list for summer sleep-away camp.

A box of tissues. Hand sanitizer. A sleeping mat and blanket for nap time. Two boxes of snacks. Crayons. Markers. Paper, three kinds. Fat pencils. Child's scissors. Glue. And more. Mei probably left most of these supplies at home or at her school in Fayetteville, but he had no time or thought to gather them. Now, she'd have a whole new set for a whole new school. Perhaps it would put her in a good mood for her first day at Cornerstone. He needed all the help he could get.

They completed a hurried trip to the big box discount store for her trunkful of supplies. Then bath time without direct supervision. He'd been trying to construct a plan where Mei would be totally on her own to bathe without being left to her own devices. Tonight he launched his plan, hoping to find a rhythm for bedtimes without also feeling like a five-year-old's personal valet or getting anywhere near her.

First, he cleaned the tub, something he rarely did. Then he set out all the equipment: towel, washcloth, a cup, shampoo, soap, her underpants, and pajamas, where they would be within Mei's easy reach. He drew the water into the tub and called Mei in.

"Mei, you need to take your bath. I'm going to stand outside the door and talk to you. First, get undressed, then, like a big girl, give yourself a bath." And he left and closed the door.

Following the second hand on his watch, he waited for the first minute. "Mei, are you in the tub?"

"No."

"What are you doing?"

"I take clothes off."

"All right."

A minute later. "What are you doing?"

"I in tub. I wet."

"All right."

Two minutes later, he called again. She was playing this time.

"Wash your hair. Pour water over it—with the cup. Use the shampoo."

"I can't."

"Yes, you can. You're a big girl."

Two minutes later. "Are you washing your hair?"

"Yes."

"With the shampoo?"

"Yes."

He waited. "Can you pour water over your hair now? Close your eyes tight."

"Okay."

"Do it four times."

"What?"

"Pour water over your head four times"

Another minute. "Are you washing?"

"No."

"Wash. Put soap on the cloth and get clean."

He decided to give her five minutes. She beat him to it. "I clean. I finished."

"Can you get out of the tub?"

"Okay."

He waited four minutes. "Are you dry?"

"No!" She sounded exasperated. He gave her some time.

"Ready?"

"Yes, I put on jamas."

He opened the door and she emerged, her hair dripping wet. She wore pajamas with what appeared to be an Asian girl on them.

He figured the no-touch policy didn't have to extend to hair. "Your hair is wet. Here." He grabbed a towel from the closet and rubbed until her hair was just damp. "Do you want me to blow your hair dry?"

"No. I no like. Too hot."

"All right." He inspected her. "Who's on your pajamas?"

"That Mulan. She Chinese, like me. We fight bad guys." She made a jerky jump and then punching movements as if mimicking martial arts.

"Is she a superhero?"

"No, she warrior. Like boy."

"Oh." No telling what that plot's about, he thought. "Let's at least comb your hair." He handed her a comb.

"Why you not help me take a bath?"

"Uh, you're a big girl. You just took a bath all by yourself, right? So you don't need help."

She offered the comb back to him. "You comb my hair."

He relented. Hair drying and combing would have to be acceptable, but he was no hairdresser and succeeded only in pulling too hard at the tangles and evoking complaints. He'd have to ask Felicity or one of the women at the office how to keep little girl's hair from bunching up like this.

"Momma help me take bath."

"I know. I'm not Momma. It's not good for men to help you take a bath. You remember that."

"Why?"

"You'll understand when you're older."

"That silly," she said, putting her hands on her hips and wagging her head in good-natured defiance of his house rules.

"No, it's not. And it's the way it's going to be in my house. Now, brush your teeth. You should be asleep soon."

"You read me book."

He sighed. How did parents do this day in, day out, and with more than one kid?

She got her way on the book reading, but he was hardly a third of the way through a book about a moose and a muffin and other animals when he heard her regular breathing and gently snuck out of her room.

At 9:30, he checked his phone for the last time that day and collapsed into bed.

Chapter 24

Tuesday morning the alarm chirped at 5:30. He had 90 minutes to prepare himself, wake Mei, feed her, and leave for the drive to school, which started at 8:00.

Who decided children had to be in school earlier than most adults had to be at work?

He'd seen enough lame movies or TV shows about adults forced into parenthood to know about the worst mistake: assuming children moved fast, and compliantly, especially in the morning. He already saw how his own walking had to be slowed to a snail's pace for Mei to keep up. Children were capable of fast, frenetic movement, he figured, just not when directed by adults.

To this point, he hadn't seen Mei with other children. A sudden anxiety snatched at his stomach. "What if she has a terrible first day? What if it's a total disaster despite Mr. Benson's best intentions and exuberance? What if she's a ball of screams when I pick her up?"

You just crossed over, dude, he said to himself in the mirror. You're doing the parent thing now. Even still, he knew his motivation—satisfy his mother and do no harm.

Mei was, like any other child, prone to dawdling in the morning. Badly. He'd made the mistake of not putting out clothes for her to wear the night before. The evening before was all such a flurry with the shopping and re-mote-control bath and bedtime. Now they battled over what she would wear. He grabbed a tiny green skirt and smocked, flowered top that appeared to coordinate.

"No. I wear pants."

"Okay." He dug through the suitcase for a pair of jeans. "Here."

"I not like that shirt."

"What's wrong with it?"

"I not wear it with pants."

"Okay. Pick something out, then."

She bent over the suitcase. "When you make dresser for my clothes?"

"Soon. Not today. Just pick out a shirt."

She seemed distracted and looked out the window.

"Come on, Mei."

She moved some clothes around and found a light blue top with words on it. "What these words say?"

"It says, 'Can I be your friend?'" He wondered why Sabra bought her clothes with messages, but he guessed the question appealed to Sabra's communal spirit. "That's a good message for the first day of your new school," Kevin suggested, reminding himself the other children most likely wouldn't be able to read the words.

"Okay, I wear that."

"Now, Mei, I'm going to fix breakfast. You take off your pajamas and dress yourself. Here are the socks and undershirt. Bring your shoes into the kitchen and I'll help you with them."

"I do my shoes myself."

"All right. Now, please don't start playing with your toys or tablet. Just get dressed, okay?"

"Okay," she said half-heartedly and sat on her bed.

Maintaining the no-touch, no-dress, and no-bathe policy with her was going to be hard, he thought. It would be easier to jostle her into her clothes instead of leaving her to dress herself; it would be faster, too. But he had no choice.

Ten minutes later she did appear, somewhat disheveled but fully dressed in the friendly blue T-shirt, yellow jeans, and her flashy shoes. This time, she had followed the "tag in the back" rule. He negotiated with her about cold cereal or instant oatmeal or toast; she obediently drank her juice and took her vitamin. After running a comb through her disheveled hair and finding a barrette to keep it out of her face, he supervised teeth brushing. Already exhausted, he commandeered Mei out the door at 7:39 for the commute to her school.

Dropping Mei off at the elementary school meant a long line of cars, inching his Acura up to the entrance, and realizing 7:39 would not work as a departure time from his apartment. With Mei still in the car, the digital clock on his dash told him only three minutes were left before the school day began, a bad way to start. Then the truth hit him: he couldn't just let Mei out of the car to fend for herself at five years old on the first day, especially with all these supplies in the box in his trunk. What was he thinking? Already late, he moved out of line, received an angry honk from somewhere and screeched his brakes, cursed softly so Mei couldn't hear, and found a parking space.

"Why we stop here?"

"I need to take you in, you will get lost."

"I can find way."

Was that stubbornness or fearlessness? He wondered. "No, I don't think so. You don't know this school."

"It look like my other school."

"I'm sure it does. Hold on."

He released himself and walked to the passenger side and opened the back door. He set her free from the bulky car seat. "Climb down." She obeyed, surprisingly. He reached for her book bag and handed it to her, and then retrieved the box of school supplies from the trunk.

Kevin felt humiliated he couldn't even get her to the school on time the first day, but he figured this would be the first in a long line of embarrassments. They dodged the last few cars in line and walked toward the main entrance. A young woman greeted them but firmly stopped their entry.

"I'm sorry, we want the children to be dropped off in the line or come off the bus. School policy."

"Uh, this is her first day. She's new. She just—um, moved here from another town. I wanted to walk her to her room."

"I understand, sir, but that's not policy. Who is her teacher?"

"Mr. Benson."

"And her name?"

"Mei Timothy."

"All right." The young woman pulled a walkie-talkie from her back pocket. "Mrs. Traylor, could you come to the front entrance? We need your help with a new student, first day, Mei Timothy."

She turned to Kevin. "Could you stand over there? The paraprofessional for Mr. Benson is coming to escort your—student."

Kevin didn't know whether to feel aggravated or disciplined, but he obeyed and walked Mei over to where he'd been directed, a section of the lobby. At least he'd led her as far as into the building, if not the classroom. This was not a good way to start, but he talked himself down from his aggravation. The school obviously had to have tight security, rules, traffic flow, and all that. No reason to give anyone a hard time about it. This was a new normal, a phrase he'd always hated as the ultimate oxymoron. He'd better get used to it.

In less than two minutes Mrs. Traylor, a chubby, short, middle-aged woman waddled up, spoke briefly to the door guard, and came over. She smiled broadly. "Hello, are you Mei Louise Timothy?"

Mei nodded energetically and smiled, glad to see a motherly-looking woman.

"I'm Ms. Traylor, and I help Mr. Benson. You can come with me. Okay?"

Kevin knew the parapro had certainly been informed about the new student and the circumstances. This seemed like a concierge level of service; it also seemed like overkill in the caution department.

"Thank you, Ms. Traylor. I'll drop her off in the car rider lane tomorrow. I was just, uh, concerned, you know, first day and all." He realized he sounded penitent, as if he'd transgressed every protocol in the book. Mrs. Traylor was more relaxed than the keeper of the entrance.

"No problem. It's pretty common for parents to do that the first day. She'll be fine," she reassured him. "Say goodbye, Mei, and let's go start school."

Mei was too distracted to obey and just followed this new woman whom she would probably end up calling "Momma" at some point soon.

"Oh, wait," Kevin remembered. "Uh, here's her box of supplies."

"I'll have one of the office staff bring those down," offered the doorkeeper, now helpful. She turned away to deal with another parent whose child forgot a sack lunch.

Kevin watched Mei and the cheerful parapro stroll down the hallway, neither in a special hurry.

Chapter 25

While he planned to spend several hours in the office trying to reconstruct his schedule and responsibilities, he knew to call Linda first and then have a talk with Sabra. The evening before he had not spoken to his mother when he called his aunt; he tried to remember why, but yesterday was a blur. Linda hadn't even asked if he wanted to speak to his mother. Perhaps Sabra was asleep or had instructed her sister to leave her alone. Either way, today they needed to talk.

"Hello?"

"Aunt Linda, this is Kevin."

"Hey, there, honey. Let me arrange myself. Hold on."

After about sixty seconds of silence from Linda with echoes of hospital sounds and a closed door in the background, she was back. "I'm in the bathroom. I didn't want to disturb Sabra."

"Sabra? Where did you sleep?"

"Here in the hospital, on this little bed."

"Oh, Aunt Linda, I wish you hadn't done that. Couldn't you have gone to Mom's house?"

"I didn't want to, Kevin. She needed someone with her."

He had to wonder if this was a dig at him, intentional or unintentional. No, he couldn't be with his mother now. He was doing what she wanted, elsewhere. "Why? Is she worse?"

"No, not really. She's just—sad. She cries a lot."

"Mom?" He'd never seen his mother shed tears.

"Yes. But we'll talk about that later. Not now. The doctor has already been in this morning. I'm still on Denver time—what time is it here now?"

"Almost nine. How did it go with the doctor?"

"He asked her if she had decided about the treatments, and if she had talked about it fully with you and me."

"And?" He held his breath. He still held a sliver of hope. Maybe his mother would come to reason. Maybe she could make it through this. Maybe . . .

"She said yes, she had talked with us, although I'm not sure I'm satisfied she and I have talked it through enough. She said she had firmly decided against the treatments and would like to go home."

He let his breath out. He felt the horrible tension in his jaws and cheeks that meant tears, a rare feeling now becoming more common. He couldn't speak.

"Kevin?" he heard Linda's voice.

"Yeah, um." He wiped his eyes. "What did the doctor say to that?"

"That he understood and it was her decision. That he would make the arrangements with the hospital for hospice care. He said some people—a social worker and representative from the hospice organization the hospital recommends—would be in to see her today."

"How do you feel about it?" he said.

"Not good. I wanted the doctor to try to reason with her."

"He already has. When I was there. And before."

"All right," Linda said. She didn't speak immediately. "I guess the arrangements and paperwork and all that will be done, and I'll take her home tomorrow or Thursday."

It all sounded so final. "And then?"

"We wait. We watch her die."

He wanted to talk to his mother. He wanted to say something kind, intelligent, appropriate, and supportive. He also wanted to tell her he was holding up his end of the bargain, and she wasn't. But it was too late. The decision had been made and the end-of-life care put into motion. He wanted to tell her—what? He really didn't know, not this morning.

"Listen, Aunt Linda. I wanted to talk to her, but I'm not ready to yet. When do you think I should call back?"

"Try half an hour, maybe."

"Sure. Aunt Linda, I can't say—I can't thank you enough for coming. I—couldn't do this without you. I couldn't—I . . ."

"I know, Kevin. You would be here if you could. If it was just your momma dying, it would be one thing. But she's asking a big thing out of you right now. You couldn't take care of a little girl and take care of your momma, and to be honest, it's best a sister do that. It's going to be—harder than you can imagine right now. I took care of my mother-in-law in her last days. I know what to expect."

"Yes, ma'am." He couldn't say more right now.

"Call back in about 30 minutes or so, okay?"

"Sure." She must have sensed his need to shed some tears, to have some quiet. Kevin was thankful for a private office. He wasn't ashamed to cry; he had good reason, but he didn't want it seen. The stress of the last five days came out in gulps and sighs. In a few weeks, perhaps, his mother, his complicated, unpredictable, giving but selfish mother, would be gone. He didn't know what to do with that prospect. It was one thing to forget her and postpone calling or visiting for all those years when she was well and living her own life and he living his. Now, all the time he always assumed they would have to make their relationship right was compressed into a few weeks.

Kevin answered emails, studied his calendar, and signed some contracts, taking about forty minutes before he could settle his mind to call his mother. This time he dialed her hospital room number.

"Yes." He did not recognize the feeble voice.

"Mom?"

"Yes, Kevin."

"Hi, Aunt Linda said I could call now."

"Yes, I can talk a bit."

"How—are you?"

"The same, Kevin. Very tired. Not hungry, though I should be. It's weird. You know I always had a healthy appetite."

"Yeah." His mother had always carried extra pounds on her large frame. In her middle age, she had seemed to stop caring about maintaining a certain size.

"But you should eat something, even if it is hospital food."

"It wouldn't matter if it was a rib-eye steak or Rocky Road ice cream. Nothing would appeal to me." He smiled; at least she remembered the joys of eating her favorites. "How is Mei?"

"She is fine."

"What does that mean?"

"She eats, she complies, and she went to school today."

"Is she happy?"

"She doesn't seem unhappy." He refrained from explaining his at-a-distance bath regimen. "She's slow in the morning. She doesn't like my fashion choices, but she eats my cooking. She likes cherries. Her wish is my command."

"Ha!" Sabra's laugh surprised him, and he felt he'd accomplished something. "So you got her to her new school."

"Yes, but not on time and not without some drama. I thought I'd take her to her class, but no go. The parapro came and got her. But the parapro is a woman, so that's a plus."

"Schools can't let just anyone roam the halls."

"So I gathered."

"No meltdowns?"

"From me or from Mei?"

"Very funny, Kevin."

"No, so far she's actually okay. I'm trying to hire a nanny. And I spent a ton on school supplies for her."

"So. How are you?"

He wanted to say overwhelmed. "Tired, but it doesn't matter. I want to know what you are going to do."

"Go home and let the disease take its course. I know you and Linda don't like it. I understand."

"You're right. We don't like it, but it's your body and your decision."

"Kevin, don't you remember what I used to do when you were younger? I was a social worker in a hospital. I helped people go to hospice, like someone is going to help me do today. I know what this is about. You and Linda think I am depressed and don't know what I am doing. I know perfectly well what is going on in my life. I have read the studies and protocol on my condition. I could spend months in heavy chemotherapy. I'd have no quality of life. I couldn't take care of Mei as she needs. I couldn't work. I'd be in and out of the hospital and maybe get half a year longer of life."

"Mom, you don't know that."

"No, Kevin. I do. And I'd rack up hundreds of thousands, maybe millions of dollars in medical bills—"

"Nobody cares about the money, Mom."

"I do. I want to leave some money for Mei, for you. I don't want the hospital and the medical establishment making money off of me while I grasp for a little bit longer life. No. I'm going home. Linda will take me and be with me when I need to have my crap and vomit and blood cleaned up and little bits of liquid spooned into me until I can't take in anything. I know what is coming."

She had reverted to her real, earthy, blunt self, the one that hid behind the academic and professional Sabra and the cool, compassionate social worker Sabra. The tears he'd shed earlier were replaced with clenched teeth. She would have her way. It was, after all, her life and her body.

"I don't like it."

"I know. I didn't say I liked any of this, either. I don't know why I'm sick, what purpose it serves, why my pancreas and the rest of me decided to go haywire. But it did. I am dying, Kevin."

She spoke as if she wanted to be cruel, but it was really only anger, and he happened to be in the way of her words.

"What do you want me to do?" he said quietly.

"Come to see me as soon as you can."

"I will."

"I love you, Kevin. I know you don't like my version of love, but I do."

He paused. "I know that, Mom. I never doubt it. I love you, too."

Chapter 26

After he ended the call with Sabra, he really wanted a stiff drink. A couple of shots of vodka would do it right about now, but it was 10:30 a.m. Alcohol would soften the blows she had just inflicted. Instead, he would have to absorb them, take them in, and turn his attention elsewhere. For the next three hours, he wrote reports, made phone calls, answered more emails, gave his assistant Naomi some directions, delayed lunch, and made every effort to keep his mind off the picture of his mother forming in his mind. That of an emaciated frame, a lined, pallid face, growing more and more unaware of her surroundings, unable to speak, as the rogue cells converted her life and energy to their own killing purposes.

At 1:30, he told Naomi he'd be leaving early for a few days and left to pick Mei up from her school. They would miss the traffic of the other pickups since the Pre-K children and the kindergartners were released earlier than the older children. He'd been so absorbed in work and grief he'd forgotten lunch. His stomach growled, but he didn't need fast food any more than Mei did. He pulled into the parking lot, obediently maneuvered his car into the line of mothers in SUVs waiting for their five-year-olds, and waited.

When he inched to place, the parapro in charge rapped on his window. "Who do you want? Where is your hang tag?"

"My what? I need Mei Timothy. She's new. It's her first day."

"You're supposed to have a hangtag up with her name and her teacher's name."

"Oh. She's in Chad Benson's class."

"You need a hangtag. It helps us keep this orderly. Otherwise, it takes too long and really, anybody can get a child. We'd be in big trouble without those hangtags."

He thought briefly that anyone bent on trespassing in the school and kidnapping a child could find a way to steal a hangtag. But this was not the time to argue about the logic of school rules. "Where do I get one? They didn't tell me about that when I registered her." He knew he sounded defensive.

"You'll have to go into the office."

"Can I get Mei first?"

"No. You would have to show identification. We can't give a child to just anybody." Her facial expression signaled she considered him a "just anybody."

This meant parking his car, as he had in the morning, trying to reach the inner sanctum of the school, and possibly being excluded again. He sighed, pulled over to park, and made his way to the office. After assuring the parapro on guard duty that he was a legal guardian here to pick up a child, he was allowed to go to the office and obtain a hangtag. The parapro used her walkie-talkie to call for Mei Timothy in Mr. Benson's class. He breathed out in relief, realizing his panic. Had he thought they would keep her, or turn her over to Child Protective Services?

Mei walked slowly down the hallway, by herself, so tiny, as he waited by the doors. He couldn't tell what her demeanor signaled. Was she sad to see him, mad he had left her there with even more strangers, or just tired and wary? He walked her to the car, holding her hand to shield her from the vehicles of the last of the mothers picking up their small children.

"Goodbye, Mei," said the attendant, making a point not to say goodbye to Kevin. Oh, well, little slings and arrows. He was more concerned about Mei.

"Mei, can you buckle your seat belt?"

She didn't answer, but fumbled with it. He climbed into the back seat beside her to help.

"So, how was school?"

She only peered back at him, wordless. Was she confused? Her expression telegraphed befuddlement with this man she was supposed to obey.

"Are you going to talk to me?"

"I want to see Momma."

"I know. We can't today. We will go in three days to see her."

"Why not now?"

"It's a long drive. We can't go all the way there and come back tonight."

"I want to see her."

"We can't, Mei. I'm sorry."

"I want to see her! I want to see her! I want to see Momma!" For the first time since he had met her, Mei showed intense emotion. That was the nice term for it. In reality, she screamed at the top of her lungs. She pulled with all her strength at the straps of her car seat and kicked her feet violently. Her voice reached a piercing level, and he scanned the area around his car to be sure no one heard it and came running to investigate the child's distress.

"Mei, calm down!" She began to wail, tears streaming.

"Mei, what's wrong?"

She sobbed some more, sucking air. Her face turned red, and she finally managed to get out chunks of words between cries. "I want my Momma. Momma is supposed to pick me up. Where is Momma?"

"Momma is in the hospital, remember?"

"Why she in ho-pi-tal? She come get me."

"Mei, you're staying with me now, remember?"

"No, no, no, no, no!"

He really had no plan for this, no resources. For four days Mei had gone along with him, even if it made no sense. All he could figure was, for some reason, her five-year-old brain promised her Sabra would be there to pick her up, like always, at the close of school.

"Mei, Mei. You've got to stop crying."

But why? Because he didn't want to be embarrassed and didn't know what to do? The kid deserved to cry, for Pete's sake, even if she didn't know all the reasons why. He climbed out of the back seat and re-entered the driver's seat, turned on the ignition, and let her express all the frustration and emotion she could on the way back to his apartment.

At home, Mei wanted to be left alone with her toys. The deep cries had exhausted her. After thirty minutes he checked in on her, and she was in a fetal position on the floor. He put a blanket on her and left her alone.

His phone rang about 3:00. He didn't recognize the number. "Hello."

"Hello, this is Chad Benson. Is this Mr., um, Elcott?"

"Yes. Thank you for calling, Mr. Benson."

"Oh, call me Chad. Just the students have to call me Mr. Benson, you know."

"Sure. So . . .?" He waited for the shoe to drop. If Mei had been that upset for him, there was no telling how she had acted in class. Maybe Chad was calling to tell him to try a different school or something.

"I wanted to let you know Mei had a pretty good first day."

"Oh, really. I'm surprised."

"Why?"

"She had a meltdown when I picked her up. A total fit. I was pretty flummoxed about what to do, but she seems to have calmed down. As in falling fast asleep."

"Oh, that. Well, you know, she was the last one left in the classroom. She seemed kind of, um, worried by then."

"So I guess I better get there earlier, right?"

"Yeah, that might be a good idea."

"That would explain the meltdown. She screamed for her momma. That's my mother."

"Oh, really?"

"Yes. Believe it or not, she's my sister. Obviously adopted, but legally my sister."

"Oh. I didn't know."

"Yeah, I guess you didn't. I'm glad you called. I'd prefer to talk to you face-to-face about this, but that's the deal. It's complicated."

"Sure. But I have time. I always use this time to call parents about any issues the students have during the day, and you're the last one."

"Before I tell you my life story, did she do all right today, other than screaming at the top of her lungs in my car?"

"She was quiet, but she went along with the other students. At game time she mostly watched . She knows her alphabet and numbers pretty well, considering. Her expressive English is behind her age level, but she didn't have problems with understanding and following along."

"Yes, she's only been in the U.S. for seven or eight months. My mother adopted her then from China, from an orphanage, although I've since learned her biological family is still alive, which is a sad circumstance. I'll cut to the chase. My mom is the kind of woman who likes adventure and to do her own thing, her own way, and she didn't inform me about the adoption until last Friday. I went to visit her in Fayetteville, where she lives, because she asked me to. We don't see each other much. I'll leave it at that. She has stage four, metastatic pancreatic cancer, and her prognosis isn't good. She left Mei to me."

"Oh, man. Are you serious?"

Kevin overlooked this response as unprofessional because it was honest. "Yes. I wish I weren't. I'm single and clueless about how to raise a kid. My mom has decided to forgo treatments. I'm all Mei has. But there it is. So, if Mei got through the day with you without bursting into tears or throwing a fit, I'd say it's a win-win."

Chad didn't answer immediately. Kevin figured he was struggling to know how to respond. "I'm sorry to hear about your mom, Mr. Elcott."

"Thanks. And please just call me Kevin. I'm kind of overwhelmed. You should feel complimented, though. Mei doesn't have much to do with men. If she got through the first day without telling you that, it's a miracle."

"Actually, she did ask me about my beard again. She said I looked like a man in a book she had. I asked her what his name was. She said 'Giant Man in the clouds who chased Jack and wanted to hurt him.'"

"Ha! I think she catches on pretty well. But she's been through a lot, and I don't know what's going on in her head. It may be a while before I do."

"Don't be too hard on yourself. It's not every day someone becomes a guardian to a five-year-old they've never met."

"Thank you for saying that. Listen, I appreciate your calling. I'll do whatever I can to help you get her situated. It sounds like she did better than I expected. So that's good news."

"Sure. I'll be in touch. We'll schedule a conference soon."

"Great. Goodbye."

Well, Kevin thought. That's at least something positive. He dealt with some emails on his laptop. Soon Mei stood by him.

"I hungry."

"Okay. What do you want?"

"Cookie. Milk."

He fixed it for her and she sat across from him at the kitchen table, nibbling at the Chips Ahoy and watching him type, gazing over her glass..

"What you do?"

"I'm working. But I'm almost finished." He pressed send on an email and closed the computer. "Your teacher called."

"Who? Man with hair on his face?"

"Yes, Mei. It's called a beard."

"Beard. He looks funny."

"Some people like beards. I think he's an L.L. Bean kind of guy."

"Beans? Like Jack?"

She definitely has an issue with that story, he thought. "No, not like Jack and the Beanstalk. Never mind. Do you remember his name?"

"No."

"It's Mr. Benson, Mei. You need to remember that. He said you had a good day at school."

"We say letters and numbers. Af-bet. I already know them. A, B, C, D, F, E, G, H, J, L . . . "

"That's pretty good. Can you say the rest?"

"I no want to now. This not school."

"Okay. How was your other teacher, the lady?"

"She not teacher. She pairpo. She help teacher."

"Is she nice?"

"Yes. She fat, too."

"True, but that's not something you should say. It will hurt her feelings."

"Why? Fat not bad."

"Some people think it is. She will think you are making fun of her."

Mei dunked the remaining half of her cookie in the milk and sucked on it. "Where CeeCee?"

"I guess she's at work."

"I like her. She nice. She pretty."

"Yes, she is."

"Can she come see us?"

"I don't know. I can ask sometime."

"I go play now, I watch cartoons on my tablet."

"Okay. You've had a big day."

She slid off the chair and returned to her room. The hysteria of two hours ago seemed healed. Was this common, for children to forget and go back to normal? Perhaps if she didn't explode with emotions once in a while it would mean something worse. He shook his head. Maybe he better read up on little kids.

Chapter 27

He didn't have to call CeeCee. Felicity's number appeared on his screen as the phone buzzed and danced. For someone who had broken up with him, she was calling him awfully soon. "Hello. We were just talking about you."

"Oh, really?"

"Don't worry. It's all good. Mei said you're nice. And pretty."

"Ah. Well, tell her the same. I'm just calling to see how it's going with your, um . . ."

"My new way of life? I've gotten her to school one day, and she eats. That's a breakthrough, I think."

"Yes, it is. That was fast—with the school, I mean."

"She needed something like school as soon as possible. If nothing else, to not be bored. And I need to work some time."

She paused, waiting for him to say more. "So, how's it really going?"

He sighed. "Do little kids sometimes just go ballistic for no reason?"

"Yes and no. They go ballistic. They have a reason."

"Fair enough."

"Kids go through more stress in this hyped-up adult world than their little heads can absorb sometimes."

"That's true for her."

"Absolutely." She paused, as if she expected something.

"So, Felicity," he said. "Could you come over here for dinner tonight? I'll get anything delivered you want."

"How tempting. I would like to see Mei. Sure. I can't be there till 7:00, though."

"That will be great. What do you want to eat?" He hoped he didn't sound too happy.

"Anything's fine."

"See you at 7:00 then."

"Yeah, bye."

What was he supposed to think? Did she really just want to be moral support and see Mei? Yes, she probably did. Felicity, of all the women he'd ever dated, was the least likely to play games. She had set the ground rules—friendship and help through this transition—and she was playing by them. End of story.

He decided to keep it a surprise that Mei's new friend was coming. He also decided to order in plain old American food from a local Mom-and-Pop place that delivered. Meat loaf, potato casserole, salads, cobbler. That sounded stable, familial, safe, and carbohydrate-full.

Felicity arrived a little early. She wore her typical work uniform: navy blue light wool suit, cream-colored silk blouse, two-inch heels, and neutral hose. Her firm demanded conservatism in everyone's dress. The women who worked there sometimes reminded Kevin of corporate Stepford Wives. Ten- or twelve-hour days were not unusual for Felicity. She'd probably gone in at 7:00 that morning.

She greeted him with a "hey," and no physical contact. "Can I take my shoes off? On my feet more than usual today."

"Be my guest." Felicity removed her pointed-toed pumps; he wondered for a fleeting second why women agreed to wear those torturous shoes. "Mei, come see who's here," he called.

Mei wandered out of her new room but accelerated when she saw Felicity. "CeeCee!"

Mei ran to her newest friend and wrapped her arms around Felicity's thighs. "I happy to see you!"

Felicity held her close. "Me too, Mei Louise Timothy. I missed you."

"Where you go?"

"I have to go to my job. I work for a bank."

"I go to school today," Mei announced, proud. Kevin hoped his face didn't show his confusion or exasperation. After the screaming jag in the car, he'd feared Mei was scarred for life. All that was gone now.

"So Kevin told me."

"I liked it."

"You did?" Felicity made a face meant to say, "I'm impressed," but gave Kevin a sideways glance that communicated, "See, nothing to worry about."

"Yes."

"So, tell me about it." Felicity sat down on the couch and pulled Mei toward her. Mei was happy to snuggle with this pretty lady.

Mei started to tell Felicity about her teacher, the room, what they did, and a couple of little girls who befriended her. Kevin caught Felicity's eye and mouthed a thank you. In a few seconds, the doorbell rang. Kevin tipped the delivery guy generously for getting the food there more quickly than he expected.

"Looks like we've got food," he announced. "Give me about two minutes to get this on the table and set up. Mei, go wash your hands, okay?"

"Okay," she said agreeably and climbed off the couch.

"Man alive, you're a miracle worker," he said to Felicity after Mei left the room. She followed him into the apartment's small dining area while he put out plates and silverware and opened the food containers.

"No, I'm not. She just needed a new person to entertain."

"She talked more in the last five minutes than the whole time I've known her."

"She just relates more to women, I think. Did she say her teacher is a man?"

"Yes, but he's not weird or anything. Normal guy, married, a few years younger than me. I figure he's doing this elementary school gig to become a principal eventually. Not a bad move, when you think about it. Easier than teaching high school algebra."

"True," she said. He could tell she was tired.

"Long day?"

"More or less. Right now they're all long."

Mei reappeared. "What we eat?"

"Meat loaf."

"What that?"

"Kind of like a hamburger, and this one has ketchup on it." He dished her out small portions of the meatloaf and potatoes and set it down before her. Then he and Felicity served themselves and they began to eat. Mei ate without complaint and listened while the adults chatted without saying anything too personal.

Kevin was glad to see Felicity and wondered if her calling him meant anything more than a friendly follow-up to the trauma of the weekend. Half way through their plates, she turned to another subject.

"So, how is your mother?"

"She's not going into treatment. My aunt Linda from Denver is with her, and they will start hospice within a day or so. Linda will stay with her as long as, you know . . ."

"I'm so sorry."

"Thank you. I don't know what I'd do without Linda coming. But she couldn't talk Mom into treatment any better than I could."

"I didn't really have any time around your mom. She probably thought I was some kind of goofball, tagging along with you but not adding much." Felicity shook her head at the thought.

"No way. Please don't think that. You saved my—no, I mean, you kept me focused. I really appreciate it."

"Thanks, but I don't know how. When will you see your mom next?"

"Friday, for the weekend. I'll go there every weekend until, well, I can't. That's all I know. That's the plan."

"Under the circumstances, it sounds like a good plan." She smiled. She did not reach for his hand. Any physical contact they had had before was curtailed. She sent strong signals of friendship, and nothing more. "This food is pretty good. What place is this from?"

"Carole and Joe's Diner on North Wendover."

"Hum." She continued to enjoy her dinner, as did Mei, for which Kevin was glad. Mei willingly complained about food she didn't like.

"There's desert, cobbler. Do you want some coffee? I can make a pot."

"Actually, I would. A little. Otherwise, I might nod off, and I need to hear the rest of Mei's story about her new school."

Chapter 28

Wednesday morning ended up slightly less hectic than Mei's first school day, and Kevin arrived at work somewhat less frazzled. Basking in the afterglow of a visit from Felicity, Mei complied with all of Kevin's orders to get moving and even wore what he set out for her. Could they be settling into a rhythm already? Was he an idiot to think that was even possible? Yes, he was. But he better accept his luck when he could get it.

After his own five-hour workday, he went to pick her up again. The logistics were smoother, but Mei was not happy again. While she didn't scream, overflow with tears, and struggle in her car seat like the day before, she did start to whine, then become unhappy with Kevin's attempts to placate her, and progress to tears and breathing hard.

"What is wrong, Mei?" he pleaded, peering at her in the rear-view mirror.

"I don't like this new school."

"What's wrong with it?"

"I want to see Momma."

"We can call her, and you can see her on the phone. Do you want to do that?"

"I want to see Momma real."

"We will soon. Let's call her when we get home."

"That not my home."

"I know. But it's where you stay now."

This set off more tears, but he steeled himself. She wore herself out and nodded off before they reached his complex.

Maybe she's just tired. Sleeping seemed to help yesterday, he thought. "Come on, Mei, let's go get you a nap." He made her walk, not wanting to pick her up and carry her. Sleepy, she wobbled and knocked into him repeatedly on the way to the apartment door and then to her room.

While she slept, Kevin called Nannies Inc. and asked to speak to Isabella Greene. He was told she would return his call, which she did within five minutes.

"Hello, Mr. Elcott. I was just about to call you when I got your message."

"You had said there would be three candidates to interview tomorrow."

"Yes, Mr. Elcott. We actually only have two who can really fit your specifications, but they are experienced nannies and very good candidates. Did you still want to meet them tomorrow?"

"Yes. As soon as possible, really."

"You'll have to come to our office, of course."

"They can't come here, to see the apartment, and meet Mei, and all that?"

"There would be, well, liability issues with meeting off premises. You can come here, can't you? About 3:30 until 5:30? April Garcia will meet you at 3:45, and Mia Flynn at 4:45. I'll need to meet you at 3:30 for an orientation and let you look at their resumes."

"Oh, sure." He didn't want to sound stupid, but he had no idea what he was doing. A week ago he had never given nannies a second thought. When he was younger, a nanny seemed like something used by rich people who didn't like their kids. "I can be there at 3:30, but I have to bring Mei."

"Mei?"

"My—sister, I mean, the little girl I'm guardian for."

"Oh, yes, excuse me. Definitely, bring her. The nanny candidates will want to meet her."

Of course, he thought. We're being interviewed just like the potential nannies are.

"Good, I'll see you tomorrow."

He hung up. That done, he attacked his work via his laptop until Mei woke up and wanted a snack.

Later that evening, he called his mother's hospital room. There was no answer. He tried Linda's phone. Again, nothing. His heart beat harder. Where were they? He wondered, concerned. Third, he tried his mother's cell. Linda answered.

"Kevin?"

"Yes, Aunt Linda. What's going on?"

Linda sighed. "Nothing. Your momma's lying here, half asleep. I had my phone on silent so as not to disturb her, and I forgot about her phone being on."

"Mei wants to, I mean, needs to talk to her. Can we do FaceTime?"

"What's that?"

"Hold on." He hung up and called Sabra's phone back with the other app. He could see Linda's blurry image this time. His aunt had aged, but the resolution on Sabra's phone, an older model, probably didn't help.

"Oh, I can see you. What's this called?"

"FaceTime. At least on this brand of phone. Can you wake Mom up?" He called to the other room. "Mei, come here."

"Yeah, here she is." The next image he saw was the increasingly haggard and gray face of Sabra Timothy, eyelids drooping.

"Mom, this is Kevin. Mei wants to talk to you."

"Is she all right?" Sabra's voice sounded like she was under the influence.

Having eaten dinner, Mei played a frog and fish game quietly on her tablet at the cleared dinner table. "Who that?" she said.

"Talk to your momma." He handed her his mobile phone.

Mei brightened and grabbed it. "Momma!"

Sabra's voice gained some energy. "Mei, honey. I miss you."

"Momma, I see you. Momma, I miss you too. Where you at?"

"I'm in the hospital, honey. You remember."

"When you come see me?"

"You are going to come see me soon. Kevin will bring you."

"When?"

"In two days, Mei," Kevin interrupted. "When school is over on Friday."

"This man say two days." Kevin couldn't help rolling his eyes that she didn't use his name. But it wasn't like he reminded her over and over.

"His name is Kevin, Mei. I told you all about him. Kevin is your brother."

"Okay. I forget his name. CeeCee came to see me."

"Oh, that's nice." Sabra's voice strength diminished. "So, did you go to school? Do you like it?"

"Yeah. It okay. I already know my letters. Some kids not know them."

"Well, you be kind to them. Remember, we talked about being kind."

"Okay."

"Mei, I love you. I can't wait to see you. You be good for Kevin."

"Yeah, I do that."

Kevin took back the phone. "Thanks, Mom. I promised her she could see you tonight on the phone."

"So . . . how is it going?"

Kevin could tell Sabra wouldn't be alert much longer. "All good. Almost. She seems to have problems at the end of the school day when I pick her up. She's crying, upset, and really tired. I guess she needs more sleep and I need to get her to bed earlier."

"Yes, no later than 8:00."

"Uh, yeah. 8:00. Sure." He had thought 9:00 was early enough. It wasn't like Sabra gave him an instruction manual.

"I'll give this back to Linda. I'm really . . . tired. I'll see you soon."

The screen became a whoosh of color before he saw Linda's face. "I don't think I like this Face thing. It probably makes me look ninety years old."

"It's her phone. It's an older model, and the resolution isn't very clear," Kevin offered, thinking the phone wasn't totally responsible. "Can you talk a bit, Aunt Linda?"

"Yeah, let me go out in the hall. She's drifting off to sleep."

He could hear the heavy hospital door open and close. "Is she that tired?"

"They gave her something new for pain. That's why. It must be stronger. I'm surprised she talked as long as she did. But she's said several times today she wanted to talk to the little girl."

Forgetting names seemed to be the theme of the evening. "Mei fussed about the same thing. So it worked out. But what else? What's next?"

"She's discharged tomorrow under hospice care. They've already delivered the bed, the oxygen, a wheelchair, and some other things. The nurse will meet us tomorrow when I take her home."

"Oh."

He heard Linda sigh. "Yeah."

"Are you going to be all right with this, Aunt Linda? This is an awful burden for you."

"Like I said, I've been through it before, not that it really helps any. But I know what to expect. I've known Sabra and loved her as long as anybody, and I know how wonderful and how aggravating she can be. Your Uncle Bob is coming back east as soon as he can to be with me, with us. He has some time off he can take. So I'll have someone with me."

"That's good. What does the doctor say?"

"We will make her comfortable. That's all. She'll eat until she can't."

"Don't they put in a feeding tube or something, like intravenous?"

"No, Kevin. You need to talk to the hospice nurse when you come. She can explain it better than me."

"She starves to death?"

"No. Not starvation. Cancer kills her. Her body is dying, Kevin, so the food doesn't matter. That's what happens."

After he ended his call with Linda, an overwhelming sense of dread settled on Kevin. What had he thought about the dying process? He'd been so fixated on Mei and trying to get her through the day that he'd put his mother's reality aside.

Getting Mei's care had seemed like an answer. If he took care of Mei for a while, Sabra would . . . what? Take the treatments? Change her mind? Miraculously get better and rise from her hospital bed to . . . take Mei back and let him return to his own life?

Or was it something else? Was he trying to say, "Look, I did something for you. I'm good enough. I am a good son." Why did he have to prove that? Was there some dark reason that never came out in those counseling sessions that he thought she left the family because of him? How could he think that after all these years? But he was fourteen at the time, a kid, and a pretty naïve one, he recognized.

Maybe the childish fear of his own wrongdoing wasn't it; maybe he didn't know what it was. But it didn't matter. Despite his resistance and defensiveness, Mei was his, permanently. In a month, weeks, there would be no Sabra, no Momma, for her to go back to.

Once Mei was asleep—after directing her bath through the door, after supervising teeth-brushing and fashion choices for the next day, after reading a few pages of a *Curious George* book in her collection, after switching off the TV because there was nothing worth watching on, he decided this might be the time to wander into the legal documents Sabra had given him. To this point he had believed everything she'd told him. He didn't suspect her of untruthfulness, but of incompleteness, especially in her anxious and exhausted mental state. He found the thick portfolio of official documents providing legal proof of Mei's short life and began at the top.

First, the court documents about the adoption, dated from March of that year. Then the copies of Sabra's application for the adoption, a sheaf of papers from an organization called Hands Across the Waters International Adoption in Fayetteville. These papers included the home study report. Then Sabra's passport. He spent some time there, noting the stamps for Italy, Ethiopia, Cameroon, Cambodian, Peru, Egypt, and finally China. He noticed the passport would soon expire.

Below those were Mei's Chinese passport, her American birth certificate with Sabra listed as parent, and Mei's new U.S. Social Security card. Then, a section of documents in Chinese. The only thing he could decipher here were dates, in British style, and photos. One document was dated February almost six years before--that would be some kind of birth certificate. He noted Mei's birthday: February 27. Another document was Mei's photo as a two-year-old, dated over three years before, which he concluded was related to her being placed in the orphanage by her parents, or maybe by the authorities. Most American kids had piles of photos of their baby and toddler years. The file had three of Mei. The file included a photo of her at three and at four; he guessed the children were photographed every year for some kind of bureaucratic purpose. Mei had lived there for more than two years. How terrible. And somehow Sabra found her.

The next section of documents told the story of Mei's life since the adoption. Her vaccinations and a medical report stating she was healthy enough to attend school. Some paperwork from her former school in Fayetteville, which she had only attended seven weeks. Other odds and ends, followed by the last group of papers, the ones she had given him in the hospital and he had stuffed into the portfolio quickly the weekend before. First, her will. There it was, on the second page: "I name my biological son, Kevin Timothy Elcott, of Charlotte, North Carolina, to be guardian of my legally adopted daughter, Mei Louise Timothy, a minor child."

Mei was not the end of her legacy to him. She bequeathed her home, car, belongings, and accounts to Kevin as well "for the purposes of material support for Mei Louise Timothy and his own discretion."

But one more document remained. Kevin's tired eyes blurred as he tackled the small print and legal jargon on that one. The lawyer had drawn up a separate document stipulating the conditions for his taking custody of Mei in case of Sabra's illness and inability to care for her. Sabra had signed it and seen it notarized.

And there was an empty line—one for his signature.

Chapter 29

Thursday. Would this be another replay of Tuesday and Wednesday, with everything fine until he picked up Mei? The morning progressed smoothly. He had a lunch meeting with a potential donor to the museum but excused himself early, hoping this was the last time he would have to skirt offending someone with money in order to collect Mei. He did explain his life circumstances had changed dramatically in the last week and he had responsibility for a family member's child now. He knew it could have sounded like a really lame excuse. He also knew the donor might have thought he'd been slapped with a paternity suit and the "family member's child" was his own. He hoped he had maneuvered the luncheon professionally enough otherwise, and the gallery picked up the tab.

On Thursday afternoon Mei gave a less dramatic replay of Tuesday and Wednesday: whining, tears, apparent exhaustion, and nodding off. But this time he let her sleep in the car and drove around for a while to kill time before arriving at Nanny Services. He sat in the parking lot and answered emails on his phone and returned calls.

The delay gave him time to mull over that empty line on the custody document. Either Sabra had forgotten about his need to add his signature, or she had chosen to forget, thinking this would give him an out if he knew about it. He gave her the benefit of the doubt, although the doubt lingered. Where did that leave him? Was he technically *not* Mei's guardian, at least not until he signed? Did the will make up for the omission of his signature? Would he get into trouble for having Mei in his house and car without the finalized document? Obviously, he needed to see a lawyer. He made a note in his phone's calendar app to address that next week and then realized the appointment time at Nanny Services had arrived.

At 3:20, he roused Mei and helped her out of the car. She yawned and tried to maneuver into the office. "I'm tired. I want something to drink."

"Yeah, I know. Look in your backpack, there's a snack for you," he urged her. She dug around and found a juice box, but he had to open it for her. The plastic around the box fought him; then he had to hold the tiny straw just right to puncture the foil on the top. Who designed these things? he thought. Mei accepted the normalcy of ironclad, high-security juice boxes. She sucked on the straw as he told the receptionist he was there for the appointment.

In a few minutes, Isabella Greene, as fresh and athletic as three days ago, ushered them into a conference room. For the next twenty minutes he talked a lot, probably more than he should have. He dumped the whole story of his past seven days on the first nanny candidate, April Garcia. April, an olive-skinned young woman with long black hair and deep dimples, smiled a lot and looked no older than fifteen. She listened and nodded through his monologue. Finally, he shifted to interview questions. "So, tell me about your experience as a nanny."

She described her previous three clients, giving details that showed she was much older than she appeared. Her last family had moved away two weeks ago, back to Mexico City, so the father could continue his professorship there. "I'm bilingual, Spanish and English, so that worked out really well."

"Oh, that's great." Too bad it's not Chinese, he thought. "What age of children are you most comfortable with?"

"All are fine with me. Mei is five, right?"

"Yes. But she probably looks younger."

"I can understand that. Everyone thinks I'm younger. I'm twenty-four although I guess I'm not supposed to say so. I'm three-quarters through my Master's in Social Work at UNC-Charlotte."

He knew the questions he wasn't allowed to ask, and he skipped quickly over typical personal ones like "do you have a boyfriend?" to find one that fit. He really hadn't prepared for these meetings—he'd had so little time. "So, why social work?" he asked, trying to learn more.

"That's a great question. Do you have about an hour?"

He was taken aback. "Excuse me?"

"Oh, sorry, that was too much. I'm really not that, um, direct. Let's just say my parents were immigrants, and we've seen a lot I think could be, well, corrected in this country for certain groups of people. Don't worry, though. I keep my politics out of everything having to do with the children."

He nodded, his mind reeling. He appreciated her honesty; maybe she'd have more empathy for Mei's situation thanks to her own background. "Tell me what a typical day, or afternoon, with Mei would be."

"I would pick her up from the school bus stop."

"Oh, you can't drive?"

"We're not allowed to have the children in our vehicles. That's a huge insurance risk."

"Oh." Could Mei handle the school bus every afternoon? She was having such meltdowns at the end of the day.

"Then we would return to your home, and I'd assess her needs. Children her age may still need naps."

"She does, or seems to."

"Right. If she wanted a healthy snack, we would do that. Then I would play with her to the extent she wants me to, review any school work she has, and give her my full attention until you arrive at home, which I understand to be 5:30?"

"Yes. Could you prepare dinner for her if I have to stay late for a meeting or event?"

"Of course, but I would need knowledge of that before-hand."

Kevin glanced at his watch, mostly because he didn't know what else to do. He had interviewed applicants for many jobs at the gallery. This was not the same. A nanny would spend three or four hours a day with Mei, and while he didn't consider Mei his sister, she was still a little human he had responsibility for.

"So, do you have any questions for me?"

"Actually, I'd like to talk to Mei for a while. Is that all right?"

"Oh, sure."

All this time Mei had sat at the other end of the confer-ence table, dwarfed by the black adult-sized swivel chair. She played with her tablet quietly. She acted as if she had grown used to this man who dragged her from place to place, talking to people she didn't know and who mostly ignored her.

April rose from her chair and went to Mei. She held out her hand. "Mei, my name is April. I'm glad to meet you."

Mei looked up. She reciprocated the gesture, wary but not afraid. "Hello."

"Shaking hands is what friends do, and I'd like to be your friend."

"Your name is April?"

"Yes. What is your full name?"

"Mei Louise Timothy."

"That's a beautiful name. My last name is Garcia. Can you say that?"

Mei repeated it slowly.

"Can you tell me about the game you are playing?"

Mei began to explain how the rabbit tried to find the carrots but they moved around and she only got points if she found one, and lost points if she looked in the same place twice.

"That sounds hard."

"It is." Mei sighed. "But I have 25zerozero points now."

"Very good."

"I have two friends at school already. Emma and Maria. They both have yellow hair. I have black hair."

"Yes. I have black hair, too."

"My teacher is a man. I think I like him now. I didn't like him first day."

"I see."

Mei began to warm up and tell about the naughty boy in her class who wouldn't play right at physical education time and had to sit in time out.

"Do you know CeeCee?" Mei asked.

"No, I don't think so."

"She's my friend, but she's a big lady."

"Ah." April said it as if Mei had revealed important ancient wisdom.

"She came to our apartment and ate meatloaf with us. I liked it."

"I like meatloaf too."

"Yeah."

Mei paused. Kevin glanced at his watch and saw that their time was coming to a close.

"Ms. Garcia . . ."

"Please call me April," she smiled and returned to her original seat across from Kevin.

"I think our time is up, April. Thank you for talking to us. I don't know what the next step is."

"Don't worry, Isabella will tell you all about that. Thank you for the interview. Bye, bye, Mei." She sent Mei a little wave, received one in return, and left.

Kevin put his head down. He was tired. Gosh, he was tired. He would take Felicity's advice and Sabra's direction and get Mei to bed earlier tonight; maybe that would help with the tearful outbursts at the end of school. But he had one more interview, and he really didn't have a point of comparison. April seemed totally qualified, honest, calm, forthright, warm, and passionate. If she had any flaws, she'd concealed them well.

Isabella Greene entered the room. "Mr. Elcott, are you ready to speak to Mia Flynn, the next applicant?"

"Oh, yes, send her in."

Mia Flynn struck him as the polar opposite of April. Tall and slender, Mia bounced into the room, her blonde hair in its ponytail bouncing with her. She greeted him and shook his hand with so much energy he felt like an old man. She immediately introduced herself to Mei, who sat up and grinned as she did for all young, pretty ladies. "Hi!"

Mia was a junior in college, studying art therapy. She had been on the track team her first two years but had to give it up due to injuries. She'd nannied for one other family of three girls, but the job ended when the mother decided to work from home. She liked to play with the children outside, taking them to parks or on walks if nothing more athletic could be arranged. "They just don't get enough physical education time in the schools, you know."

Kevin asked her a different set of questions from April; he was winging it anyway. Whereas April was calm and measured in her answers, as would be expected from someone expecting to be a licensed social worker and dealing with all kinds of people in all kinds of situations, Mia seemed like a cheerleader. What approach did Mei need? Did he even know? Of course, he didn't.

He thanked Mia for the interview, and he and Mei were left alone.

"Who was those ladies?" she asked, justifiably puzzled by the happenings of the last ninety minutes.

"They are nannies."

"Nannies? That's funny name. Nannee, nannee, nannee," she chimed, wagging her head side to side. "What a nanny do?"

"They take care of children. One of those ladies will take care of you."

"No, I don't think so. Momma take care of me."

"Mei, Momma is very sick. Do you understand?"

"She get better. You said we see her soon."

"Yes, tomorrow. I promise."

"Good. I want to see her bad."

"Momma might not get better. Mei, Momma is very sick. She may have to—" he stopped himself. How in the world was he going to explain death to a child? He'd tried before, and she clearly didn't understand because she kept asking the same questions.

There and then he decided he wouldn't. That was one thing Sabra would have to do herself.

Isabella Greene entered the conference room and sat across from Kevin. "Do you have any more questions about Mia or April?"

"Is this where I'm supposed to pick one?"

"No, you don't have to right this moment. You can think about it and let me know, say, tomorrow."

"I don't have a clue, Ms. Greene. They both seem to be great human beings. Beyond that, I confess. I'm ignorant of how to pick the better one for Mei."

"That's understandable."

"Should I ask Mei?"

"I don't—recommend it, really," Isabella made one of those faces that tried to hide how foolish she thought his question was. "Children aren't very good judges of qualifications. However, you can take into consideration how she responded to them."

"She was slow warming up to April, but I think that was just because April was first. Mia is . . ."

"Energetic, I know," Isabella smiled, understanding his hesitation. "Her last job was with three somewhat rowdy little girls who all played soccer and softball. They loved her."

"I can imagine. But she's young . . ." he paused. "I think I lean more toward April."

"You don't have to make a decision today. Why don't you sleep on it and call me in the morning? Then we'll go from there."

"When can the one I pick start?"

"Sometime next week."

"I had a question. April said Mei would have to ride the school bus."

"Or she could be in a carpool with other children. It's too big a liability for our nannies to take on for them to have the child in their car. They can drive your vehicle, but not their own. "

"Oh. I have a light truck. Could whoever I pick drive Mei in that?"

"Yes, as long as your insurance is in order and you have the right kind of child restraint."

"Good." If he had to pay more for insurance on a second driver, fine. He couldn't imagine Mei riding a school bus by herself.

In the end, Kevin called Isabella the next morning and hired April, who seemed more maternal and stable. Of all things, Mei needed calm stability more than enthusiastic athleticism. April would be able to start on Wednesday of the following week, which gave him a few days to deal with the new arrangements. Before that, his weekend would be filled with travel, helping Aunt Linda, and insisting Sabra explain her death to Mei.

Chapter 30

Friday meant he had finished a week as a—what *was* he, anyway? He could think of a number of titles, some descriptive, some cynical. Sometimes he felt like he was the servant of Mei's whims. Other times, a protector and provider. Other times, the guy who chauffeured her around. So far he had all the responsibility of parenthood and none of the joys. Mei didn't seem to care what he thought. She didn't understand or use the concepts of "please" or "thank you" or general politeness. She didn't use his name and referred to him as "that man" or "mister." She didn't brag to him about her work at school or show him a picture she had drawn just for him. The best he could ask for now was acquiescence.

In the morning he worked, planning future meetings. The Christmas and New Year's holidays were major fundraising times, and he needed a nanny as soon as possible for those late-evening events. He called Isabella to confirm his decision about engaging April. Isabella said she would initiate the paperwork and he would have to come by Monday to complete the transaction and sign the contract. Wrapping up the day in his office early, he ran to the apartment to pack some clothes. Mei still had enough clothes at his mother's home. By 2:00, they were on the road.

"We go to hospital?"

"No. We're just going to Momma's house."

"That MY house," she reminded him, pointing at her chest. He didn't respond. At least today, with the promise of home and Momma, she limited her after-school emotions to crankiness rather than frenzied, uncontrollable crying.

"I am thirsty." He noticed her use of verbs occasionally improved.

"Really?"

"Yes. I want Coca-Cola."

"No, not now. I'll get you some water in a bottle." When he saw a convenience store, he pulled over. He probably shouldn't give in to every one of her wants and demands, but they both needed some hydration for the trip.

She drank for a while, but the car ride eventually lulled her to sleep. He pulled into his mother's driveway a little before 4:00. He quieted the engine and sat for a while in the car, thinking and letting Mei finish her nap.

He'd made it. He had spent a week of his life with no regard for himself. A new experience. He didn't like it. It didn't feel generous or noble. It only felt necessary for the present. For now, he would put one foot in front of the other and smile and make his mother know Mei was cared for. He couldn't be by Sabra's bedside all the time, but he was doing what his mother requested.

Sitting there, his mind wandered over the last seventeen years. At this stage of his life, he was less distant from his dad than from his mom. Kevin realized he had not called his dad about Sabra. Tom Elcott should know about his ex-wife's condition, even if his marriage to Sabra was far in his past. Yeah, he would call soon. It would not be an easy call. His dad had remarried a few years after his divorce and moved to Memphis for work. Nancy, an attractive woman with two young boys, the widow of a cop who died in the line of duty, was a woman who needed his dad in her life, and his dad needed Nancy.

A strange late model car with South Carolina plates sat in the driveway; that must be Linda's rental, he concluded. She'd want to return it to the company and use Sabra's car and save money; he'd help his aunt with that chore. This weekend would be a long string of errands and long-delayed, sorely needed conversations.

"Aunt Linda? Mom?" he called into the house. The door was unlocked and he'd pushed it open wide. He'd have to warn them about locking the doors. He sometimes categorized Sabra's neighborhood as "a little sketch;" not crime-ridden, just in need of some renovations and a strong neighborhood watch. "Anybody home?"

Linda came from the bedroom. "Oh, Kevin. It's been so long."

They gave each other a hug, longer and warmer than he deserved. From those brief times he had spent time with his aunt, he remembered her as supremely normal. Neither pretty nor ugly, neither heavy nor thin, neither bright nor dull, but always warm, helpful, and capable of making him feel comfortable and as normal as she was. Linda's more common name symbolized her personality in contrast to her exotica-loving sister with the unusual name.

"Is Mom . . .?"

"She's awake. She's been anxious about you getting here all day."

"Well, we're here. Mei is in the car, still groggy. I wanted to scope out the place. I didn't know what would, you know, be going on."

"I wanted to have the bed in the living room, I thought it would be brighter for her. She said no, she didn't want Mei to see her home as a hospital ward and she didn't want her in bed to be the first thing visitors saw. Her room is dark; I guess that's better for her rest, too."

"Linda, are they here?" Sabra's voice came from down the hallway. Her master bedroom with its own bath lay at the far end of the house.

"Yes, honey, they're here."

"I want to get up."

"Hold on."

Linda and Kevin entered her room. He was unprepared for what met him, although he wasn't sure why. A basic hospital bed, a sort of discount, less elaborate version. A drip bag with some kind of medication. He heard a low roar and traced the long, clear tube across the floor to his mother's nose. Oxygen. She was already using oxygen. Even in the hospital, she had been breathing fine or at least seemed to be. He let himself take in his mother last. She had aged five or ten years in a week. Her face was thin, almost skeletal, her eyes sunken deeper, her skin pale with some kind of grayish hue. Her hair, in need of a cut and now gray since she had stopped coloring it a while back, spread out wildly from her head on the pillow.

"Kevin. Hey, honey. I'm glad you're here." Sabra tried to move and sit up, but only managed to adjust herself a little.

"Hi, Mom." He bent over and kissed her forehead. It was dry, almost scaly. He took her hand. The hand felt dry and scaly, too, but warm. Her hand also seemed frail and light. He didn't remember his mother being so small. She never was before.

"I know this is a lot to process. Linda's taking care of me. I don't know where I would be without her."

Alone, he thought. He pushed back thoughts about where she would be without him, too. Not now. He forecast her next question. "Mei is in the car. She slept on the way. I'll go get her if you want."

"Yes, please. When you can."

He left the room, Linda following. "What's in the drip bag?" he asked under his breath.

"Something to help with pain. Not morphine though. It helps her sleep, too, but not all the time."

"She needs oxygen?"

"Yes. Some."

He walked outside to the car. He had left the windows down on this breezy fall day, and Mei had started to wake up. As she often did upon awakening from a nap, she moved slowly from a state of confusion to anxiety to clarity. She rubbed her eyes and squinted.

"Where we?"

"We're here, at Momma's house."

"Momma?"

"Yes. Come on."

She unbuckled herself and hurried to jump out of the car seat. Now home, she ran inside, Kevin taking big steps to get ahead of her. She stopped abruptly on the porch. "Oh, I forget my picture, of horse. I show Momma."

"All right, stay here." He retrieved her artwork from the back seat and they entered.

Inside the front door, Mei stopped and confronted Linda, a stranger in her house. "Who are you? Where is Momma?"

"Mei, this is your Auntie Linda. She has come all the way from Colorado on a plane to see us and help Momma."

"Where Colorado?"

"About 1000 miles away," Linda said. "It's nice to meet you."

"She can be very direct," Kevin said, keeping the sarcasm out of his voice. "I think it's a language thing. Or maybe a five-year-old thing. Maybe just a Mei thing. Don't ask me."

"I see Momma. She in her room?"

"Yes, but Momma is very sick, so you have to be gentle with her," he reminded her.

"Okay."

They walked together into Sabra's room. "Momma!" Mei did not seem to notice the new and bigger bed, the tube in her mother's nose, the medication coming through another tube into her hand. For five days she had endured a strange man, a new school, a teacher with hair on his face, and a different bed. Now she had her mother back, the woman who had rescued her from the orphanage, who had brought her to America and lavished her with attention and clothes and toys for six months.

"Oh, Mei, I'm so happy to see you. Come up here."

Sabra let Mei crawl into bed with her. "Look, Momma, I make picture for you."

Sabra glanced at the large colorful page, barely taking it in, more concerned about Mei than the art. Kevin could see her wince just from moving her body in the bed. "Oh, you worked so hard on it, I can see. I like it." Linda hovered, concerned that Mei was being too rough on Sabra in her joy to be home.

"Mei and I would like to be alone for a minute," Sabra said, firmly but with a weak smile that revived her face. Linda and Kevin left obediently.

Chapter 31

"So, how has it gone this week, as a new father?" Linda asked as she poured him a glass of iced tea and they sat at the kitchen table. The house was cluttered, somewhat in disarray, but not because Linda was a bad housekeeper. Sabra often joked her homemaking style was controlled chaos.

"Please. I don't know what I am, but I'm not a dad. I'm a servant, maybe. If you had told me a week ago I'd have a five-year-old girl in my life, I would have laughed my head off. Somehow we got through it. She's not horrible, but she knows her own mind and tells me what she thinks. She's probably learned survival instincts. She definitely hasn't learned any manners. I might be doing everything wrong, but she seems okay so far."

"You're a saint."

"No. I didn't have a choice, Linda. None at all."

"Are you going to keep her?"

"What?"

"Kevin, what Sabra did to you was wrong," Linda said, lowering her voice almost to a whisper. "For someone who has been so all-fired self-righteous in her life about ethics and that kind of thing, she blew it. You don't just dump a child on someone who has no background with children."

"Right now, I don't know what else to do. Later, I'll think about it. As long as Mom is alive, I'm Mei's guardian. End of that story."

"It's just wrong. It's wrong for the child, it's wrong for you."

"Maybe. I'll let you know later. Now, we wait and do whatever we can." He paused. "What about you? Is this hard on you?"

"No. She's not a hard patient. She watches TV, talks to some people on the phone. Sleeps. Eats some broth and oatmeal and pudding, not much. We talk about the old days, growing up, being girls. It's all right. I'd rather be here as a guest, sure, than watching her die."

"Has she said anything about why she didn't want the treatments?"

"She says different things. She says she doesn't believe they would work. That it would be too hard on everyone."

"And this is easier?"

"People say things, Kevin, when they are dying, things they don't mean but think they do. I think the word "cancer" made her freeze her life. When I try to talk about her condition, she just changes the subject."

They sat for a few moments, when Mei walked in. "Can I have drink? I thirsty." Back with her momma, her grammar reverted to more simplistic English. Maybe, he thought, she has a hard time knowing what's expected of her. That would make sense.

"Sure, honey," Linda said. "You want tea or juice?"

"I want Coca-Cola."

"I don't have any, darling."

"Mei, Coke isn't good for you. It's only for special times. Tea or juice?"

Mei made a face at Kevin, as if he were a killjoy who always stopped her from getting what she wanted. "Juice."

Linda stood up to open the refrigerator. "I have orange? Is that okay?"

Mei nodded and climbed into the kitchen chair. She drank her juice quickly. "More." She held out her cup.

I really need to start teaching her the 'please' thing soon, he thought. "In a little bit, Mei. Did you talk with Momma?"

"Yeah. She sleep now. She say she tired."

"Yes, Momma *is* tired." He emphasized the verb to remind Mei.

"Momma said she go to heaven."

"What?"

As if Kevin didn't understand English, Mei changed to more correctness. "Momma say she is going to heaven. With God. She very sick and she going to die."

"She told you that?"

"Yeah."

Kevin held his breath. Well, that was one conversation with Sabra he wouldn't have to have. His mother's good sense had prevailed and she had explained death, in a way, to Mei.

"Do you understand what she said?"

Mei nodded.

"Are you sad?"

"Yeah." Mei said this in a dreamy, distant way.

Linda and Kevin exchanged glances. "We can talk about it any time you want to, Mei," he said.

"I know. She say I have to be brave girl and be happy with you. You will take care of me." But she didn't sound convinced.

"Yes, I will." Even as he said it, Kevin wondered if he could keep his promise.

The weekend was a melee of sitting with Sabra, running errands for Linda, packing more of Mei's clothes and toys, renting a trailer to haul back her dresser and belongings—he'd return the unfinished IKEA project, thankful not to have to wrestle with it—completing paperwork related to hospice care and legalities, and occasionally entertaining Mei. He wished Felicity were with him, but he reminded himself again he needed to forget about their future together.

Mei acted quiet and reflective, as reflective as a five-year-old could be. She tried to help her mother. She retrieved items for Sabra and brought her food or drinks when asked. Sabra's face seemed to lose a few years of age and decline by having Mei around. She spoke kindly and gratefully to Kevin about his care for her. Mei lay in bed with her and they watched children's television together for a while. Linda was happy for company she knew, rather than neighbors or Sabra's friends, and a break from full-time caregiving. On Saturday afternoon one of Sabra's colleagues from the social sciences department, a forty-ish woman named Sandra, came by. The visit was awkward but Sabra appreciated it. Sandra seemed like the college's scout who would go back and tell the rest of the faculty whether they should attempt to visit a dying woman. Sandra did bring a frozen chicken casserole Linda cooked for Sunday dinner.

Late Sunday afternoon they all exchanged hugs and he drove Mei back to Charlotte. Mei continued her general silence and agreeableness; somehow she seemed to understand this man named Kevin would take her Momma's place, at least for now.

Chapter 32

By the end of the second week of caring for Mei, the two had reached a sort of rhythm, a sometimes-uneasy way of being together. April began as nanny on Wednesday, and Kevin escorted her through the routines of their day. On Thursday, April took over. He checked in with her twice, but he liked the ability to stay at work until 5:00 and attend to the work that had been neglected in the past two weeks. On Friday he and Mei returned to Fayetteville, and their visit was very similar to the first, except that Sabra slept more and spent less time with Mei. Her decline did not seem as dramatic because he had grown used to it the first weekend.

Week three ran smoothly, except April reported Mei continued to be irritable and upset when picked up from school. Juice—she guzzled it so fast April had two juice boxes ready for it--and a snack and one-hour nap helped. Afterward, she was a different child, and soon Mei was so happy with this new lady, devoted to her needs, that she rarely brought up CeeCee's name.

Felicity checked in with him a couple of times, thoughtful, inquisitive, willing to listen, but they did not see each other except for a quick sandwich lunch the week after April took over.

The eatery was packed and not a place for intimate conversation. They sat down with their food at the smallest available table in the middle of the room.

"So. . . how's your mom?"

He told the truth. "Maybe three weeks or a month left. My aunt Linda and now her husband Bob, who just flew in from Denver, are doing the real work with that. She's a treasure. I'm glad Mom has someone in the family who can be there for her."

"Oh?" He noticed Felicity was back to her noncommittal answers. He wasn't sure whether she wanted more information, but he plunged on to answer her question.

"She has another sister in Flagstaff, Arizona but I don't know what her problem is. Marjorie came up with an excuse not to come. Otherwise, Mom has no brothers, cousins too distant, and no kids but me. Kind of sad, in some ways, but I'm thankful for Linda."

"Yes. Sisters like that are . . . like you say, treasures. Both of mine are, I think. Too bad about the other one, I mean, your other aunt."

"Yeah." He paused. "And you?"

"Overworked."

"I'm sorry about that."

"It hasn't changed from when we . . . you know."

"Yeah, about that . . ."

"Yes." She hadn't touched her sandwich, he noted but did take a sip of her lemoned water. "I'm sorry I laid all my life on you. It was not great timing."

"Felicity, there is no need to apologize. You could have just said, 'Let's call it off.' You were completely honest." And it was weird timing, he thought, but when would have been better to reveal the worst parts of her past? She was what they called a "wounded person". She hid it well. No one would guess.

"That's good of you to say. I'm not sure I was completely honest—I don't know how I could be. I could have told you before, I guess."

"No, please don't get onto yourself about it."

"To add to the being honest part, you are the first guy I saw for any length of time since . . . you know."

He wanted to say, "Oh," like she did, but opted for a "Hmm."

"I mean, sure, I had a few dates, but they were total lo—, well, you know. I could tell from the beginning. More into themselves and their careers than anything else."

"I can imagine."

"They would not have wanted to even speak to me after what I told you."

He wondered if this was a compliment, or something else.

"I guess there are guys like that out there," he said. Where was she going with this? He thought. He noticed he had only taken one bite from his own sandwich.

"So, I mean, thank you for not acting like I had a disease," she said. She finally lifted her sandwich, bit delicately, and chewed slowly. After a pause. "How's Mei?"

He answered. At first, it was choppy and hard to express. But he warmed up, sharing more and more of Mei's daily words and actions, even getting a laugh out of the reserved and almost somber Felicity. She had wanted to clear the air and that's why she asked him to share lunch with her. Perhaps being around Mei had been more painful for her than he could understand.

"You seem to be getting along with her," she observed.

"Maybe. That's the best I can do."

"Of course. Don't be so hard on yourself. You're going through something unbelievably hard."

"Thanks. I do need to remind myself of that sometimes."

"Kevin, if I didn't make it clear before, I'm not walking away from you as a person. Just as a . . . you know, whatever we're supposed to call it nowadays. I'm dumb enough to think men and women can be friends without the other . . . stuff."

He had no reply to this and didn't want to say something stupid and awkward. "Thank you" almost came out, but thank her for what? He didn't know if he was capable of saying, "That's good to know" without sounding sarcastic. "Me too"? No. He landed on the words he thought women were supposed to like. "I understand."

She seemed satisfied with his words, and dug into her sandwich as if she had to say her piece before eating. He ate too for a while.

"Sandwich okay?" he finally asked.

"Um-hum." She chewed. "It has an interesting herb on it. Good. New. To me at least."

They began to chat about inconsequential things, at least as compared to the previous topics. The gallery. Some renovation to her apartment. The price of gas. They needed to get back to their jobs. He didn't want to leave yet, partly because he enjoyed her company, and partly because he had something else to say.

"Felicity, I'm glad you agreed to have lunch with me. If we're clearing the air, or whatever, I want to say, uh, friendship is great and all, and I appreciate it and you want to know about Mei. But, in the long run, that won't be enough . . . for me."

She averted her eyes, not her usual reaction in a conversation. "Yes. Thank you for being honest, Kevin." She picked up her purse and put her raincoat back on, which she had lain over the third chair at the table. "I've got to run. I hope to see you again, soon, and Mei. I'd like to meet April. I bet Mei's fallen in love with her."

She hung her purse on her shoulder, clearly in a hurry to leave now. "Please let me know . . . about your mom . . . and if and . . . when she passes," Felicity said.

And she was gone. He didn't doubt her sincerity, despite her sudden departure. As he watched her leave, he saw her wipe something from below each eye as she left the restaurant.

He did not look forward to the third necessary weekend visit. Linda's husband Bob had arrived the previous Monday, so she had help and companionship. The house was crowded now. More people in the neighborhood and from the college came by. Sabra met briefly with each, smiled as best she could, and fell asleep after each visit. She took small doses of morphine now for pain. She ate a few bites of pudding and spoonsful of broth once a day. She couldn't let Mei in bed with her anymore. And she told Linda she wanted to talk to Kevin privately.

"Yeah, Mom," he sat down by her bed. "Can I get you anything?"

"No, honey. I just wanted to talk a little."

"Sure." He wasn't sure why he was trying to sound upbeat. It was kind of pointless.

"How are you, Kevin?" she asked. Her voice was weak, breathy. He could tell conversing, even just speaking, sapped what little strength she had.

"Mom, I'm fine."

"No, really."

"Okay. I'm overwhelmed. But I try not to think about it."

"I know. Me too." She turned her face away, as if to watch the world on the other side of the window. He followed her eyes to a tree, maybe an oak or poplar. Kevin wasn't sure because he'd never really learned tree names. A few of its leaves, almost brown, floated downward in the waning late October sun. They could hear an ambulance siren a couple of streets away.

Sabra finally spoke. "I want to say thank you."

"Sure, Mom. But you don't have to."

"Yes, I do. Thank you for coming back on the weekends and bringing Mei."

He wanted to say he didn't have a choice, but he checked himself. It would sound petulant, and that was neither what he needed nor wanted to be at this moment. With that edited from his words, he didn't know how to respond. As if she knew that, Sabra went on.

"I think you're taking good care of her."

He wanted to say, "How would I know if I were?" Instead, "I try."

"She likes you."

He snorted and regretted it. "I think she tolerates me right now. Maybe sometime in the future there will be something else. She likes Felicity and her parapro and the nanny and the lady who delivers the groceries more than me."

"No, she said, 'I like Kevin.'"

"Hmm. Did she give you a reason?"

"She said you were funny and she liked the food you give her and you don't fuss at her and she likes your car and your truck."

"Well, that's something. If she thinks I'm funny, she has a weird sense of humor. And she must laugh behind my back."

"She's five. Who knows what funny means to her, especially when she has only been around English and funny-looking Americans since March."

"True." He remained silent. He wanted Sabra to talk.

"Kevin, I might as well be honest and real here. When, or if you come next week, there's no telling how I'll be, what shape I'll be in."

"We can hope for the best." Lame, Kevin, he thought.

"No, there is no 'best.' I might have a short revival of strength. That kind of thing happens, but I don't feel like it now. I might be like this for some more weeks, or I might be unconscious in six days."

He knew there was no reason to argue with her or try to put a good face on her condition. She had spent years as a social worker in a hospital. She would not have spoken to a patient like this, but to herself, she wouldn't hide the truth.

"I'm sorry," was all he could say.

"I know I've done things in our relationship that have made you resent me," she said, moving on to what she had only a little strength left to say.

"No, Mom, I don't resent you. Not as an adult. I can't say I understood you, and sometimes I was a turd, ambivalent, and all about me and a crappy communicator, but resentment was not part of it."

"I wouldn't blame you much if you did have some re-sentment, but that's not the point now. I know asking you to be Mei's guardian was more than could be expected . . ."

There was asking? he thought. I got the impression I was told. But he listened.

"But there was no one else who could do it. No one else I would trust."

"I suppose it's true, Mom," he spoke quietly, but without a sense of reassurance, agreement, or joy. Only accep-tance of what had come to pass.

"I trust you. You will raise her well. You will take care of her, make sure she is educated right, make sure she knows how men should treat her. I don't think, no, hon-estly, I know I couldn't have done that. I would have spoiled her, given her too much. I would have let her have her way too much. I might have taught her to dislike and distrust men, maybe indirectly or unintentionally. And even if I had not gotten cancer now, something might have happened to me later at my age."

Kevin wanted to say, why didn't you think of these before adopting a child? Why did the decision have to be about you? But somewhere in these words of Sabra's were two messages. First, an apology, which he doubted she would ever explicitly give because she would never admit her choices needed forgiveness. And second, a kind of compliment to him for being an adult qualified to take care of her child.

"I appreciate you believing that of me, Mom." He said after an uncomfortable pause. If he wanted to spew any anger and frustration, he knew it was too late. Perhaps in a week, she would be beyond conversation, beyond reaching. He could not tell her the truth, not now. He should have done that many years ago, but it would have meant building bonds with her, stepping over fences and walls he hadn't wanted to cross in the past.

"I know, deep down, you want an apology," she said, as if she were reading his mind. Was that what he wanted? Not now. "But I can't give it. Maybe in a few days I will call you and ask forgiveness, but I don't think so." Yes, she was honest, forthright, bold, and infuriating in her self-knowledge. "I only hope I see you and Mei again."

"You have explained to Mei what will happen, haven't you?"

"Yes, as best I could. I'm not religious, as you know, but I opted for that. It works with children for them to think of their adults in a happy place. I am going to be cremated, so there won't be a cemetery plot for you all to visit. If you like, you can spread the ashes in some place meaningful to you. I like Grandfather Mountain, it's beautiful, but I don't know if they allow folks to spread ashes there."

"I'll try to fulfill your wishes as much as I can."

"I've talked to Linda and Bob about the memorial service, what to do. Sandra from my department at the college said she would help. It will be informal, but I'd like you to come."

"Of course, Mom. I wouldn't miss that."

"Have you talked to your father?" This was an abrupt change of topic from Sabra, and he hoped she didn't pick up on the surprise on his face.

"Actually, no. I've tried. A few times. I couldn't get into the right frame of mind. And when I was, Mei needed something, so I put it off."

"You should when you can, but I've already talked to him."

"Oh." This surprised him.

"What was said is between us, but he knows."

"All right." He didn't want to imagine that conversation. His father had never spoken well of his mother since the circumstances surrounding their divorce.

"My life insurance and accounts all have you as beneficiary. It won't be much, but it will help for a few years with Mei. I'm all right with her going to public school, of course. Private is too big of an expense, although I think she'd do well there. Save money if you can for her to go to a good college. I think she's smart. And please get her back into her music lessons."

"Yes," he said. This was not a promise, only a way to respond.

"Thank you, Kevin. You'll take care of her well, I know. I trust you. And I love you." She sighed. "Could you get me some more ice chips?"

"Sure, Mom." He picked up the Styrofoam cup and plastic spoon she used for chips. She could still spoon a few into her mouth. He walked to the kitchen and found one of the frozen bags the hospital had provided. On returning to her room, he found her fast asleep. He set the cup of ice down and sat by her bed for a while.

He knew people prayed in this situation, and he tried, but he was out of practice and not exactly sure of what the point would be. His faith upbringing was hazy and superficial. His dad had been a pretty consistent Episcopalian. Sabra had been an agreeable agnostic who allowed her son to be baptized as a baby and confirmed at twelve because Tom Elcott wanted it that way. Kevin had dallied with campus religious groups in college and high school, searching for something solid. Some of it stuck. But sitting there, he could only ask God to make his mother peaceful at this time and not be in pain. The drip into her IV was answering the second request. As to the first, Sabra would have to make her own peace with God.

Chapter 33

On Sunday evening Kevin and Mei drove back to Charlotte for Week Four of their lives together. It seemed normal now, less strange, but still not right. He was thankful for April, who helped Mei with her baths in the evening so he did not have to. April was also physically affectionate, which Mei needed. She tried to sit on his lap, to snuggle up to him. He gently put her in another chair or moved away when she did.

The truth was, he was afraid of her. He was afraid she would mistakenly and innocently say something that would lead her parapro or even April to conclude the worst. He knew it wasn't healthy for a child to be deprived of physical touch, but he didn't see his action as depriving her. He was protecting himself, and what would happen to her if he were falsely accused, if she was taken into the child welfare system due to a misunderstanding?

Yes, what would happen? What would happen after Sabra died? In the few times he thought about the future, he would have confessed it terrified him. What would

Mei be like at eight? Eleven? Fourteen? And one day he wanted to get married and have his own children. How would that work? How would a wife respond to Mei's presence in his life?

How could he possibly do this?

Kevin did call his father during the fourth week. Tom Elcott confirmed he had talked with Sabra, but it was all he offered.

"Did she tell you about Mei?"

"What happened in May?" said Tom.

So like her, Kevin thought. "You might as well know, since the next time you see me I might have Mei with me. Mei Louise Timothy, five years old, born somewhere in China. Mom adopted her less than a year ago. She's my legacy. A little sister, the sibling I never had."

"You're putting me on."

"No, Dad. I have a sister now. I'm this little girl's guardian."

"That's not possible."

"I'm afraid it is."

"Who would be stupid enough to allow your mother to adopt a kid?"

This hurt, and Kevin winced at his father's bitterness after all these years. "I don't know, but it's legal. And now she's legally mine, without my knowledge. Or sort of. There might be some legal technicalities to work out."

"That's wrong. How could she do this to you?"

"She did. And I wasn't exactly in a place to say 'Forget it.'"

Tom paused on the line. Kevin knew his father was trying to keep from exploding. "What the hell are you going to do? You can't raise a child."

"I probably can't, but right now I am. Once Mom is gone, I may rethink this whole plan. I can't think about it now. She will probably be passed in a couple of weeks, Dad. I've got to get through that first."

"I'm sorry you're losing your mother, Kevin, even if she expects you to clean up after her decisions."

"The problem is, her decision involves an abandoned child, so it's not that easy. Anyway, how are Nancy and the boys?"

"They are fine. Our older boy, Dustin, graduates from UT-Martin in December. Hunter started at U of Memphis this semester. So we get one done about the time we have to pay for the second."

"Good deal. Well, say hello to them for me. Can I come see you all at Christmas for a few days?"

"Of course, any time."

"I'll have extra baggage."

"Oh, yeah, the little girl. Well, Nancy will probably get a kick out of that. Does she speak English?"

"Oh, yeah. She's smart, and not a bad kid as kids go. Just not what I expected to be doing a month ago."

"I bet."

"I'll see you later, Dad. I'll call when, you know, happens."

"Sure, Kevin. Bye, I love you."

He hung up. He knew he was a lot like his dad, for which he was thankful. His dad had not let himself inflict his own pain over a dead marriage on Kevin the teenager. Tom had not remarried until Kevin was in college. Kevin wondered how his parents had gotten together and stayed married as long as they had. They were as different in values and temperament and politics as two people could be, and those differences only grew after their divorce.

These thoughts occupied Kevin for a few minutes after the phone call with his father. Soon his attention was diverted by Mei wanting a drink before bedtime. She reminded him she needed to take some money to school tomorrow, but she didn't know how many dollars.

On Thursday night of the fourth week his aunt Linda called at 10:00 p.m. He knew immediately something was wrong.

"Yeah, Aunt Linda?"

"Are you coming tomorrow?"

"Sure."

"Can you come early?"

"Why?"

"It's the end soon, I think, honey. The hospice nurse thinks so, too. If you want to see her alive, you should be here in the morning."

"Is she conscious?"

"Barely. The morphine doses are pretty heavy now."

"All right. I'll do my best. Thank you. I'm sorry. You've been great. She needed you so much."

"She's my sister. I couldn't let her go through this alone."

"I know. I'll see you in the morning."

This meant taking Mei out of school for a while. He'd make calls in the morning. He'd pack tonight to leave early. They could be there by 10:00 a.m.

What would be his last words to his mother, a difficult woman whose love was never in doubt but never predictable?

Mei whined a little about missing school. Something special was supposed to take place; she wasn't sure what but she was supposed to take some money. He fished in her book bag and found a flyer about a fundraiser selling school supplies with the school's logo on them. "We're going to see Momma now."

"Why now?"

He kneeled down by her at the breakfast table and put his hands on her shoulders. "Mei, you know what Momma told you about how she was going to go to heaven and be with God because she is very sick?"

Mei nodded but looked away. "I don't like that."

"I know. I don't either. But Momma is very sick. She will go to heaven very soon. We have to go say goodbye to her."

"Will she come back from heaven?"

Kevin felt his tears forming. Sorrow was a rare emotion for him. His infrequent attendance at funerals or viewings shielded him from the rawness of grief. "No, Mei. When somebody goes to heaven, they never come back." He could hear the undercurrent of anger in his voice, anger that he had to explain death to a small child, that he could not endure his own loss alone but had to drag Mei, whom he barely knew, along with him.

Something had broken through to Mei, despite the language, her age, and her typical morning mood. "Never come back? Momma not come back to us from heaven?" Her dark eyes glistened.

"No, Mei. That's why we have to go, now. We have to say goodbye to Momma. I need you to help me and be a good girl for now, for many days, okay?"

She nodded. She turned to her bowl of Cheerios and dangled the spoon. "I not hungry."

He didn't need her to dawdle, so he agreed to let her skip breakfast so they could leave. "All right. Go brush your teeth and we'll leave soon."

She submitted to his directions. After quick calls to work and Mei's school and after throwing suitcases in the back of his car, they were on the road one more time, perhaps the last for a while.

Chapter 34

When they arrived a little before 10:00, Linda met them at the door. She wore her housecoat and nightgown.

"It's been a long night. A lot of pain. The hospice nurse had to come and give her a heavier dose of morphine."

"You do look exhausted, Aunt Linda. Why not go get some rest?"

"I've just had a nap. Bob is with her, in case something happens. But I'm glad you're here. She's been calling your name."

"Really?"

"Yes, of course. But I can't say it makes sense."

"Mei, you stay with Auntie Linda. You probably have to use the bathroom, don't you?"

Mei's wide eyes and quiet nod told her fear. She seemed to know something was different this time. The mood of the house was hushed, all the blinds drawn. "Go ahead then, and I'll come get you after I talk to Momma."

He entered his mother's room slowly, inching the door open. "Oh, hi, Kevin," said Bob, standing up. A head taller than Kevin, Bob shook his hand. "Glad you made it. Your mom's not doing well, not at all."

Bob was an affable, heavy man, one who took over a room with his size but not his demeanor. He'd been an insurance adjuster for forty years and had learned to approach life, even sitting by a deathbed, with a calmness that was comforting but unnerving at the same time. Nothing seemed to intrude on Bob's composure.

Kevin knelt down by his mother's bed. She lay on her side, staring. "Hey, Mom."

"Kevin?" her voice was raspy, barely a whisper.

"Yeah, Mom, it's me."

"Kevin, I'm sorry."

"About what, Mom?"

"About the ball hitting you in the head."

"What ball, Mom?"

"The baseball. Even though you wore the helmet, that boy threw too hard. It knocked you out."

Kevin recalled the time in rec league baseball when he was ten. The pitcher, widely known to be a jerk of an older kid, tried to brush him back from the plate and threw too close. The fastball knocked his helmet off and Kevin landed in the dirt, dazed. He never was that good at baseball. If he had a sport as a kid, it was soccer, and he ran track in high school one year. In fact, he only played baseball one year, and was glad to be done with it. He wasn't knocked out, but that was how Sabra remembered it, now, more than twenty years later. A memory of his childhood was what her confused, traveling mind had settled on and what she wanted to apologize for as she faced death.

"That's okay, Mom. I hadn't thought about that in years. He didn't hurt me. Embarrassed me in front of my friends, but he was a piece of crap anyway."

"Oh. How old are you now?"

"I'm thirty-one Mom."

"Do you have children?"

He paused. "No, Mom."

"What happened to that pretty girl you were going to marry?"

"What girl, Mom?"

"The girl . . . I don't remember." Her voice was so soft he had to bend his ear down to a couple of inches from her mouth. Where is . . . where . . .?"

"Where is who, Mom? Mei?"

"Where is Tom? My husband Tom."

Kevin felt tears on his cheek. He hadn't expected this. It wasn't dementia, but her mind processing, somehow, her life in her last moments. He didn't understand it. If he had been a good son and had made the time, he would have read about death, the literature from the hospice organization, and would have known what she was going through right now. He would have known, but wouldn't have been able to help. She was being sucked away from them now, sinking into a place of oblivion, and he could only watch.

He decided there at her bedside that, unless she called for Mei, not to put Mei through watching the woman she called Momma now be wrenched from her. At five Mei had been through more than most adults had been. The least he could do was shield her from watching Sabra die.

Sabra grew quiet. She still breathed, almost imperceptibly, and her eyes stared ahead, but she did not speak. He sat in the chair Bob had left for him. He closed his eyes and tried to release the tension in his body. He was unsuccessful. He felt the sobs come up through his chest and he let them come.

Why hadn't he spent more time with his mother, why had he gone so many months without seeing her? Was his life and work so important? He ran an art gallery, for crying out loud. He wasn't a brain surgeon in the third world. He'd spent plenty of weekends out with friends, going to ball games at Chapel Hill, or with women who eventually bored him. He'd even skipped the last holidays with her, preferring to fly to Memphis to see his father and step-brothers than drive the few miles to see Sabra.

Why would she think, then, he was fit to raise a little girl? He wasn't. So far he had escorted Mei; fed her; made sure she was warm and protected, in school, watched, unharmed. That was not raising a child. Some time in the future he would have to face the truth and either change himself or change the situation, but he couldn't think about the future now.

Sabra had closed her eyes and appeared to be sleeping; her blanket rose and fell slowly, and he could hear rushes of air. In these last days, the oxygen tubes had been removed, and no machine hummed. He left the room, wondering how many hours more she would suffer.

Sabra's suffering did not last much longer. Sometime in the afternoon—perhaps around 2:15, the time the hospice nurse later recorded—she stopped breathing. Linda was with her, holding her hand, and praying her sister would find peace in another world. Linda's presence beside her was probably as it should be. Linda, seven years older than Sabra, had seen her sister brought home from the hospital fifty-six years before. She knew her best and probably loved her best.

Kevin stood firm that Mei would not see Sabra, dying or dead. He asked Bob to take Mei somewhere, anywhere, for an hour or so when the funeral home came to retrieve the body for cremation. Bob complied and took her to a park down the street. Mei agreed to be pushed in the swing and to climb the slide but had taken on the mood of the adults. Mei had not asked about her Momma and had watched TV when Kevin abandoned her to say goodbye to Sabra. She had given one-word answers to the grownup questions, had nibbled at a sandwich, and went into her old bedroom to play with the few toys left there. Kevin wanted to help but didn't know how. He was inexperienced in his own grief, much less shepherding the sorrow of a child. He let Linda and Bob, experts in grandchildren since they had five of their own, tend to her.

Later in the afternoon, after two heavy-set men wearing dark suits and somber ties, employees of the funeral home, came to the house and removed Sabra's body, he realized he had not spoken to Mei for hours. He found her in her old room. She was pretending to read to herself, telling stories about the figures in a Doctor Seuss book. He couldn't understand a word of what she said. She spoke Chinese, something he had not heard her do since the first days he took over her care four weeks before. Her voice sounded angry and frustrated and she pounded her delicate fist at the drawings of Horton the blue elephant, who absorbed her outbursts in stride.

Chapter 35

Kevin realized how sheltered he had been from death, from the rituals of it, the business of it, the legalities of it. On Saturday morning he and Linda made arrangements with the funeral home for a memorial service the following Saturday. He called Sandra the colleague—he couldn't remember her last name, but she'd left her phone number—and asked her to organize the part of the service that would involve people from the college. He would have to speak. Dad would not come, of course. Linda contacted some more distant family members in the Charlotte area and in the Carolinas. He called Felicity to let her know. She promised to attend on Saturday, offered her condolences sincerely and kindly, and asked about Mei. He couldn't tell if she was coming because she had promised earlier or for a deeper reason. Details like where donations should go for flowers needed attention. He remembered the name of the adoption agency she had used to find Mei, an international one connected to a small denomination, and put their name on the obituary for the "in lieu of flowers" line.

On Monday he made an appointment with a lawyer who was recommended to him by the funeral home to help him execute Sabra's estate. On Tuesday he met with Lydia Bridges, whose photo on her card showed a woman ten years younger. But Attorney Bridges treated him professionally, listened to his story, and raised some questions he didn't anticipate.

"Your mother named you guardian of a minor child she'd adopted, but she didn't tell you?"

"No, she didn't. Not until she was very ill. She gave me the papers, and they looked legal. I have Mei's birth certificate, passport from travel, immigration papers, everything from the governments of China and the U.S. To be honest, this has been such a rush, such a change, that I haven't read them thoroughly. I haven't even figured out what part of China she came from to learn what language she speaks. When I say Mei was dumped on me, I don't mean it to demean the child. I mean she was handed to me with a briefcase of papers, and I've looked through them enough to get her in school and hopefully not get arrested for having a minor child I'm not related to."

"Let's just stop there. Legally, she should have secured your notarized signature on those papers agreeing to become the little girl's guardian."

"To be honest, I wondered about that." He fished through the portfolio and handed her the document with his missing signature. "I found this with her will."

Lydia Bridges perused it. "Yes, you were supposed to sign it. Otherwise, the minor child could be in danger of becoming a ward of the court."

"But she put it in her will that I would have her."

"Yes, but in what capacity? You aren't a blood relative. Are you planning to adopt her yourself? This is not my main expertise, adoption law that is, and what I'm about to say will sound very harsh at this time, but your mother did not do you any favors."

"So that means my guardianship of Mei might be questioned?"

"Possibly. Again, you need an adoption lawyer. I suggest you consult one as soon as possible."

"But what would happen?"

"I'm not in a position to give you legal advice on that, Mr. Elcott. But if you haven't agreed to take Mei, you can't be expected to continue as her guardian."

"I can't give her back." But in the back of his mind, a voice said, "Can't you? Is this the best for her and you?"

"Again, I'm speaking off the record here, but adoptions can be reversed. It's rare, of course, but sometimes adoptions do not work out and parents change their minds. Then the court decides what's in the best interests of the child."

Kevin could only stare at Ms. Bridges. His mind raced. He could lose Mei; at the same time, he could ask her to be placed elsewhere. He felt sick. "I wasn't ready for this. I apologize. I'm shocked."

"I apologize, too. This is a difficult time for you, Mr. Elcott. No one should make decisions during times of loss and grief. And I'm only giving you advice to get a second opinion from someone with adoption law expertise. Let's move on, if you don't mind, to your mother's financial assets."

He realized lawyers were busy and he had engaged her for one purpose, not to offer him personal counseling. He also realized they billed by time and he did not want to throw her any more money than needed. But he felt like a sort of lifeline had been thrown to him, and it was attached to nothing.

He didn't like keeping Mei out of school for a whole week any more than he liked missing work. However, he wanted to tend to as many of Sabra's estate issues as possible and not have to return to Fayetteville multiple times. The week filled with new experiences and sensations. On Tuesday, the same day he spoke with Lydia Bridges, the funeral home brought the urn with Sabra's ashes. He also made appointments with a real estate agent to put her house on the market, with an estate agent to sell the furniture and household goods, and with the bank to create an estate account. Events moved fast. He preferred it that way. He could avoid Mei, whom Linda and Bob seemed content to care for, just as Mei seemed content not to deal with him. And he could avoid thinking about his mother, the fraught years of their relationship.

In many ways, he hoped to end this stage of his life, and more and more he wondered if he actually had an out to raising Mei, if what Lydia Bridges said gave him permission to find another way, to arrange for a better home for her than living with him.

Chapter 36

On Thursday Mei gave the first indication she understood Sabra was gone and it disturbed her. Or maybe it was just the first indication Kevin had bothered to notice. He had managed not to be alone with her since Saturday. Linda and Bob had gone out for the afternoon for a well-deserved break. Linda had arranged to meet a friend from her younger days in North Carolina who lived in Lumberton. She and Bob planned to fly home on Monday after the memorial service.

"Why Momma go to heaven? Why she die?" He was working on bank documents. Mei approached him defiantly, as if she were hunting for the person responsible for Momma's death.

I don't know, he wanted to say. I don't have a clue. She was only 56. She was relatively healthy, I always thought, beyond the typical mid-50s stuff like cholesterol. Nobody else I know of in our family has had that kind of cancer. They all die of self-inflicted diseases. She just got sick and died. Why are you asking me?

Of course, he kept the torrent of words back. "She was very sick, Mei. Her body was tired from fighting the sickness. She couldn't fight any more. When our bodies get that tired, we die."

"Who take care of me?"

"I will, of course." Why did he feel like he was lying? "You'll live with me. In *our* apartment. We will go back there on Sunday, in four days, and you'll go back to school, to Mr. Benson's class, and Miss April will take care of you. You like Miss April, don't you?"

She was not to be distracted. "Where Momma go?"

"Do you mean, where is her body? Her soul is with God in heaven. Her body, we sent it to a place called a funeral home, and they take care of her body." Even he knew the concept of cremation would scar Mei deeply and probably cause terrifying nightmares. He wasn't sure he was on board with the whole cremation thing, but it was what Sabra wanted, probably to save money and from thinking it was better for the environment. It was too late to question any of that now anyway. On second thought, though, he didn't think the idea of her momma in a box underground forever would comfort Mei very much either.

"I never see her again?"

"No, Mei. I'm sorry. On Saturday, in three days, we are going to have, sort of like a party, but a sad one, and people are going to come and talk about Momma and why they loved her and how they will remember her. You can come and say something to the people if you want."

She thought about this and looked away, then let out a deep breath. "I bored."

Interesting she knows that word, he thought. Where did she learn it? He hadn't heard it from her before. "I know. I know you should be in school, but we had to stay here this week to help Aunt Linda and Uncle Bob and do some other adult things."

"What is 'dult'?"

"Grown-ups, I mean. Big people. I had to go to the bank and talk to people about Momma."

"Can I have drink?"

"Yes, I'll get you something."

He sighed, thankful she didn't dig for more answers he didn't have. "Maybe I need to take a break here. After we get some tea, let's go for a walk, Mei. We need some fresh air, and that park down the street looks kind of nice. You'll need to wear your jacket. It's chilly."

The week was a slow walk to Saturday when they would gather at the funeral home for a memorial service he had very little say in. He would speak for a few minutes and share some personal memories, as seemed fitting. Many neighbors came by with food, mostly things easy to heat up quickly or eat cold. The refrigerator was full of fried chicken, pulled pork barbecue, potato and macaroni salads, baked beans, and casseroles, and the kitchen counter was laden with deserts. Linda proved a gracious enough hostess to offer dessert and coffee to visitors, which helped reduce the stash of heavy Southern food from the well-meaning.

He knew he had to write his remarks, but he resisted putting anything on paper. It wasn't until Friday night that he sat at his laptop and wrote and wrote, most of it not appropriate for a public service, most of it far too personal, some of it irate, fuming, explosive at God, at cancer, at Sabra. When he had finished three pages single-spaced, he scrolled through it, noticed the profanity he didn't even remember typing and stood up to clear his mind. Linda and Bob and Mei were watching TV; Mei was in love with this surprise aunt and uncle who understood children and grandchildren and indulged her with the right amount of boundaries. She was cuddling with Linda as they watched a Disney animated movie on a DVD, one about animals who talked or something. The cable service had been cut that day; he'd returned the devices, so DVDs and local stations were all the viewing fare they could enjoy.

He went outside into the cold, damp November air to stretch. The real estate agent had already installed a "for sale" sign but would not show the house until next week. He hoped he wouldn't have to return to Fayetteville until the house sold, although the attorney may need his presence at some point. The drive was short enough that he could do it in a day and April could take care of Mei. What a lucky break April was. Of course, she was paid well. Even this week, with them gone, he paid her. Or, really, he paid Nanny Services, Inc. well for her, and they got their cut. His mother's estate would help with those expenses until . . .

Until he decided what to do about Mei. Looking in on her with Linda and Bob, seeing her enjoying a pair of adults who knew how to mold their lives and speech around a small child, convinced him Sabra's plan for him to have custody of Mei was foolish, insane, irresponsible, maybe immoral. Deep frustration, maybe even fury, over that belief came out in his first draft of a speech for the memorial service, which he reminded himself he needed to get back to and finish.

Back at the laptop, he surveyed his draft, highlighted all but a couple of paragraphs, and hit the delete button on the rest. He would play it safe. Tell the story of his early years when she was a devoted, if quirky, mother. Talk about her care for clients and love for travel and her students. Stay away from the subject of Mei, of the cancer, of the family split, or everything but the cheerful and sunny from her life.

Chapter 37

The memorial service at 11:00 on Saturday morning in the 100-seat chapel of the Babcock-Ziegler funeral home drew about sixty people: neighbors, faculty colleagues, a vice president of the college, and several students. A few relatives from the central North Carolina region and into Upstate South Carolina came. More than once Linda noted Sabra's other sister could not make the trip, and Linda made no excuses for her sister, "that self-absorbed Marjorie," who couldn't get on a plane to see her sister once before she died and be with Linda and Kevin at this time. "She can go to Vegas to gamble easy enough when she wants and sit her rear in front of a slot machine." Linda kept her comments to herself, Bob, and Kevin, but otherwise didn't hold back.

Sandra the colleague (he finally remembered her name, Dr. Sandra Falco) arranged a somber but fitting service. She had a student play a tune from a musical on the violin. She asked a theatre professor whom Sabra had befriended to read a poem about loss. The vice president for academics spoke of Sabra's commitment to students and contribution to the college. Others chosen by Sandra shared anecdotes, and Kevin was invited to speak before the service was opened to reminiscences by those attendees.

Kevin read his remarks. He knew it wasn't the most sincere approach to talking about his mother at her memorial, but he also figured family members were under no obligation to speak at such events. He also didn't want to risk ad-libbing and saying something unscripted. On a table in front of the platform sat photos of Sabra from various stages of her life, a few with him and two with Mei. None of Mei and me together, he thought. That's fitting; we aren't really family. In some parts of the world, especially the South, mourners came to view the deceased in an open casket, and the family even kept the coffin open during the funeral. He was grateful Sabra had insisted on her remains being physically absent.

He also saw the wisdom of reading his speech when he saw Felicity, by herself, sitting three pews from the back on the right side of the chapel. She had promised and fulfilled. She wore an elegant basic black dress with a gold chain, her thick straight hair pulled back, and she smiled slightly when they made eye contact.

The service lasted over an hour, and the more or less potluck luncheon afterward lasted another. Felicity said hello, squeezed his hands, whispered it had been a lovely service, and managed to exit without eating or being seen by Mei. Wonderful Uncle Bob shepherded Mei for the time being. She seemed to think this huge, balding man was her knight in shining armor, her protector from all these strange people. Linda and Kevin greeted, chatted, thanked, accepted condolences, wiped away a few tears, and sipped coffee while the others ate quietly in groups. All of it exhausted them.

By 2:00 they arrived home, ready to be quiet, alone, and undisturbed. He hoped he would never have to go through such a day again in his life, but it was the cost of family, of being loved.

On Sunday evening Kevin and Mei returned to Charlotte. Linda and Bob spent Sunday evening in a hotel near the airport so they could catch their 9:15 flight to Denver. They all returned to a much-altered normalcy.

It was a week of readjusting. He put Mei back on a schedule despite her complaints. He caught up on neglected duties at the Gallery and called Fayetteville several times to talk to the lawyer's paralegal, the real estate agent, and the estate sales company representative. Then he was able to think about his future.

He had never heard from the Gunther Museum of American Art in New York about the position he had applied for prior to Sabra's illness. Well, that wasn't correct. He had heard from them in a short email that they were considering other applicants and the process was taking longer than they had planned. But that was over six—no, was it seven?—weeks before. He had expected better of them. Granted, these were big decisions, and he was up against, well, he didn't know who, but he figured some strong competition. Still, the professional thing to do was inform applicants the position had been filled with someone else, some temporarily anonymous person whose name would appear on the website soon.

No use holding his breath, though. The Fordyce Gallery job was a very good one. He knew it well without being bored by it, not yet, and he still needed to address the larger concern. He had to take Lydia Bridges' advice about seeing another lawyer seriously. He had too many questions about his and Mei's legal status. He made two appointments for mid-November. One with an adoption lawyer who specialized in Chinese adoptions, the other with the adoption agency Sabra had used.

Chapter 38

The adoption lawyer advised him to sign the custody agreement document immediately, in front of a notary, of course, and scolded him in an indirect way for not doing so already. Kevin didn't appreciate the criticism from someone he was paying. But Kevin had a bigger question. What would happen if he didn't sign the paper, or more to the point, if he decided he didn't want to continue as Mei's guardian?

"She becomes a ward of the court."

"She goes into the system, like foster care?"

"No, what would happen is the adoption agency would become involved. They would work with the court to find another placement for the minor child."

"That simple?" When he asked it, he realized the lawyer would have a condescending comeback. Kevin didn't care. He already didn't like the lawyer and had to keep glancing at his nameplate to remember his name—Lloyd Coleman. He might as well get his money out of the guy by asking stupid, crass questions.

"No, it's not simple at all. It's a long process. Is this something you are considering?"

"I wouldn't say that. But put yourself in my situation. In early October my mother called me to come visit her, as soon as possible. She has made this big decision, to adopt a child, then another, to put me in charge of the child in case something happened, and then something does—she gets terminal cancer. One in a million situation, but it happened. I'm unmarried, not looking to get married any time soon, have no kids, and would like to move out of the region. If you were me, what would you do?"

Mr. Lloyd Coleman sputtered a bit, trying to answer. "I would hope I would . . . I mean . . ."

"That's what I'm saying. You don't know, and I didn't, I just did my best and went with it. But I might have second thoughts. Then what?"

"All I can say, Mr. Elcott, is you need to sign the paper. My legal assistant is a notary, of course, and we can take care of it right now."

"Thank you, Mr. Coleman. I'll be in touch."

He wasn't sure if he left that way because the lawyer was such a jerk, if he wanted a second opinion, or if he really wanted to see Mei adopted by another family. He wanted to talk to the adoption agency first. A few more days without his signature wouldn't change things, he figured, unless Coleman reported him or something.

Yet he was more concerned about Mei. She was a different child now. She had managed, in her five-year-old way, to hold in her emotions and survive through the week in Fayetteville after Sabra's death. However, returning to Charlotte, school, and a supposed regular life meant a transformation in mood, temperament, and emotional stability. She was not an angry, upset little girl. Not everywhere. Not all the time. Not with everyone. Just around him.

She started by adopting the habit of talking to him in Chinese. He of course would say, "Mei, you know I can't understand when you talk in those words. I can only understand English." More than once she shot back, "You dumb, then. I am five, and you big man, you should know what I say." Other times she just turned and walked away, rolling her eyes. When she sat in her room pretending to read to herself, she spoke in Chinese. Sometimes she just regarded him with frustration for his stupidity.

In fact, frustration described more and more of Mei's daily life, which meant more frustration for him. Mornings went even more slowly. She refused to wear the clothes he put out and insisted on choosing them herself, but she cried when April picked her up because the other children made fun of her outfits. Neither April nor Kevin were surprised; a flowered T-shirt with a plaid skirt and mismatched socks would cause any kid to tease another. Kevin found it easier to give in to the wild combinations. This was a job for April, he decided and put it out of his mind. Wise April soon solved the problem by hold-ing a daily negotiation with Mei about her next-day's wardrobe.

Chad Benson called Kevin one evening to say she had been withdrawn in class but still did her assigned work; she frequently said she didn't want to play during the physical education time and preferred to sit on the side-lines by herself, but he could sometimes cajole her into it, with some effort. He reported that on the previous day she had burst into tears over an art project gone awry because the color was not what she really wanted it to be. "I want the color of my Elsa blanket" but none of the available markers met that standard. Ms. Traylor the parapro comforted her by finding another box of markers in the supply closet that contained a purple Mei approved of.

Her frustration toward Kevin was the most obvious and sometimes outrageous. Along with labeling him "dumb," for not knowing Chinese, behavior he knew should be disciplined, she escalated to "stupid" one morning when she disagreed with his fashion choices. "Mei, that's not a word we are going to use around here."

"I not care. You *stupid*."

"Mei, I will have to discipline you if you keep using that word, especially towards me. That's not right."

"You stupid, you stupid. You dumb." Her voice was ris-ing in volume.

"Mei, calm down." He couldn't put her in time out—they were already running late for school.

"I not come down," she screamed, misunderstanding. "You stupid. I hate these clothes." She picked up a skirt and threw it on the floor. "I hate this place. I hate you! I hate you!"

"Mei! That's enough."

She let out a high-pitched scream. "Go away!"

He felt slapped in the face, and for the first time, he wanted to spank her. It was all he could do to leave, slamming her door behind him. He couldn't let a tiny, 35-pound five-year-old do this to him. He had to get away.

He walked out of his apartment's balcony, which he had kept locked since she arrived. This morning was a wash; there was no way they would get to school on time, so he might as well forget it. He had to clear his head and collect himself.

At first, he resented that she exhibited such ingratitude. Didn't she get what he was doing for her? He resented his life being upended this way. He resented his mother, his dead mother, his mother who had suffered so much in her last month. Yeah, resentment. He had a lot of it. He might as well face it. He resented just about everything in his situation.

But when the mature part of him took over he knew Mei had no part in the circumstances that made him resentful. If she acted ungrateful and bratty and out of control, it was probably because no one had bothered to teach her anything in her life, and definitely not since she had come to the U.S. Sabra had probably pampered her. He had made sure she was clothed, fed, housed, and in school but hadn't gone anywhere near the idea of manners or human civility. What was the expression his paternal grandmother used? "Home training." "Those people never got any home training, that's what's wrong with them" is what she'd say to anything she saw on television she didn't approve of.

No wonder Mei was acting like a hellion. She'd been in an orphanage for over two years, transferred to the home of a middle-aged woman who thought she wanted to raise a Chinese orphan, and then sent to a clueless guy who until this moment hadn't even thought about discipline or politeness. No wonder she was frustrated and acting out, reverting to her first language (who wouldn't?), and bursting into tears over a purple marker.

On top of that, Mei was sucking her thumb now when sleeping, a new behavior or at least one he hadn't noticed before. Instead of picking at her food, she couldn't get enough and asked for seconds, and drank three glasses of juice or water at every meal. He didn't mind to feed her more. She could stand to gain weight and wasn't getting any heavier. When Felicity called one Tuesday night to say hello, he asked her advice.

"Kevin, has it ever occurred to you to take the child to a doctor? Does she even have a pediatrician? She might need vaccinations or something."

"I have her medical records. Mom gave them to me. They say she's caught up with shots."

"All right. But you're still going to have to find a doctor for her. I'll ask around for a referral."

Pediatrician. Referrals. Would it ever stop? But he said, "Thanks, Felicity. I don't know what I'd do without you."

"Ha, me neither," she teased. "Although honestly, Kevin, this is going to sound, I don't know, nosy, but I think this is getting to be . . . a lot for you."

"Yes, it is," he confessed. "It *is* too much. I keep thinking, when the legal stuff is done, when the house is sold, then, what? I'd like a vacation. I want to go see my dad at Christmas, and I want to go out for a beer with friends, and to one of the bowl games. Stuff I should be able to do. Get away. I sound like a whiny college kid, sorry."

"Don't say that. I'm not one to give advice. Tell you what. I can spend a Saturday with Mei. Give you a break. You're with her a lot, and that's hard on anyone. Let's say this Saturday. There's probably some new movie for kids coming out, and I can take her to that for you. Maybe you can just watch a game with someone."

He agreed that would be great, and then he took a chance. "Where are you spending Thanksgiving?" he asked. The holiday was two weeks away.

"I'm driving to my Mom and Dad's in Louisville on Wednesday, but coming back Friday."

"I just realized when I asked you. I don't have anything planned."

"Oh, for Pete's sake, Kevin. Don't plan anything. Let her watch the parades and go out for dinner. She doesn't need the stress any more than you do. She's a little kid going through a terrible time. And you are a big kid going through even worse. If you don't eat turkey and dressing one year, the world won't fall apart."

"That doesn't sound like you."

"What do you mean?"

"Felicity, you're so together, so corporate, so driven. You're giving me permission to be lazy for a day."

"Maybe I'll start taking my own advice. The winds are changing for me, maybe. I gotta go. I'll come by Saturday morning at 11. Eat Hawaiian pizza or something crazy for Thanksgiving. It will be a nice change."

He said goodbye. Her words only soothed him temporarily. Felicity was right. Mei didn't need any more stress and change and confusion. But she needed something else, and he was growing convinced he could never provide it. Mei had been so happy with Linda and Bob and had clearly preferred their company to his. Of course, they indulged her, cuddled her. Big, space-taking-up Bob even carried her. Mei sensed Kevin's distance, his lack of touch. Whenever she tried to sit close, he stiffened. Uncle Bob knew better than to push a child away.

Chapter 39

Talking to Felicity added another item on his parenting to-do list; take Mei to a pediatrician, soon. Or eventually. For now, he was more concerned about her outbursts, withdrawing, and insistence on speaking Chinese. He feared these behaviors had to be signs of deep psychological trauma, a condition he was in no way prepared for. He and Mei needed someone who spoke Chinese to help them communicate and for him to understand her life and past. Finding someone like that in Charlotte seemed daunting. Maybe just finding someone, anyone, who spoke her dialect of Chinese would do. He studied her papers to learn what province she came from, or at least in what province her orphanage was located. The adoption papers mentioned a government orphanage in the city of Changde in the Hunan Province. According to Wikipedia, his go-to for geographical research, Xiang was the first listed dialect for the Hunan province. He had no idea how to pronounce the word and took it to be something like "shee ang."

Asking at a university where students from China, or where possibly Chinese was taught, was his next step. After three long, awkward, and overly disclosing phone calls, he obtained the email address of a young woman studying at the University of North Carolina at Charlotte. Yihuan Sun, a graduate student and teaching assistant in mathematics from the Hunan province, spoke Xiang. He typed her a long explanation of why he needed her help, and she called, agreeing to meet them in a coffee shop right off the campus on the Saturday before Thanksgiving.

He entered a little before 10:00, holding Mei's hand, and scanned the shop for someone who might fit the description of a young Chinese woman. Apparently, this shop was a meeting ground for many international students from Asian countries, but most seemed to be huddled in groups around computers or laughing about images on their phones, or in the middle of intense, eye-locked coffee dates. One young woman sat by herself near the entrance, looking up occasionally to see who had entered. Their eyes met; Kevin saw her shift her gaze to Mei, smile in recognition, and stand. Kevin approached her, holding Mei's hand.

"Hello. Are you Yihuan Sun?" he asked, feeling obvious.

"Yes. You are Mr. Elcott?"

"Please call me Kevin. Let's sit down. Can I get you anything?"

"No, I have tea. Thank you." They sat down at her table.

"So," he started. "This is Mei."

"Hello, Mei," she said in English.

Mei's facial expression changed into a sort of instant connection. She saw someone, for the first time in her recent memory, who looked like her. "Hello."

At that point, Yihuan shifted seamlessly but calmly into a Chinese dialect. For a while Kevin could only sit and wonder what was going on between them, and watch Mei's face and hands. At first Mei looked—was it quizzical? Confused? Yihuan spoke for a while, without a break, but slowly, as if she knew to ease Mei back into hearing what she had known for the first five years of her life. Then Mei nodded, and smiled, and then spoke, and they conversed. Mei spoke quietly and haltingly at first, but she became more animated over the course of four minutes, then six, then almost ten, and more words came.

"Can I interrupt?" Kevin asked.

"Yes, Mr.—Kevin," said Yihuan.

"What, I mean, can you tell me what she is saying?"

"Oh, let me explain," said Yihuan. "I said to her at first, 'Mei, I want to tell you a story.' And I told her a folk tale from my province. It is like, what do you call them, fables with animals. She listened. It is not a long story. Then I asked her . . ."

"She ask me if I know what she say her," Mei broke in. "I did. I had to think hard. Then I understand." Her face and body showed a joy Kevin had never seen in her.

"You see," said Yihuan. "Then, ah, we talked, um, about her school, and such things."

"Such things?" asked Kevin.

Yihuan averted her eyes, shyly. "Yes."

Kevin took this to mean something they had said was not for his ears. "Yihuan, I really appreciate this. Now I know what dialect she speaks." He turned to Mei. "Did you like talking to Miss Yihuan, Mei?"

She nodded. "This is how I talk before I come to live with Momma. I not forget it. English is hard to learn. Everything was hard when I come to live with Momma."

Yihuan, though smiling and deferential, spoke honestly. "Mei should be able to speak Chinese with other children. I will see if there is a class or, what do you call it, club, for Chinese children in this city. Many Chinese live here; they go to the university, or have chosen to live here. Some of them are from Hunan."

"That would be great."

"Mr. Kevin, may I speak to you, privately, sometime?"

"Of course, email or call me on the weekend. If I can't speak, I'll call you back. Here's my card. My cell number is on the back."

"Thank you. I must go now. It was nice to meet you." She turned to Mei and said something in Chinese. Mei waved goodbye with a short phrase in Chinese, and Yihuan excused herself.

"She make me happy," said Mei. "She pretty. Not like CeeCee. Yihuan sweet, and that make me think she is pretty."

"That's a very kind thing for you to say, Mei. I am glad to see you smile."

Mei sighed, as if she were a balloon full to popping and now deflating. "I want doughnut here."

"I don't think so. Let's go home now."

As they walked back to his car, he said, "You know that I don't understand when you talk Chinese, don't you?"

"Yes. No one here know Chinese. I talk to Momma that no one understand me. She tell me she love me but I can't speak Chinese, must learn English. That make me sad."

What a weird thing for Sabra to say, he thought. "You can speak it whenever you like, Mei. I don't want you to forget it." He wanted to say, "You'll be able to write your own ticket in the business world when you're a bilingual adult, too," but held that in.

"That good," she said, and remained quiet until they arrived at his apartment.

Yihuan Sun, true to her promise, did call him Sunday afternoon. "Kevin, I did not want to repeat what Mei said in front of her. But I think she needs, what do you call it, um, a psychologist?"

"Oh?"

"Yes, I am very sorry, but she said she is sad. Her Momma went to Heaven, is what the adults told her. She misses her. She wants a mother and father. She doesn't understand why in America she can have a mother, but she died, and then she lives with a man who is not her father. In the orphanage they tell the children, and she remembered, if they go to America, they have a mother and father. And that's not true. The children in her school have a mother and a father."

"She told you all that?"

"Yes, in a Chinese way, and not in that order. I am saying it in English in a way that makes sense to an adult. She said it like a child, and she has lost some of her Chinese. She learned it until she came to America, and then did not learn more, and we can forget, so she speaks Chinese like a child younger than she is. But she still understands it."

Kevin listened. He didn't have the right to argue with this young woman who was only trying to help him, as he had asked her to. "Thank you, Yihuan. I think you are right. She should have a mother and father and even brothers or sisters. I did not have siblings, and it was lonely sometimes. You have been very helpful to us. But why do you think she needs to see a therapist?"

"That is only my suggestion. I am not an expert in such things. I know mathematics, not psychology. But, how can I say this; she was in an orphanage, correct? It cannot have been good for her. And then your mother and you take very good care of her here in the United States, but it is all strange. She says she is sad, and that is all I know.

Maybe there is something else she needs. More friends? I do not know."

He let out a long breath. He wanted to know more, although he sensed Yihuan's reluctance to cause him embarrassment, to lose face. "Did she say anything about the orphanage? Other than what they told the children about having a mother and father in America?"

Yihuan paused. "Yes. That is another reason why I think she needs to see a psychologist. That is all I can say. It would be wrong of me to say more."

"Then I will have to make decisions about her care, Yihuan. Thank you again. If you can learn of any organization where she can be with other Chinese children, I would like to know about it."

"Yes, I will ask other Chinese about it. I am sure I can give you ideas."

"Thank you."

They ended their call. Was there no end to this feeling of inadequacy and failure? He'd been putting it off, with so much to do, but he would have to talk to the adoption agency as soon as possible. Mei had to be placed in a different home, before it was too late.

Chapter 40

Between Mei's care and running the gallery, his days were full. Despite Felicity's occasional offers to take Mei to a movie or for "girlie time" as she called it, he had precious little time for fun or to think of anything beyond the immediate. And despite Felicity's advice, he had not engaged a pediatrician. His immersion in the flurry of everyday activities was why the phone call on December 1 from Xavier Giuliano shocked him. He had met Giuliano, the Vice President of Operations at Gunther Museum of American Art, during his interview visit to New York. Xavier, handsome and pure New York, did not seem impressed with Kevin at that time—more a reason for Kevin to be astounded by the call asking him to come for a second interview.

"I'm very interested," Kevin said, "but as they say, timing is everything. When would you like me to come?"

"Not until after the New Year," Xavier said. His accent was thick; Kevin wondered if he sounded as bound to his region as Xavier did. "The holidays are not a time we do hiring or anything operational, anyway. Fundraisers and parties. Would the fifth of January work for you? It's a Tuesday; you could fly up Monday, spend the day with us, and get a late flight out."

Examining his calendar, Kevin decided he would make it work no matter what. He had given up on the Gunther and New York. He couldn't help being suspicious about their calling now, but the position was worth another trip to New York at their convenience and on their bill.

"That will work great."

Xavier gave him some directions about being reimbursed for his tickets and lodging, and ended the call at a typical New York pace.

He would have to work it out with Nanny April to spend the time with Mei. It would mean double overtime pay for her, but he'd deal with it. School did not start until Wednesday of the week after the holiday break, for some reason. School schedules didn't seem arranged to align with those of parents. Mei would be out of school for Christmas on the twentieth, two weeks from today, he thought, clicking through his mental calendar.

He stopped himself. What did it mean that his first thought after getting off the phone was about Mei?

In early December, Kevin took a day off to drive to Fayetteville for a 10:00 meeting with the Director of Placements for Hands Across the Waters Adoption Agency. He didn't want to make that trip again, not without more than one reason. He could check on the real estate agent while there. The house had not received any bids, so maybe the price should be lowered. He didn't want to keep paying the mortgage much longer. He had access to his mother's accounts, but months of mortgage payments would deplete those soon. Of course, someone at work had mentioned that Mei, as a minor child, could possibly receive Social Security benefits in Sabra's name. Those payments would help with finances, but it meant another task in a long to-do list, and dealing with the federal government in the process. And if he was going to have the adoption reversed, Social Security was not an option . . . These thoughts cycled through this mind on the drive to Fayetteville.

Hands Across the Waters Adoption Agency was located next door to a large, stately Presbyterian Church, an impressive, traditional brick building with a marker stating it was constructed in 1895 and on the National Registry of Historical Places. The agency, however, occupied an obscure one-level house on the other side of the church's parking lot. A modest sign with a logo of, what else, two clasped hands over a stylized globe announced the agency's presence. Kevin made it to his appointment just in time.

The house that served as the agency's headquarters had undergone minimal renovations to qualify as an office. The former living room was the waiting room. The conference room had been a dining room. Bedrooms were now offices. Kevin concluded this agency was neither large nor well funded. He hoped his face did not show his wariness when he began his appointment with Mary Donnelly, the director, who proved to be his mother's age, more or less, plain but friendly. In the absence of a receptionist, she came out to introduce herself.

"Good morning, Mr. Elcott. Let me extend my condolences about your mother's passing."

"Thank you, Ms. Donnelly. "

"She was a lovely person to get to know, and very excited about giving Mei a home."

"Yes, she was." He tried to smile at this remark, wondering if he was missing a subtext to her words.

After settling in her office, he started. "It is about Mei, of course, that I am here."

"Yes. Do you need more information about her?"

"Not at this time. I recently got in touch with a Chinese woman studying at the university in Charlotte. She is helping me with the language and some cultural issues. She has given me some background and Mei was able to speak Chinese with her."

"You encourage that?"

"Of course. I think it would help Mei if she kept her first language."

"That's not really necessary."

"Excuse me?"

"The children need to assimilate, not be reminded of their home. Mei was barely five when your mother adopted her. Needless to say, a Chinese orphanage is not the best place for a preschooler. Your mother tried to help her forget."

"Oh. All right. That's . . . an interesting approach. Anyway, let me get to why I'm here. I have to tell you the whole, unvarnished truth, Ms. Donnelly. My mother did not tell me about adopting Mei until October. By that time she had been sick for a while and had decided to leave custody of her to me without my knowledge. That's something I've since learned was not really, let's say, entirely accomplished, legally. I have not signed the paper agreeing to this arrangement yet. So, imagine my shock when my mother tells me she has terminal cancer, she has an adopted five-year-old, and I'm the guardian."

Mary's face did not hide her surprise. "That would be . . . quite a . . . thing to take in." Kevin noticed the woman's use of understatement.

"Yes it was. First, I'm not married. I've really had no dealings with children. I don't know what she was thinking or why she considered my guardianship a good idea. That said, I've had Mei for over two months now. It's been a difficult time. She tries, I try. She goes to school, where she is learning pretty well. I feed her, take care of her, buy her things, put a roof over her head. She has a nanny for part of the day."

"That sounds commendable, Mr. Elcott. Your mother would be so happy to know you and Mei have bonded."

"That's just it, Ms. Donnelly. We haven't. Not at all. Mei is not happy. She's grieving, like a little kid would, but she's lonely, and I think she's angry and frustrated, confused and maybe on the border of serious depression. And me, I am uncomfortable around her. To be honest, I'm scared I'm going to be accused of something not so, I guess, appropriate, because I'm a single male and I'm not really even her relative, even though my mother wanted me to be her big brother, I guess."

"We have a network of counselors that help with the children adjusting to their lives here," Mary said.

"That's great, but it's not why I've driven here today. I am not sure my mother should have been granted adoption of Mei in the first place, but I can't dispute it if it's your policy. But I know I can't raise Mei. I know, actually I'm convinced, she needs a mother and father and a real home, hopefully siblings and a dog and all the normal stuff. I was given no choice in the matter. I don't believe that was fair or wise. I've done the right thing since my mother . . . gave Mei over to me, and she's a great kid, but I'm not the one for this job."

"So what are you saying?"

"I've talked to a lawyer. I want to have the adoption reversed and Mei granted to another family, a better family."

"Are you sure?" Kevin tried to interpret Mary's expression. Was it just surprise, or panic? Confusion, or judgment?

He paused. "Yes. It would be better for her in the long run. Maybe not immediately, but she's been through so much in the last eight or nine months, I guess her whole life, it makes more sense to me she gets re-adopted by a good, stable, two-parent family now than to put her through it later."

Mary Donnelly contemplated him, as if she were trying to hold something back, something harsh and biting. "Your mother thought you would take care of her."

"How do you know that?"

"We discussed it."

He felt his anger rising. This woman's demeanor struck him as—what was the word, he thought— condescending? No? Superior? Like she knew things he didn't. Apparently she did.

"Really? Could you fill me in on that? It would have been good to know about it before all this happened."

"She came to me, let me think, in September," said Mary Donnelly, studying an open calendar on her desk. "Yes, September fifteenth. She said she was ill, and we discussed what she should do. I told her she needed to talk to a lawyer immediately."

"But she didn't talk to me."

"She said she would, soon. She said you were her only close family member in this part of the country."

He sat back. "I have some hard questions for you, Ms. Donnelly. First, did you think it was wise to let a single person my mother's age adopt a child?"

"It's not that unusual, Mr. Elcott. I mean, it's not rare. When it comes to older people wanting to adopt, usually it's a couple in their fifties, but sometimes singles do. Your mother was healthy at the time of the process. She had a steady job, and she was willing to take an older child from difficult circumstances."

"By that you mean Mei's biological parents are still alive."

"That's one of them."

"You vet the people here who get children, but did you vet how the orphanage got Mei? I mean, how do you know she wasn't trafficked, or stolen from her parents? I've been reading up on these kinds of things since they concern me pretty directly now, and you can't tell me there isn't corruption and crime around these adoptions sometimes."

"That's a very severe charge. We do thorough checks on the orphanages we use. Mei's parents gave her up because of the one-child policy. They already had a child, a son."

"How do you know that for sure?" Now his anger was not only rising from deep within him, but also in his voice. Mary was ready to match it.

"We are a reputable, accredited adoption agency, Mr. Elcott. We do our homework and everything legally and ethically. I have to ask, what exactly do you want me to do for you?"

"I was given custody of Mei without proper knowledge. My mother was dying and Mei had nowhere else to go. Since late September, I have been responsible for her and done a pretty damn good job. She has everything she needs and almost everything she wants, except things I can't give her, like two parents and the kind of affection a child requires. My mother died. I did what I could. Now, it is clear to me my mother was wrong, or at least misguided, to leave Mei to me, and I would like the adoption reversed and Mei placed with a stable, approved family."

"Very well. Are you prepared for what this means?"

"I will have to be. I cannot keep Mei. It is not best for her. She's unhappy. The young woman I mentioned, the one who speaks Mei's first language, a dialect of Chinese, told me how Mei feels. Mei had no trouble telling this woman the truth, and she's obviously a frustrated, grieving, and demoralized kid. No, my keeping her is not what's best for her."

"Or for you."

"That's not any of your business."

"You'll have to go to court, relinquish all rights to contact the child, and other things. There will be fees."

"So, there'll be fees. I'm paying a big chunk of my paycheck to take care of her now."

"Is the issue money?"

"No, it's not. Anyway, my mother left money for her care. That's not the point, and again, none of your business. Whether you believe it or not, my concern is about Mei's long-term health, well-being, whatever you call it."

"Very well. We cannot really help you until you petition the court through a lawyer to start these proceedings."

"Do you have a family that could take her quickly? One that's waiting for a child?"

"She'll have to be fostered for a while. We have a network of approved families for that, until she is placed permanently. It's possible one of the foster families will decide to adopt her."

"Is that ideal?"

Mary Donnelly made a sound he took to be a short, sarcastic laugh. "Nothing is ideal in this circumstance, Mr. Elcott. I think you need to think about it more. You've been through a huge shock and difficult time in your life. I can't say your mother did everything the way she should have. She should have informed you of the adoption when it happened. I don't understand what your relationship was like that she didn't do that."

"Again, not an issue here. I loved my mother, she loved me and trusted me, obviously. And really, beside the point. I am single and have no experience with raising kids, but I have a good job, a clean record, education, all the stuff an adoption agency would want. Your organization would probably approve me if I got it into my head to adopt a child. But you should know my mother could be eccentric, let's just put it that way." Self-centered was closer to the truth, he thought, but eccentric would do for now.

"Understood," she said. Was she shrugging her shoulders? he thought. "Still, I think you should think about it more. If—since Mei is the main concern, she's better off with someone she knows than to be moved around, maybe twice, to new schools, different environments. Plus, how do you think she is going to feel about being rejected?"

"I'm not rejecting her. I'm looking out for her happiness and stability."

"That's easy to say. Look at it from her viewpoint, especially as she gets older. Her biological parents preferred a boy to her. Her adopted mother died. Her, well, guardian or stepbrother, sends her back after a few months. She stays with a foster family until something better comes along."

"Which it will."

"You can't be sure."

"That's your job, isn't it?" he countered. "Don't you pick the next family?"

"Maybe. We can't be sure what the judge will decide. Anyway, even the best of two-parent families have problems. People adopt children and they divorce. It happens. Your parents divorced, didn't they?"

"Yes. I guess my mother told you that. Again, not the point." This woman infuriated him. She seemed more interested in protecting her organization's reputation than dealing with his request about Mei's welfare.

"I'm just saying you know how hard that is," she said. Mary paused for a long minute. She moved her gaze out her office window to the street, as if she were searching for a new approach to this unpleasant man. She sighed.

"As I said, if you are convinced, you'll need to see a lawyer and start the proceedings. We don't do that, although we can be involved. Still, I think you need to wait. Get through the holidays, let yourselves find some normalcy, a pattern of life, after the difficult time of losing your mother."

"That's good advice, and I will wait until the new year to take action about this, but I don't think my mind will change, Ms. Donnelly. No, I should say I know it won't change. Things might be more complicated than I want to discuss here." He moved his weight as if he were ready to leave.

"Can I ask you a question?"

"Sure." He steeled himself for another intrusive query.

"What are your feelings toward Mei?"

"My feelings?"

"Do you like her?"

He thought for a moment. If this was a debate, a parry of some sort with this strong-minded, combative woman, he didn't want to give away too much. He could see her using it against him in court. He had probably revealed too much already. "Yeah, really. She's . . . cute, bright. Funny. Easy to get along with, most of the time. She isn't a pushover. She likes the nanny and some of my friends, gets along with them. Sure, I like her. She's not that crazy about me, but I can't blame her, everything considered. That's not the point in all this."

"Do you love her?"

"No," he said. "If you really want the answer to that question, I do not love her like a family member. I have concern for her as a child. I'm a responsible person trying to do what I promised my mother when she was dying, but I don't love Mei. To be honest, I don't have a reason to."

"Do you think you could grow to love her?"

"That's not relevant here, Ms. Donnelly. What's relevant is her getting a better situation to grow up in. I know I'm not that person." He stood up to leave and offered his hand. "I will be in touch, ma'am. It will be in January, but I'll definitely be in touch. Thank you for your time."

He didn't want to sit in the agency's parking lot to check phone messages and email. The encounter had sucked energy from him and put him in a foul mood. He pulled out and found a fast-food restaurant for an early lunch and to deal with his communications.

Kevin wasn't sure what he had expected at Hands Across the Waters. Giving back a child was not something agencies or the courts would encourage, of course, but his circumstances were different and Mary Donnelly seemed unable and unwilling to understand that. He didn't look forward to the whole court battle thing, but he had lived in an alternate universe since September, anyway. One more weird experience wouldn't matter.

One theme kept recurring as he contemplated his inability to raise Mei, which he knew accompanied his lack of desire to do so. Her mood swings and superficial lack of manners might mean something deeper. Mei had been neglected in her earlier years. At least from two to five, she lacked a family and home. What damage had been done because of the deprivation she came from? She seemed happy, at least with April and CeeCee and at school. Would this last? He feared a mental health crisis was on the horizon for Mei, and he knew he was not the one to help her through it. All the more reason for her to be in a two-parent home rather than with a single guy with no background in child-rearing and his own unresolved family issues.

Chapter 41

For Christmas, he really did want to see the other half of his family. He needed to talk to his dad and be around the normal, sweet, unassuming Nancy. That meant a long car trip through the "villes"—Asheville, Knoxville, and Nashville—to Memphis, a journey of nine hours. He contemplated ordering plane tickets, but three obstacles arose: availability, timing, and price. Or really, price, price, and price. First, he had to get two, so double his normal price. Second, he'd waited too long. The only tickets left were either for red eye flights or cost twice the regular price. Third, by the time they left to travel to the Charlotte airport, spent the two hours or more waiting to board, landed in Atlanta, waited another hour or more to board again, flew over an hour to Memphis, and rented a car, not that much time would be saved in flying. Fourth, he'd have to rent a car with a child seat, anyway. If he weren't looking at lawyer's expenses and potentially a move to New York, paying extra for the flight might have made sense. But all things considered, they were up for a road trip across Tennessee. He could do most of it in the dark and let Mei sleep.

In early December he had let her know, and the conversation was revealing.

"Mei, we are going on a trip."

"Where?"

"A city called Memphis. We'll go in the car. It's kind of far."

"Why we go to Mefis?"

"Mem-phis. We are going to spend Christmas with my father and his family."

"What is that?"

"Christmas? Don't you know about Christmas?"

"No."

"You will. Christmas is great. Kids love Christmas. It's the biggest holiday of the year."

"You have father?"

"Yeah."

"He lives in Medfus?"

"Mem-phis. Yes. He has a wife and two sons there."

"I no understand."

"I know. But you'll have fun. They are nice."

After that exchange, he dropped discussions about Christmas with Mei, since she didn't need his tutelage. Soon she was coming home from school telling him all about Christmas. April, a member of a conservative multi-ethnic Baptist church, made sure Mei understood the holiday wasn't about the birth of Santa Claus. Otherwise,

April encouraged Mei to enjoy the legend and all it meant, and along with her classmates, trained Mei in all things Christmas.

The school arranged for a local man who impersonated Santa Claus to come and take pictures with the children. Kevin had to pay for them, but Mei was so excited he couldn't burst her bubble. She wanted a tree and decorations and lights. He felt like the Grinch for not wanting to buy a tree, just another expense, but April found an artificial three-foot one at a thrift store for five dollars and donated it. She taught Mei to make decorations from colored paper rings and popcorn, and Kevin broke down to buy some lights and a star for the top. Mei sat and stared at it for hours, and used her tablet to find all the toys she wanted Santa Claus to bring.

"He doesn't bring everything you want, Mei."

"Why not?"

"He can't carry everything for every child in the world. So he'll bring you some of them. The ones he thinks would be best for you." Kevin was proud of his creative lying to keep Santa Claus' reputation intact.

In fact, as he looked back over the last several weeks, he had to give himself a better than passing grade on being a makeshift parent. He made mistakes, but usually not. They were only noticeable because most of the time, he got it right. He couldn't say he enjoyed it, though. Nothing against Mei; he just wasn't sure parenting a surprise little sister from the other side of the planet was the best way to ease into the responsibilities of the job.

So when he thought about his meeting with Ms. Donnelly to initiate some sort of adoption reversal, he could truthfully say he hadn't failed at this unexpected assignment, but he hadn't embraced it. And he didn't plan to.

They left for Memphis at 4:00 the day before Christmas Eve. All the gallery galas and festivities, school parties and holiday concerts were over and it seemed that the world, or the world he could see, had gone into a hibernation to observe Christmas in their own way, in families or alone. It took about two hours from Charlotte to Asheville, which he planned as a good place to stop for dinner. Thirty minutes outside of Asheville, Mei glanced up from her tablet.

"I'm hungry."

"I know. We'll stop in half an hour."

"I'm hungry now!" He was glad to notice her grammar was improving, even if her manners weren't.

"Mei, we can't just stop every time you want food. This is a long trip. It's 5:30 now. We usually eat dinner at 6:30. You'll have food in your stomach by then."

"I want to stop and get food now!"

"Mei, you're being rude. Let's not start this trip that way."

She started to whine, then cry.

"Mei, calm down. I brought snacks." He fished around in a tote bag in the front seat. "Here, have some goldfish." He handed them to her in the back seat.

After a few seconds, she said, "I can't open them."

"Give them back to me, then." He reached back, trying to keep the car on the road without slowing down too much in traffic. He tore the bag with his teeth. "Here, don't spill them."

That kept her happy for the next thirty minutes. He fumed. "She really needs to learn some manners," he mused. "I hope she doesn't act this way around Dad and Nancy and their sons. That's one area where I get an F on this experience."

They stopped and ate at a chain restaurant. Mei drank a glass of lemonade and then asked for some more water. "More?"

"I'm thirsty."

"You ate all your chicken strips. I guess you were hungry."

"Can I have ice cream?"

"All right, but we'll split it. You're going to get fat if you keep eating like this, Mei."

"That mean thing to say."

"Well, you're right. It is."

He ordered some vanilla ice cream. He figured she was going through a growth spurt or something. Felicity had mentioned those happened to children at certain ages. She still seemed smaller than the other children in her class, at least the girls, even though she was technically older than most of the others. He noticed it at their holiday concert. Children in all the grades, Pre-K to second, had performed a couple of songs and then combined for a big finale. He watched, amused; Felicity came and sang Mei's praises. She elbowed him to take some pictures on his phone, which hadn't occurred to him until she mentioned it. "All the other adults are," she whispered. "She'll feel left out."

Felicity was certainly a better parent than he was even when she kept her distance. She was true to her word not to forget Mei, but she remained on platonic terms with him. She just knew more about kids from being in a big family. Kevin didn't allow himself to dwell on the truth: Felicity had planned to be a mother twice, had geared her heart and life toward that role and had it stolen from her.

He thought about Felicity a lot. Too much. He didn't think she was dating anyone else, but she wouldn't have told him if she were. For himself, even if he had been in a position to meet a woman, he had no time to date anyone. Maybe when the adoption reversal proceedings were over . . . He hadn't mentioned his plan to April or Felicity, or to anyone. He'd have to, eventually, when it happened. One day he would just have to say to April, "Thank you for your great service, here's a gift for yourself that Nannies, Inc., won't know about, between us, and have a great life." He'd have to tell the school and Mr. Benson and Ms. Traylor, two people whom Mei had come to believe did no wrong. And Linda and Bob. And the employees at the gallery. What would they say? Surely they would understand when he said she would be with a real, stable family. Of course they would.

Felicity would be a different story. He'd have to break the news to her slowly. She'd been with them from the beginning. She might let him have it, tell him he was a creep, an ingrate, a piece of crap, but since she wasn't interested in anything permanent, why would she care or have a say? Well, that was unfair. She was attached to Mei. Maybe more than he was. It would be wrong to break them up, sure. She would just have to understand. In the end, it was his life.

Then why did he feel a sense of darkness about the decision?

Chapter 42

Mei managed to sleep from 8:00 to midnight. By then he needed to stretch his legs and gas up the car in a town past Nashville. They'd arrive at his dad's about 2:30 at this rate.

"Mei, wake up."

This startled her. She shook, squinted at him, then her gaze darted around the dark gas station parking lot. She began to cry in big, gulping sobs.

"What's the matter? It's me, Kevin." He hoped no one would hear and think he was kidnapping her. That was one thing he wouldn't miss. The constant sense people were looking at him and trying to figure out what he was doing with a small Asian child.

She wiped her eyes and started to breathe regularly. She said something in Chinese.

"English, Mei."

"Where we?"

"In Tennessee. It's a big place. Do you need to use the bathroom?"

"I scared."

"It's all right. I'll carry you in there and I'll stand by the door so nobody can go in. Were you having a dream?"

"Yeah."

After taking care of bathroom needs, filling the car with gas, and letting her have some juice, they resumed their trip. At 2:45, he pulled into his father's driveway in the Memphis suburb of Germantown. Nancy and Dad met him at the door as he carried Mei in. "She'll be in the guest room. You'll have to sleep on the sofa bed in the den."

"That's fine. Anything sounds fine now. I'm wasted. Listen, I'll set my alarm for about six. I want to get up before she does. Otherwise, you'll have a screaming little Chinese girl on your hands, babbling in Xiang. She won't know where she is."

"It sounds like you've got this guardian thing figured out, Kevin," said Nancy, as he laid Mei on the guest room bed. Nancy arranged the covers around her and took off her shoes. "She's really cute. Not that it makes the whole thing any easier."

"No, it doesn't. But we're here. Thanks for making space for her. At least I can give her a Christmas before I try to find another home for her."

"Are you sure that's what you'll do?"

"I have to. But we'll talk tomorrow. Good night."

Kevin's phone roused him at six. He rubbed his eyes. He'd shower and get to her room before she woke up to a big bed, a room she'd never seen before, and strangers.

He'd need coffee first. To his surprise, Nancy and Dad were sitting at the breakfast table hearing all about Santa Claus from, of course, Mei.

"Nancy, you're a miracle worker."

"Actually, your dad got her up."

"She thought I was you," his father assured him.

"I always said you all look like brothers," Nancy said. "Mei agrees with me."

"Mei, do you know who these people are?"

"Yes. She is Nancy," she pointed. "He is Tom."

"And who are they?"

Mei shrugged. "They live here. You say we come see them."

"You weren't scared this morning?"

"No, I like the bedroom. Very pretty."

"You crack me up, kid," Kevin shook his head. "I can't figure you out."

"Go back to bed, Kevin," said Tom. "You look like you're coming off a drunk. Get some sleep. She'll be okay with us."

"I hungry."

"She eats all the time," said Kevin. "And drinks, too."

"Really?" asked Nancy.

"Yeah. Not when, you know, at first. In the last two months."

"Have you asked her doctor about it?"

"Uh, that's not . . . really, she doesn't have one yet."

Nancy glimpsed at Tom with concern. "She needs a pediatrician."

"Sure. Listen, um, I'm going to go back to bed. She'll amuse herself. Her toys are in the car. The keys are in my coat pocket."

"Oh, we'll be friends and have fun," said Nancy.

He staggered back to the den, thinking what a find Nancy was for his dad.

At ten he woke up, feeling more human. A shower and coffee would help. He decided to skip shaving for a week before he had to go back to work. Later, he found Mei helping Nancy bake cookies. "Mei needs to be with people like them," he thought. "She deserves it. Maybe they wanted to start all over with the kid thing . . .. No, I don't think either of them wants a permanent reminder of Sabra Timothy, and Dad was almost fifty-seven himself. Nancy is ready for grandchildren, though."

"What you doing, Mei?" he asked.

"Nancy and me bake cookies. See, we put colors on them," she held one up, ecstatic at her rudimentary decorating.

"Nice. Don't eat too many, though."

"I just have one."

"Breakfast is basic today, Kevin. Cereal and such."

"Sounds good." He poured himself corn flakes and sliced a banana on them. He watched quietly as Nancy, the mom to beat all moms, talked Mei through cookie baking.

The rest of the day stretched on, relaxing hour after relaxing hour. He and his stepbrothers shot hoops in the driveway. They watched the family traditional shows: *Elf* for the boys, *It's a Wonderful Life* for Nancy, and *National Lampoon's Christmas Vacation* for his dad, who still had a goofy and somewhat warped sense of humor. *Elf* fascinated Mei because of Santa Claus, and she could hardly contain herself when the sleigh flew through the air over New York. She stood up and clapped her hands and jumped on the sofa. "Santa Claus! Santa Claus! Yeah!" Dustin and Hunter treated Mei like big brothers were supposed to, but that was easy for them. She was the cute little houseguest, and they didn't understand the family dynamics that made Mei's presence awkward for their parents and Kevin. They just knew Kevin as their stepbrother. Their step-dad had been married before to a woman in North Carolina, who had died recently.

Kevin was glad to let someone else entertain Mei while he slept and ate through the holiday. His trunk was full of presents he would put under the tree for Mei after she went to bed. She would receive a third of what she'd put on her list, which consisted of everything she could find online for a little girl her age. A complete set of dolls from Disney movies. Two different princess outfits. A dollhouse. Clothes. New shoes. A pretend stove and refrigerator and kitchen sink. Kevin drew the line at the child-sized kitchen appliances, more than one princess get-up, and most of the clothes.

Nancy, the consummate hostess, held an open house for the neighbors to drop by from seven to nine on Christmas Eve. At 11:30, the family attended a midnight service at St. Barnabas Episcopal. Kevin stayed home with Mei, as it was too late for her to be out. She didn't want to go to sleep because Santa was coming, but 9:30 was her limit. On Christmas morning she tore into the presents, as if she were on a sugar high. For the rest of the day, she glowed with the realization of this wonderful thing called Christmas.

"I like Christmas."

"Yeah, most kids do."

"You like?"

"Yes, I like it."

"I like this much," she stretched her arms out.

Dinner at 1:00 looked like a magazine layout. Dustin's girlfriend, a lanky blonde from Ole Miss, ate with them. They had been together in high school and reconnected after three years at separate colleges. Mei needed a nap afterward, and he went into the room to wake her up at 4:00.

"Wake up, Mei."

"I wet."

"What?"

"I pee in bed."

"Oh, that's unusual."

"What that mean?"

"Have you done that before?"

"Yes, sometimes with Miss April."

Nancy had had the good sense to put a plastic cover under the bed for a five-year-old. "It's no big deal," she said as she handed him a new set of sheets. "This happens to kids." She lowered her voice. "Hunter wet the bed until he was seven. And I think she gets so excited, she forgets to use the potty. And she did drink a lot at dinner. You probably do need to have that checked out. Maybe it's a bladder thing."

On Christmas night, he decided to call Felicity. Mei needed to thank Felicity for her present, a pair of dressy shoes with bows that Mei had liked in a child's boutique on one of their shopping days. Mei's manners were lousy, and learning to thank adults was a step toward more polite behavior. After Mei explained Christmas and how she saw Santa Claus on television and then he came and brought her presents, she surrendered the phone to Kevin.

"So, how's it going with your family in Louisville?"

"Great. We had thirty people over for dinner today. My mom is crazy to keep doing these dinners. She loves it though. And thank you for the present."

"It was Mei's idea."

"She has pretty good taste for a five-year-old. I didn't know she was so smart about choosing watches."

"She had a little help. I wanted to thank you for all your help."

"You didn't have to. Mei is fun. She sounds like she's sold on Christmas."

"Man, is she. She's hilarious. It's too bad, though."

"What?"

"Um, I guess I should tell you this face to face, but we weren't able to get together before Christmas. I've decided to go to court to help someone else adopt Mei."

"What?" He had to pull the phone away from his ear.

"Listen, Felicity, I don't believe living with me is the best situation for her. My mom was desperate when she left Mei with me, as if she is some kind of inheritance. That's unfair to Mei, and she deserves better. She needs a real family, a mom and dad, and I might be moving to another city, New York, actually, they've called me for another interview, and . . ."

"Are you telling me you are giving her back? Like you're returning something to Walmart?"

"Come on, Felicity. That's ridiculous."

"No, *you're* ridiculous. I can't believe this. What kind of cold bastard are you? You'd give her up for a job some-where else?"

"No, that's not it."

"You haven't tried, Kevin. You don't show her love. You just buy her things and pawn her off on the nanny, who's a saint, by the way, and I know you're not paying her near what she's worth. Or you send her to school or you get someone like me to do things with her. What do you do with her? You do the absolute minimum not to get put in jail for child neglect."

"That's not fair, Felicity. Give me a break."

"Kevin, I like Mei. I like being a little part of her life. And I thought I was helping you get through a dark time in your life, I wanted to be a friend. I really thought you would rise to this. Raising a kid is tough, but you're thirty-one. You're not sixteen, for Pete's sake. I thought this would help you grow up."

"That's not your say, whether I grow up. I've done a damned good job of what was expected."

"Bullshit. You've done the minimum. A child needs love. Have you stopped for one minute and thought about sending her to another home would do to her? What kind of havoc that would play with a kid's mind and emotions? It would devastate any kid, and Mei, it could destroy her."

"Of course I have. I weigh putting up with me, who is a cold bastard according to you, with having a loving two-parent family and maybe other kids, and probably people who go to church and are involved in the community and do sports and all that stuff kids need."

"Kevin, I'm going to hang up now before I really use some words and phrases I'll be really sorry for. Thanks for ruining my Christmas. I was having a great day until you told me you're bailing on this one thing you didn't have a right to screw up. Good-bye."

The phone's beep and silence mocked him. He'd probably never speak to Felicity again. She would most likely block his calls or never return them. She thought he was a screw up, a kid. No, worse, a villain. It was easy for her to judge. Too bad. She was a great, giving person, intelligent, and beautiful. Out of his league, maybe. Maybe she believed it. It was too late now. They had crossed a line.

Chapter 43

He planned to stay until the twenty-seventh. Leaving the day after Christmas would be a little rude, but he didn't want to overstay and take advantage of Nancy's good nature. He wanted to have a long talk with his dad and managed to go for a lengthy walk with Tom the afternoon after Christmas. Winter hadn't hit Memphis yet; the bright winter sun warmed the day up to 65 degrees.

With his dad, he could be fully honest, angry, profane, candid, confessional, raw. Dad listened. He refrained from advice. "But I want some," Kevin said.

"Will you follow it?"

"I don't know."

"Part of me wants to say your mother played a dirty trick on you, Kevin. She got herself in a bind. You were a way out. But that's cruel of me to say under the circumstances and I'm letting my old bitter feelings toward your mother get in the way. She was dying, what else was she going to do? You do an okay job with the little girl, but most people would say she'd be better off with a family. That's obvious. Unless you get married, and soon, to some woman who's willing to be a mother right off the bat, I don't know how you are going to do this thing. It's not right."

Tom's support momentarily strengthened his resolve to go through with the reversal.

"Thanks, Dad. That makes me feel better, that you have my back."

"I wouldn't call it that. You're between a rock and a hard place. What I say shouldn't make you feel better. This isn't going to be easy. For either of you."

"Easier than keeping her."

"Maybe. It's not a decision I'd want to make, but I wouldn't want to be in your situation. Changing the subject, who is April?"

"Her nanny. A girl in graduate school who takes care of her in the afternoon and when I have evening events. She's great."

"Oh. And who is CeeCee?"

"A friend. We were dating, but not now. Long story, but she went with me to Fayetteville the first time, when Mom dropped all this on me. She helps me out sometimes." They walked a few yards. "But . . . I called Felicity, that's her real name, last night, and told her about the plan to reverse the adoption. She was, let's just say, pretty mad. Let me have it. I doubt I'll ever see her again now."

"Oh. Mei talks about them a lot when you're not around."

"Yeah. She likes women better than men. Or she likes women better than me. Or she likes everyone better than me, even you guys."

They walked more, talked more. He wished he lived closer to his father so they could have more of these visits. And he wished he could change the past.

Before dinner Mei watched *Elf* again, but quietly. The ecstasy of Santa Claus seemed to have worn off after four viewings. In fact, she lay on the sofa in the den, head on a pillow. Kevin could only take so much Will Ferrell in green tights, so he put on earphones and did some research on his laptop, reading about adoption laws and reviews on attorneys. He ignored Mei. When Nancy announced dinner, he closed his computer.

"Mei, Nancy is calling us for dinner. You can watch the rest of this later."

There was no movement or sound from Mei. "Mei, hey, let's go." Thinking she had gone to sleep, he touched her shoulder and shook her gently. "Mei." Nothing. "Mei!"

Mei rolled over, unresponsive. Her eyes had rolled back. Her skin was pale. He put his face in hers to check her breathing. Shallow, and her breath smelled, what was that? Like apples or something? Had she eaten apples for lunch? He saw a large dark spot of wet on her jeans and smelled the intensity of the urine. He shook her more forcefully. Her muscle tone was fully slack.

"Dad! Nancy!"

He rushed into the kitchen where his family was seated for dinner. He held Mei, flaccid, in his arms. "Something is wrong with Mei. We have to call 9-1-1. She's unconscious."

The ambulance was there in less than five minutes. The paramedics, a young woman and an older guy about forty, worked fast to give her oxygen and test her blood. "Is the child diabetic?"

"No—I—don't—think so—I don't know. Is that what's wrong?"

The young woman studied the meter she had used for the blood test. "400. Glucose level out the roof."

"What should it be?"

"Maybe 100, 120. She's probably diabetic, sir. And going into diabetic ketoacidosis. That could lead to coma. Is she your child?"

"I'm her guardian."

"Do you have medical insurance?"

"Yes."

"All right. We're taking her to Le Bonheur Children's Hospital, Emergency. You can follow us in your car."

Chapter 44

Tom drove Kevin's Acura, with Hunter following in Nancy's minivan. They didn't want him to drive, and he didn't know the way to the hospital. He sat in the passenger seat, with Nancy in the back. They asked him a few questions about her health since she had come to live with him.

"She seemed fine. I don't know," he kept repeating, mindful he wasn't holding it together and he wasn't telling the whole truth. He was scared. What would happen if she couldn't come out of this? What if she had been unconscious too long, already too far gone? He had ignored her for most of the movie. Why hadn't he checked on her?

"I'm such an idiot. I should have seen something was wrong with her."

Nancy put her hand on his shoulder. "You couldn't have known. Nobody expects this. I had a friend when the boys were growing up, the same thing happened to one of their children. It seemed to come out of nowhere. Later, they saw how they missed the signs."

"We expect our kids to be healthy," said Tom. "If we sat around waiting for every sign of them being sick, we'd go crazy. This wasn't your fault, Kevin."

"She's so little. When I picked her up, she was like a limp . . ." he hid his face. This could not be happening. Was he asleep, dreaming something horrible because of his grief or his guilt or his anger? No, that was stupid. This was his car, Dad was driving, it was dark, they were in Memphis, on streets he didn't know, and they were pulling into the driveway on the emergency side of a hospital. Tom let him and Nancy out to park the car, and he could see the ambulance carrying Mei.

Later, all he remembered of the next two hours were rushing personnel who hooked Mei up to machines and an IV and asked him to stay in the waiting area for now; talking to the admittance clerk and filling out paperwork; being embarrassed that he couldn't recall her birthday, "I think it's February . . . the twenty-seventh, and let me think." he counted back five years to give the clerk a year. The admittance clerk gave him a look of pure suspicion. He didn't want to go into the long story, but had to summarize it. "My mother adopted her. She died in early November. I was given custody. I'm new to this. We live in Charlotte and are here for a Christmas visit. I have the paperwork, but I didn't bring it. We were more worried about getting her to the hospital."

Then he faced an interview with a nurse who asked him questions about Mei's health, her eating habits, her sleeping, her moods. Thankfully, Nancy and Tom stayed with him. At first he wanted to put a good face on everything. But given that Mei was unconscious and her body was fighting itself, he realized the stupidity of painting a rosy picture, and he told what he knew. He wished April were there to verify his answers and to complete the facts about Mei's daily routines, because he knew so little. Finally, the emergency room physician came to talk to him. His identification tag said Ranbir Bhatt; he looked younger than Kevin himself. Like the nurse, he asked a litany of questions about her lifestyle and health, and Kevin tried to explain his custody of her was unexpected and sudden. Dr. Bhatt finally said,

"Mei is a Type 1 diabetic. She is a very sick little girl. If she regains consciousness . . . "

"If? Is it that bad?"

"Yes. Her body has produced too many ketones and that can turn the blood acidic. It happens because she is not producing insulin, and this has been going on a while. Some children who have this experience come through it in twenty-four hours. For others it takes, well, longer. Her life will be very different from now on. We are doing more lab work to be sure she isn't in kidney failure and that her heart is not affected."

"Her kidney? Her heart?"

"Like I said, she is very sick. She'll be here for a few days, or more. I understand you are visiting family for the holidays, and live in Charlotte?"

"Yeah. We were going to leave tomorrow to drive home."

"That will not be possible. It will be at least five days before Mei is able to leave the hospital, and even then, her insulin levels and blood sugar will have to be monitored for several days to be sure she is well enough to travel. You'll have to find a pediatric endocrinologist now to see her when you get home. Her pediatrician in Charlotte can help you with that. I would call tomorrow for a referral and to get an appointment."

"She doesn't have a pediatrician."

Dr. Bhatt frowned. "No family doctor?"

Kevin shook his head.

"That's unfortunate. She would probably not be in this situation if she had one, at least a good one." He pulled a pen from his pocket and clicked it. "However, tomorrow the hospital's specialist in Type I diabetes will come see her and take over. She can have someone on her staff call their contacts in Charlotte and arrange for an appointment with an endocrinologist there."

"Thank you."

"I'm sorry this has happened. She still has a battle to fight, but we're doing all we can. The nurse will talk to you about the transfer to the room in ICU and give you some literature about Type 1 diabetes. I'll be back in a couple of hours to talk with you."

"Can I—we—see her?"

"Yes. The nurse will show you back to where she is now, and soon she'll be in a room," Dr. Bhatt shook his hand and left, writing on a chart as he walked.

If he were a real parent, he would have halfway intelligent questions for the doctor, he thought. He would have known every minute detail of Mei's existence, would have answers ready for every question, could give the name of her pediatrician, would have noticed the changes in her eating and thirst and moods and energy level.

He would have cared enough to notice.

Why didn't he? What adult wouldn't have had the maturity, sense, or wisdom to see what was there, and to care? Did he have any feelings toward Mei at all?

What was wrong with him?

Felicity was right. Could he not choose to love Mei, even if the situation was far from perfect? Who holds back love from a child? What was he missing, what was the deficiency in himself that he couldn't even see? What kept him from giving into that love?

Love meant more than paying for Mei's needs. That was all he had done.

The nurse, a young black woman with intricate braids and a huge smile, approached him. "Mr. Timothy?"

"No, it's Elcott. But I am Mei Timothy's guardian."

The nurse cocked her head. He wasn't what she expected. "You brought her in?"

"Yes." He was getting so tired of explaining himself.

"All right. You can go see her right now, before they take her to a room in the ICU."

"Intensive care?" Nancy broke in. She and Tom had kept quiet for most of the time since they'd arrived.

"Yes, ma'am. She's very sick, so Dr. Bhatt wanted her to be there . . . for now."

"This is my dad and my stepmother," Kevin explained.

"Here is some literature for you to read about her condition. In the ICU you can only go in to see her every two hours for thirty minutes. The next visitor time is," she looked at her watch, "10 p.m."

"Can we all go back to see her right now?" Tom asked.

"Yes, but she'll be moved in less than ten minutes, so come ahead."

They followed the nurse down the corridor to a private room in the emergency ward. A curtain hung around the bed. He steeled himself; he needed to. The friendly nurse pulled back the curtain to show her thin, waifish body in what looked like a wildly oversized hospital bed. An oxygen mask covered her face; three bags of different fluids dripped into a tube attached to her lower left arm; a blood pressure cuff embraced her tiny upper right arm. Her eyes were closed, her hair splayed on the pillow, and he noticed a transparent bag of urine, dark amber, attached to the bed. He knew what that meant; she was dehydrated, despite all the juice, milk, and water she had wanted to drink earlier that day.

"She's . . ." Nancy started to say.

"In distress," the nurse finished the sentence. "She's not in a coma; you all made it here soon enough for that not to happen. But she's a sick little child. You say she's five?"

"Yeah. Almost six," Kevin said. "Yes, in a couple of months," he thought. "If she makes it. And I planned to have her with someone else by then. I planned to get rid of her. This changes everything."

The nurse excused herself and the three adults watched Mei for several minutes, saying almost nothing, searching for a sign. Mei was not able to give them one; her usually active body lay completely motionless. Kevin thought of her jumping up and down two nights before, cheering on Santa Claus. Finally the tech arrived to move her to ICU.

"You guys can go home now," Kevin said. He was so tired. "You haven't had dinner. You must be starved."

"We think you need someone here with you."

"I can't expect that. You're leaving my car here, right? If I decide to come home, I will. If I have to spend the night outside the ICU, I will. I want to see her again at ten and whenever they let me. I have to be here when the specialist comes."

"Aren't you hungry?"

"No. If I am, I'll eat out of a machine, and I guess they have a cafeteria here. It won't be the first time I rough it."

"Kevin, I–"

"Don't worry, Dad. Really. You all can come back tomorrow if you can. I'm staying here."

He convinced them to go home and that he would call them if something changed in Mei's condition.

Chapter 45

He found the medical ICU waiting room equipped with reclining chairs and clean throw-blankets for patients' families. It was 9:30. He stretched out on one across from a large wall clock to wait for 10:00 and the chance to see Mei. His stomach churned with anxiety; the thought of eating crackers or cookies from a vending machine nauseated him.

"This changes everything." That phrase sang, squawked, chanted, and called to him. He couldn't quiet it. "Whatever you thought you were going to do, whatever your plans were, think again, dude."

He'd been kidding himself all along. No, he'd been deliberately lying to himself. "She'd be better off with a couple. I can't do this. I can't take care of her." The truth was he didn't want to because she was a pure inconvenience to him. Mei, her very existence, got in his way, blocked his plans. Whatever the bizarro-world circumstances that brought Mei into his life—and he acknowledged the people he met on a daily basis had a hard time believing his story—they were *his* circumstances. He had tried to push her away, keep her at a distance. It didn't work. Here he was, the day after Christmas, 500 miles from home, stuck in an empty ICU waiting room because of Mei. He had a new choice before him. To be a rotten, spoiled kid who resented a five-year-old fighting for her life in the next room, or to be a man and figure out what love meant, what directing his attention toward a life other than his own was about.

At times he wished he were a more spiritual person. Then he could pray for his stepsister, his adopted sister, his ward, *his child*, and gain some comfort and hope from it. Instead, he got to beat himself up waiting for the ICU doors to open. They finally did, and he asked for Mei's room. It was the sixth of eight in the circular ICU ward. The other two patients, whom he glanced at as he walked by their rooms, were elderly. No one was visiting them this late. In contrast, the curtains to Mei's room shut out the gazes of visitors.

He sat down by her bed and peered at *his child*. She was his child, no matter how she got that way. Her appearance was no different from what it was in the emergency room. She was still a tiny human form engulfed by wires, tubes, and machines. Vulnerable was too positive a word to describe her. She was totally dependent on means outside of her own body to keep living. She would be dead now if . . . it weren't for these machines, for the ambulance and paramedics. She would be dead now because her body did not produce what it needed for her survival. And because of . . .

Of him. He wanted to say that. Yes, he could blame himself indefinitely. But that would not do.

It came then. He hadn't anticipated it. He didn't know it would feel like a boulder coming off his shoulders by a magical crane. That he could now relax after a long fight.

He loved Mei.

Probably because he hadn't had siblings, he was out of practice. Loving your parents didn't count; they are in a special category, these mighty adults who give you everything until a certain age when you start to be a jerk and resent them. And rebel. He had loved two girls when he was younger, both relationships that didn't last, one because he didn't want it to, the other because she didn't. One in his freshman year (he had the sense to break it off), one in his senior year (she broke his heart). Yes, he was out of practice in loving people. Granted, girlfriend love and sibling love and parental love were a little different, but a lot the same. That same part of all loves considered living for the other person's needs more important than living for one's own.

That was how he loved Mei. What he wanted, what he thought he needed, he saw now as far less important than what she needed and who she was. With the arrival of love, all thoughts of reversing the adoption left. Returning her, the same as rejecting her, was unthinkable now, just as it should have been before.

He wept for a bit, happy in this brief time the nurse had left him alone. When they kicked him out, he'd be back at midnight. And at 2:00. Maybe he'd sleep through 4:00. Maybe not. But he would be there in the morning. He would be there every morning and night for as long as Mei needed him.

At 2:30 a.m. on December 28, more than thirty-two hours after Kevin found Mei unconscious, she opened her eyes, confused, then terrified. A nurse happened to be in the room. Understandably, she struggled in the bed, but security straps held her tight. Her moans attracted the nurse, who came to remove the oxygen mask.

"Hello, sweetie. I know you're scared, your daddy will be able to see you in a little while. I'm Miss Mandy—"

A stream of Chinese met Miss Mandy, who had no idea what language the child was using to protest her imprisonment and express her panic. The nurse pushed a button for help.

"Can you speak English, honey?"

Mei continued to struggle, but less fitfully. The recognition of the other words fit into the puzzle pieces of her mind as she tried to make sense of her surroundings, the machines, the wires. "Where Momma?"

"Momma?" No mother had sat by her bed.

"I want Momma! Why I here? I want Momma!" Angry tears were forming and easing down to her pillow.

"You're very sick, honey. Let me see," the nurse checked the dry-erase board with the shift information. "Mei.

That's your name. Yes, you've been very sick, sweetheart." The nurse smoothed Mei's hair and released one of the straps so that Mei could feel some freedom.

"I want Momma."

"There is a man here. He watches and visits you. Is he your daddy?"

"No. He Kevin. I live with him. He take care of me. He not my daddy."

"Okay."

The other shift nurse entered. "Oh, good, she's conscious. Let's call her guardian in here in a minute, even though it's not time. He hasn't left since the night before last, and any man that dedicated needs a break. We need to check everything first, and do a blood sugar test. She's probably starving, too, and can have some sugar-free pudding and chicken broth."

Mei started to cry, and Miss Mandy soothed her. "We'll get your Kevin in here soon, honey. And get you some food. First, let me see your arm." Mandy deftly used a child-sized vacuum capsule to extract some blood from the IV. "We are taking care of you. You've been asleep a long time. Do you remember anything?"

"Santa Claus," Mei said. "The big elf. He was on TV."

"Oh, yes, I like Elf, too. He's so funny." Mandy finished her work and felt another presence in the room. She glanced up to see a crumpled, careworn young man with a five-day growth of beard and bleary, half-closed eyes at the door. He stopped and looked at the child, leaned against the door, and burst into tears.

"She's awake," Mandy said. In two seconds the young man had the child in his arms. The child accepted it without objection, even if he wasn't her momma.

Chapter 46

Dr. Bhatt, and his successor, Dr. Kenzie Marister, the endocrinologist, had predicted a stay of five days in the hospital for Mei. They were, of course, correct, and on December 31 she was released with a strict diet, needles, prescriptions, bottles of insulin for injections, and a store of test strips and a meter. Eventually, she could be fitted with a glucose monitoring system she could wear, but not for a while. She needed to relearn her life with this new regimen, a life where she had to eat and where she couldn't eat everything she wanted, where she had to listen to her body, rest, and know what her blood was doing all the time. Kevin would need to relearn life as well.

Dr. Marister wanted to see Mei in her office January 2 before she would release Mei for the road trip. Dr. Marister had also arranged an appointment on January 5 with Rudy Salazar, a pediatric endocrinologist at a large hospital in Charlotte. Dr. Marister promised he was the best in the region and her fellow student in medical school.

Their new life began. On January 2 Kevin called Xavier Giuliano and asked to postpone the interview for a week. "I have custody of a child in my family, and she has been hospitalized for five days" was all he said.

Xavier seemed miffed. "You're not single?" he asked.

"Yes, I am. It's a long story." Kevin kept his voice calm; questions about family were not supposed to come up in interviews. Xavier either slipped, forgetting employment law, or he didn't know it very well.

"Let me see," Xavier paused. "Yeah, we can make it happen the following Tuesday, same time."

"Thank you for the extension. I'll see you on the twelfth."

The extra time, unscheduled, in Memphis, meant long talks with his dad and Nancy, reconciling his new life. Nancy and Dad hugged him when he told them of his decision to keep Mei and eventually to adopt her legally. "We're so relieved," Nancy said. "We could see how hard it was on you when you talked about sending her back. I didn't want to lose her. I feel like I have a granddaughter now."

"It doesn't bother you, well, she was brought here by . . ."

"That's not Mei's fault or doing, Kevin. Really, it doesn't matter. She's your child, or will be. God brings people to us in ways we don't control, or even like sometimes. But they end up being great blessings."

Kevin wasn't sure God had much to do with his mother's decision to adopt Mei, but he respected Nancy's optimism. Maybe God had something to do with his own change of heart. "That's a nice way to think about it, Nancy," he said. "I'm at least grateful for Mei coming through the crisis."

He and his father had a private conversation, outside of Nancy's presence. "Your mother, you know, called me not long before she died, Kevin. Believe it or not, she apologized for hurting me. It took, what? Seventeen years. Even still, she said it was really for the best. She was never one to be too plagued by guilt."

"No, she wasn't. No apologies for me, not for what I would have expected, at least."

"Then she said she really called to ask me to help you with Mei. To encourage you. To not let you give her back, not to let you reverse the adoption."

"What?"

"She knew it was an unfair thing to do to you. I told her so, but she was stuck."

"Why didn't you tell me this before? You led me to believe you didn't know about Mei when I told you."

"Yeah, I know. I apologize. I didn't want you to know about me talking to your mom. I had my reasons."

"Does Nancy know about it?"

"No, it was just between me and your mother. I said I couldn't tell you what to do. After you brought Mei here, it was a different story. I like her. Nancy's in love with her. She's a woman who should have had daughters. We had so much fun with her. So, I was torn. Seeing a real child, I knew letting you send her away was wrong. I changed my mind. I planned to try to talk to you about it before you left, somehow, maybe after dinner that evening . . . and then it didn't matter."

Kevin didn't know whether to be angry or relieved, disbelieving or ecstatic. He didn't like people talking about him and his decisions behind his back, but he appreciated his father's candor. "I never would have believed I'd be this person. Life can be crazy sometimes."

"Sure is. And now we have a new member of the family. Quite a surprise."

He called Mary Donnelly to say he had changed his mind about trying to reverse the adoption. In fact, he wanted to sign the custody document as soon as he could arrive home and visit a lawyer. It wouldn't be Lloyd Coleman, whom he disliked, but he'd find another one who specialized in adoption law, one he could trust to guide him through the adoption process. He would become her father, which would be a clearer relationship and stop the need for explanations. Mary wanted to know what had changed his mind. He didn't believe it was any of her business. "I just have. It's best for Mei, and that's what matters."

Mei's change toward him was less dramatic. Her health had to come first, and he accepted she would still be suspicious of him. He had neglected her emotionally for these three months. He had not appreciated that a five-year-old's grief would be as intense as his own. He could not get inside her skin to know how the illness affected her thoughts and feelings. She had been through so much in her short life, and he knew nothing about her, really, before September. Sabra had handed Mei to him as if she were a blank slate, and Mei was anything but that.

Finally, he began to have some empathy for her as Mei, not just some sympathy for her as a child. She would need to associate with Chinese people who spoke her language. She might need tutoring to improve her English proficiency. If he could find a psychologist who specialized in adopted children, even those adopted internationally, he would ensure Mei had help for what she was facing. But all of that was moot if he did not change his own dealings with her. He would have to listen to her, have to stop treating her as a burden who occasionally amused him. He would have to take her to the movies rather than expecting Felicity, whom he doubted he'd ever see again, to do it. He would have to think to take photos of her with his camera, something he'd only done once because Felicity nudged him to remember. He would have to. . . any number of new actions sprang to mind.

Slowly, even while they were still in Memphis, Mei warmed up to him, now that he let her sit next to him on the couch with her head on his arm and he seemed interested in her opinions and games and toys. She started to listen to his fashion sense, and she told him to keep his beard.

"You don't mind?"

"Mr. Benson has beard. You have one, too. That good."

"You always have opinions, Mei."

"What is 'pinion' mean?"

"Good question. You know what you think and say it." He noticed her English had been set back a few months, perhaps from the long period of unconsciousness.

"Is good?"

"Most of the time. That's who you are, and I don't want to change that."

As he drove home, this time in the winter daylight, allowing Mei to see the world of Tennessee, the mountains, the cities, the sleeping fields, they talked. He listened to her babble about school and her friends and television shows, something he had left to April. She sang along to the videos on her tablet, oblivious to how she mangled the words and the tune. He played music on the radio and he sang. She told him he couldn't sing "good." He overacted being hurt, wiping away invisible tears, which made her laugh instead of apologize. When she slept, he thought of how he had missed all the signs of her condition, bouncing between guilt, astonishment at how sick she was, and gratitude she survived the crisis.

In the hospital, waiting for her to wake up, he had read all the literature he could find on what used to be called juvenile diabetes. Dad and Nancy brought him his computer—along with meals—and he read all that the Internet provided. The thirst, the hunger, the weight loss, the moods and outbursts, the fatigue, the wetting herself that he didn't know about, all were clear and classic signs of Type I diabetes. April would be upset when she learned of Mei's new diagnosis. He had only called her to say they would be staying longer than he expected and she would need to start working the afternoon of January 5.

The more he researched, the more he started to understand the science. He wanted to be knowledgeable so he could talk intelligently with the doctors. Type 1 diabetes was rare in Asians, less frequent than in European Americans. Mei had lost the genetic lottery in that regard. Mei could live a full active life but she could never take her condition for granted. He even read about dogs that could smell a child's blood sugar drop. He wasn't ready for a dog, but it wasn't a terrible idea either. Maybe it was time to buy a house.

Unless they moved to New York. He couldn't see having a dog there, and houses were far pricier and less available than in the South. But New York could mean access to better medical care for Mei, all the cultural outlets, and possibly ways to meet other Chinese. He couldn't imagine growing up in New York himself, but they could make it work, with some adjustments. If it happened. He couldn't read Xavier's signals on the phone call.

This daytime road trip meant more stops. He needed to check her blood sugar and see to injections; she needed healthy snacks and to eat better than fast food, so he would have to arrange for more cooking at home and only eating at "real" restaurants. Amazingly, he saw none of this as a bother. Ten days before he had wanted Mei to sleep during the whole drive and he had hoped Nancy would entertain her during most of the visit. Now he enjoyed her chatter, her attempts to tell jokes, and her musical interludes. She wasn't much of a singer, but he'd have to look into starting Mei on the piano lessons Mom talked about . . .

After the long drive home, he saw to Mei's bedtime and then unpacked the car. The next day would mean an early trip to Dr. Salazar, then a late school arrival for Mei, easing back into the office, making final preparations for his trip to New York, and talking to April about spending the night with Mei when he flew to the job interview in six days. But some things he didn't have to worry about in the next month: dealing with Mary Donnelly, explaining to a judge why he had to return a child, and saying goodbye to Mei. Mostly, he wouldn't have to deal with wondering what had become of his surprise little sister and living with the guilt of a stupid and selfish decision for the rest of his life. They were now together, permanently. Mei would never know that he had set in motion a plan to rid himself of her. He would do what he could to give her a healthy, if unconventional, upbringing. The new year was truly bringing a new way of being for him.

Chapter 47

He should have known flying to New York in early January was a gamble. In any hint of bad weather, Southern airports get nervous. A storm of freezing rain threatened on the morning of the eleventh, but the weather reports kept pushing back the time it would settle in. His flight at 1:00 to JFK International would precede the storm, if it materialized. If the ice storm came, school would be dismissed as well. April agreed to spend the night on the eleventh and stay as late on the twelfth as he needed to fly back. This trip would be quick and absent of any sightseeing or theatre; the best adventure he could manage would be some real New York pizza. If all went well, perhaps he would be returning soon and he and Mei would enjoy the city's riches for a long time.

He said goodbye to Mei when he dropped her off at school, reminding her April would spend the night because he had to take a trip in a plane. She knew all about planes, having come from China less than a year before; she reminded him of that, and he didn't mind.

In the last two weeks, she had assumed a whole new demeanor towards him, if slowly. For one, her moods were better because her sugar and insulin levels were closer to normal. For another, she saw, in her own way, he was trying to show affection, in his own way. He paid attention to her, for one thing. He took selfies with her. He was less distracted and dismissive. He gave her shots but apologized every time. He said he knew it hurt but it would keep her from going back to the hospital.

She hated the hospital. She had not shed the terror of waking up with an oxygen mask on her face, tethered to a bed, and with strangers in the room. Anyway, a hospital was where she found out her mother was sick and someone else was going to take her away to live in another city. Some day she would outgrow that dread of hospitals, but one thing at a time. She needed to learn daily care for her chronic disease, to learn English while keeping her Chinese, and how to be an American kid.

Kevin checked into the same four-star hotel as during the previous visit; he walked the streets nearby in the frigid air, looking for an Italian restaurant; he window-shopped and planned on getting April and Mei little presents from New York before leaving. He called about 8:00 to check on them; school was closed for the next day, just in case the storm hit late, although it was just as likely to skirt Charlotte to the north. Many thoughts occupied him, especially his last conversation with Felicity. He saw a necklace he would like to buy her before reminding himself his feelings were pointless and it was time to start considering other women. Right now most of the women he knew were his employees or not the kind of woman he would date, for many reasons.

Felicity's words still stung. No, they still felt like a stab wound. She was not wrong, he had been a cold bastard in his attitude toward Mei, and all that was changed. At the same time, that kind of judgment coming from her broke any sense that he could remain a close friend. She had shown a new, different side of herself. He didn't want to entertain the thought she might change her mind now that he planned to keep and adopt Mei formally. He didn't want her to change her mind. Not now.

Despite the extraordinarily comfortable bed and accommodations, he did not sleep well in the hotel. Too many thoughts and too much rehearsing of his answers to Xavier's questions, too much worry about how he would maneuver the interview and meetings in the morning. They would not have incurred the expense of this second trip unless they were truly interested in hiring him, so he should anticipate an offer. And he knew what he was worth and should expect.

At 9:15 he entered the twenty-foot art deco doors of the Gunther Museum of American Art in Manhattan for his 9:30 appointment. The Gunther, a 115-year-old institution, prided itself on channeling the energy of America, and it showed in the dynamic architecture and the dramatic color. The Gunther also sent the subtle message—or not so subtle—it considered New York and its history to be the epicenter of that American energy. New York-originated and New York-themed art definitely outnumbered artworks from other regions or cities in sheer volume. One of his goals, or expectations, as the next Vice President of Development, would be to raise the funds to build a more representative collection so that the Gunther showcased American artists, not just New York creators.

He introduced himself to the receptionist in the administrative offices, was escorted to a waiting room, and offered coffee or water, which he declined. After two minutes he stood up to greet the handsome Xavier and a stocky young woman with streaks of aqua in her hair, who was introduced as the curator. They were accompanied by a very slender middle-aged woman with jet-black hair and stylish glasses, whom Xavier referred to as "Genevieve" and a member of the board.

For the next hour, the four of them held an intense discussion about the history of the museum, its strategic plan for the next ten years, its financial statements, and Kevin's qualifications. Some of this was a rerun of his meeting in September, but the curator and the board member hadn't sat in on that interview. This one was more wide-ranging and mentally exhausting. They called for a break and Kevin was encouraged to get some coffee; in fact, the receptionist came to the door and offered to show him where he could find some. He took the hint;

Xavier and the two women were going to confer. After ten minutes, he returned, a little more alert with caffeine and sugar in his system.

Kevin drew the conclusion that so far, so good, which made what happened next so strange. Xavier began. "We want to get a sense of your level of commitment to this position."

"All right," he answered, trying to smile but inwardly suspicious.

"This position requires a great deal of travel."

"Oh? I was not aware of that."

"I'm surprised you aren't," Xavier's manner, rather suddenly, had turned confrontational. Was this a test, some scenario he was supposed to problem-solve like a rat in a maze?

"It wasn't mentioned in the position description, or in our previous interview."

"Wouldn't you expect that a position like this would require travel?"

"I'm not sure how to answer you, really. When you say travel, where would I be going?"

"Name it. Europe. Any part of the United States, Mexico, or Canada."

"What would I be doing on these trips? Since the collection here is of American art, I wouldn't expect there to be a reason to travel overseas. On this continent, perhaps, but why Europe?"

"You'd be going to conferences, buying trips, discussions with donors who might live in other parts of the world."

"I see. So, how much qualifies as 'a great deal"?

"Probably two five-day, give or take, trips a month."

"I see."

"And that's not a problem?"

"It's something I would have to think about."

"Additionally, the position requires many long hours. Meetings with donors, events, galas, board meetings, etc."

"Of course, I understand that. I do a lot of those duties in my current position at the Fordyce."

"But Mr. Elcott," broke in the elegant board member, "surely there is no comparison. The Fordyce is a relatively small gallery in the South. We're talking about the New York art world."

"Yes, I understand this is a much larger museum. But you and Mr. Giuliano and the board would not have sought to interview me if you didn't see a parity between what I've done there and here."

"Let me get to the point," Xavier cut in. "The position is not conducive to a person who is parenting, unless you plan to let a nanny do most of the child-rearing."

"I see," Kevin said, nodding as if in affirmation, but actually in a new understanding. Yes, this was a test.

And he decided to fail it.

"First, Mr. Giuliano, you know you can't ask me questions about my family arrangements, or dance around them, legally. Second, yes, I am the guardian of a child. She's a five-year-old adoptee from China my mother, who recently died since our last interview, left me to take care of. That's not relevant. And the reason I had to postpone this interview is that she was in the hospital for six days because she was on the edge of a diabetic coma, and we didn't know she was diabetic, and we're learning to live with that. One month ago I would have smiled and put up with you asking me an illegal question in a job interview because I thought I really wanted this job. But that was then."

"We're not asking about your situation as a parent," said the board member, trying to control the damage.

"That's all right, ma'am," he smiled. He might as well be the good North Carolina boy he was. "I just made up my mind that, while I appreciate the offer and the opportunity to fly up here again, I don't think this will work out for either of us. Thank you again. I'll leave now. I hope you find someone you need for this position. Good-bye."

He reached out to shake their hands, which each of them returned with blank expressions, and he walked out.

New York at 11:00 a.m. was not much warmer than the night before, and he sensed the unmistakable smell, or denseness of air, that says snow. A snowfall in New York would be a nice sight; maybe he could walk the city and see skaters at Rockefeller Center and get a good lunch before his 4:30 flight. He felt free. He needed to go back and buy those presents for April and Mei, and he should get something for Nancy, who helped so much when Mei was sick and just out of the hospital.

Later he would shake his head and wonder what came over him to just walk out of the meeting so abruptly and unprofessionally. He was bold and gutsy to call them on their questioning his personal life. He did not even hear them out long enough to turn down their offer, which would have given him more power and the true last word. Maybe, he pondered, he should not submit the bills for travel, since he ended the interview. But he talked himself out of that pretty quickly. He came at their request and he'd seen enough of the Gunther's financials. They could afford his overnight trip.

Kevin returned to the area where he window-shopped the evening before. He bought April a snow globe of the New York landscape and a New York sweatshirt and Yankees ball cap for Mei; he bought matching ones for himself. He chose a set of imported crystal wine glasses from an upscale shop and had them shipped to Nancy. After picking up his luggage in storage at the hotel, he grabbed a cab for JFK to make his flight, unbelievably satisfied with himself.

Chapter 48

With New York and the Gunther Museum off the table permanently, Kevin and Mei's official new life started January 13. His first duty was to straighten out his legal situation. He chose an adoption lawyer, Valerie Johnson, met with her, signed the custody agreement four months late, and started adoption procedures. That meant interviews, a home visit, and piles of more paperwork, but he'd grown used to those intrusions. He requested, under the circumstances, his lawyer do whatever she could to speed up the process, even if it incurred more costs. In late February he went before the judge in Mecklenburg County Court and became a father.

However, he kept this a secret from Mei and waited to mention it to April, saying nothing until she needed to participate in the home visit from the Department of Children's Services. Mei would not understand the legalities, and April, studying to be a social worker, would understand too much. Above all, he wanted neither to have an inkling he had planned to reverse the adoption. Since

Felicity was out of the picture, forever, Mei wouldn't hear it from her. April might have quit in disgust if she knew his plans, even plans that didn't happen. She was far too good a nanny and could probably get another situation, even a better one, quickly. No, what was past was past. Maybe, when Mei was thirty-five or forty, he could tell her the truth, or not. What good would it do? He'd made his commitment. She was safe.

In the meantime, he had to address three concerns about Mei. Her health had to always be at the forefront. Even when they learned to live with her condition, it would control her life every day. They saw the endocrinologist Dr. Salazar several times in the first six months. As she grew, her injections of insulin would change. She couldn't eat sweets at school parties, which meant sending a healthy snack so she would not be without. She had to exercise daily. At five, now six years old, she couldn't understand all the regulations and restrictions, only that eating one of the cupcakes brought by a classmate's mother would make her sick again and she did not want that. The mention of the hospital set her to trembling and pleading. She had to visit the school nurse once a day for an injection and twice or more for blood sugar checks. At night Kevin woke her up for checks and injections, which she barely remembered the next morning. He feared she felt like a pincushion. He apologized a lot for poking her. She sighed habitually.

He wondered what she thought. Although Mei accepted that now Kevin played with her, took her to movies, and showed some affection, she grew quiet and watchful of him, as if reassessing this strange new personality. The mood swings were gone, for the most part, except when she was tired and protested yet another finger stick. She began to use 'please' and 'thank you' more regularly. She still preferred April. "Why can't April come see me on Saturday?"

"April has other things to do. She goes to university, you know, big people school. She needs to study. And she has a boyfriend now. You know Claudio."

"Yeah. He's handsome."

Indeed, Claudio was a guy that turned heads. They had met him when he attended the school Christmas concert with April and had seen him at a few other events. Kevin wondered if Mei had a crush on Claudio, whose smile would charm any female, six or ninety-six.

"I miss April," she would say on weekends. Well, her attachment was to be expected. April was the mother figure in her life now. Once or twice Mei said, "Why CeeCee not take me to movies?" and he had to make some weak excuse for her. Felicity would have concluded that he had sent Mei back, "returned her to Walmart," to use Felicity's words.

Felicity could have asked, could have called. But she didn't. She was silent.

His life was full of Mei's appointments, lessons, and activities—she was starting piano again, which meant the purchase of a used piano for the apartment. It felt too early to start dating, although he swiped on a couple of dating apps. He admitted to himself he was really trying to find Felicity on them, wondering if she had put herself on the market again. She hadn't. She probably would find a rich banker type at her firm, become a CEO, and go into politics, forgetting she ever knew Kevin Elcott and Mei Timothy.

That Mei mentioned CeeCee added to his concern about her mental health. She needed a counselor, a specialist. Mei couldn't unburden herself in some sort of cognitive therapy. She didn't have the English yet, and probably not the Chinese either. He wanted to find the best, the most trained for her particular needs, which meant a lot of research and referrals. Finally, he found Rachel Chou. Rachel, third-generation Chinese, originally from Texas and in her fifties, married an engineer whose parents emigrated from China, escaping before the Cultural Revolution. She had learned to speak the Xiang dialect out of respect for her in-laws and husband. She confessed that she wasn't fluent, but she could manage a conversation with a child at Mei's level when English wasn't enough. Most of all, she knew exactly how to get Mei to talk.

Kevin's main concerns surrounded the orphanage experience. He knew coming to the U.S. was hard enough. What happened before that? Did she remember her biological parents? And he hated to say it, was she abused in a way that she wouldn't remember consciously? Rachel cautioned him about expecting Mei's therapy to yield those answers soon.

"I realize you have concerns. Mei will tell us these kinds of things when she is ready, if they are true. She may have blocked a lot of the orphanage. On the other hand, perhaps the workers in the orphanage were generally kind; we can't really know. But remember, coming to America was such a contrast, and her last year here has been so eventful, she might have experienced sensory overload."

"But does she say anything about China?"

"She does. She mentions small things, very minor things. She has some memories. None of them seem negative. But eventually, as she gets older and knows more about the world, she is going to understand why she is here, what it all means, and we want her to have the resources in herself to cope with those then. What we must work on is stability, acceptance, love, routine, things that will add to her security and foundation when the memories do rush in, if there are bad ones."

"Her biological parents are still alive, at least, they were when she was put in the orphanage."

"I didn't know that," Rachel said. "But it is not unusual."

"Should we tell her that?"

"Not now. She will eventually learn more, and she will ask questions. Let her show you the way to understand her, Mr. Elcott."

He wanted a path inside Mei's brain. Rachel Chou resisted showing him that path. "It is important she keep her first language, though," she affirmed him. "I think you're right to want that for her."

"The adoption agency my mother used advised her to discourage her use of Chinese."

"That's odd, and shows a . . . lack of appreciation for how language acquisition works. Yes, being bilingual will be a strength. It will slow down her acquisition of English some, but in the long run, she'll catch up. She's bright, and the fact she's a year behind in grade level will help for now. She might catch up to her age group later, and if she doesn't, so what? It's not a competition."

With Rachel's confirmation, Kevin pursued the third most important concern—ensuring Mei kept speaking Chinese. Yihuan Sun helped. She gave him the numbers of Chinese mothers affiliated with the university who met for play dates with their children on Saturday mornings. He felt odd taking Mei the first time, but Yihuan provided an introduction that day. "Mei, these children speak Chinese together. Their mommas want them to learn Chinese stories and games. I'll stay here while you play, okay?"

If she had given him skeptical looks before, this one bordered on sheer disbelief. He wondered if her immersion with American kids had made her want to discard her Chinese identity. As she had often done, she sighed, and walked over, a bit apathetically, to a little girl about her size. At that point, she entered a new zone and Kevin could only watch and listen. A mother intervened, addressing Mei enthusiastically. Mei answered quietly, but in her Chinese words. The mother engaged the children in a game that seemed to involve counting and a bean bag, and Mei played along, slowly catching on. The mother backed away and the children took over. Finally, Mei smiled and even laughed.

After three hours, Kevin drove her home. He remembered how his mother used to try to get him to talk when he was a teenager. She told him once it made her feel like an interrogator dragging answers out of him. He decided Mei should have to initiate conversations sometimes.

"That was fun."

"Really?"

"Yeah. I make friend. Sara. She in first grade. Her daddy is pofessor."

"Humm. That's good."

"What is pofessor?"

"Pro-fessor. It's like a teacher, but in a university."

"What is youversty?"

"U-ni-ver-si-ty. It's school for grownups."

"Oh. You go u-ni-versary?"

"A long time ago. I went to the best in the country."

"You do?"

"Oh, yeah. The University of North Carolina at Chapel Hill."

"I go there."

"That's a plan."

Their day in court arrived and began with his announcement to surprise Mei.

"You're not going to school this morning, Mei. We are going to do something else, something very important."

"What we do? Can we go to zoo?"

"I know you like the zoo, but not today. I want you to wear your best dress and shoes. We are going to see an important man. He will sit up at a high desk and talk to us."

"I don't like."

"I think you'll like this."

Although she performed her part for the judge, and posed for the picture made of all new adopted families, she didn't fully understand what happened. He tried to explain.

"Momma took you to see the judge before, don't you remember?"

"Some. I little then."

"That was just a year ago, Mei."

"Why we do that again?"

"Momma became your mother that day. Today I became your father."

"No, you Kevin."

"Yes, I am Kevin, but the government will say I am your father."

"That weird." She liked to use this recently learned word whether it fit or not.

"Yeah, a little, but in the long run it's a good thing."
"Why you do that?"
"So I can take care of you."
"Then that good." She sighed. "We go to zoo now?"

Chapter 49

The month of April in Charlotte produced spectacu-
lar weather after a wet and gloomy winter. It only
rained at night and when it didn't matter. Easter was
in late April as well, and Kevin decided that he and Mei
should try, for once, to attend a church service and see
how that worked out. April pressed them to come to
hers, promising a multi-ethnic experience with a great
choir on Easter Sunday. Kevin, a little wary of Baptists but
not wanting to disappoint April, or Mei who was in love
with all things April Garcia, agreed. To Mei's delight, she
needed a new outfit.

The Saturday before Holy Week they braved the
crowds at SouthPark Mall, mostly mothers on the same
errand. He would have to depend on a salesperson to
help. They started by scouting out the standard stores
like Macy's and Belk, getting ideas, and then exploring the
smaller shops.

Either he or Mei decided they needed a break and sat
down by a fountain. He handed Mei a small package of

peanuts for protein, and he sipped an Americano from Starbucks. After some time passed, Mei jumped up.

"CeeCee!"

Before Kevin could stop her, she was running away and towards a tall woman. Yes, it was Felicity, who embraced Mei as she ran into Felicity and grabbed her waist. He hadn't expected this today and wasn't ready for an icy confrontation, but Mei's exuberance had started a train he couldn't stop.

"Mei, I'm so happy to see you!"

"Where you been? I not see you in long time!"

Felicity seemed to be getting her bearings, looking around after Mei's embrace for some sense of where she had come from. "What are you doing here, Mei?"

"I'm with Kevin. Come see Kevin!"

"Kevin?"

Mei pulled a surprised and confused Felicity toward the fountain where he sat. He stood up as a matter of courtesy and shook her hand.

"Hello, Felicity."

"Hello, Kevin. You grew a beard. I—wouldn't have recognized you."

"Yeah. Mei likes it. It's getting hot now, though. Might be time to shave," he rubbed the wiry hair on his chin.

"Why you call her Fleese-ty?"

"That's her real name. Felicity. CeeCee is her nickname, Mei."

"Fuh-lee-cee-tee." Mei sounded it out, emphasizing each syllable equally.

"Um. How are you and Mei doing, Kevin?"

"Well. Different, but well."

"You still—have custody of her? She lives with you?"

"Of course. I legally adopted her, end of February."

"What about . . . your other plan?"

He shook his head. "Things changed. I changed. I'll have to fill you in about it one day."

She smiled. "I would like that."

"We're buying an Easter dress and shoes," Mei interrupted the adults. "For me."

"Definitely not for me. Now Mei, I didn't say anything about shoes. You're such a shopaholic."

"I like shoes. CeeCee has pretty shoes, see, look at them." She pointed to Felicity's feet, on which she wore turquoise espadrilles. "You gave me shoes for Christmas. I remember. Santa Claus brought me a lot of presents."

"Maybe you can wear the shoes CeeCee gave you with your new dress."

"Okay," she sat back down, content to finish her peanuts.

"Do you have time to sit and talk?" he asked Felicity.

"Not today, I'm, well, could we meet for coffee sometime?"

"Sure. Text me. The number's the same."

"I will. Goodbye, Mei. I'm happy to see you again. Take a picture so I can see you in your Easter dress with the shoes."

"Okay!" Mei waved goodbye.

"See you," Kevin said.

That was lucky, he thought. Or weird. Mei had good eyesight and memory. If Felicity texted him, he'd follow through. But he wasn't holding his breath. She looked pretty embarrassed to see them, or maybe seeing him.

Felicity did text Kevin in a couple of days and asked him to meet her for lunch near the gallery on Thursday, her treat. When he walked into the tearoom she had chosen, the hostess escorted him to her reserved table. The ambiance was very feminine and he hoped he could get something meaty and substantial for lunch. He was hungry, but more, he was on guard. Felicity had wasted very little time in arranging this meeting after their encounter at the mall. Maybe she just wanted to tie up loose ends. They—or she—had ended their friendship abruptly and disastrously, he with a stupid and ill-timed announcement, she with scathing insults. Maybe she was concerned about Mei. He doubted she wanted to renew anything with him.

When she arrived, exactly punctual, the first thing he noticed was her clothing, but he refrained from mentioning her corporate uniform was changed to black slacks, a mauve sweater set, and pearls, a much more relaxed look.

"Are you off today?"

"No. Oh, you're talking about my clothes. I changed jobs."

"You did?"

"Yes, actually I quit. I worked out my notice yesterday."

"What? I thought you loved that job?"

"Are you kidding? When did I say I loved it?"

"I just assumed. I guess I shouldn't have. You sure gave it everything you had."

"It ruled my life."

"Mom once said corporations like yours were monsters."

"I wouldn't go that far, but I can understand why she said it."

"So, why did you stay as long as you did? You certainly had other options with your degree." He found himself saying exactly what he wanted to say to Felicity. He had no reason to impress her with compliments or shade the truth about his own life. Not now.

"I liked the paychecks. I liked that I could spend those paychecks on a pricey gentrified apartment where I was supposed to live based on my education and career. I worked overtime to live in a place where I had to work overtime."

"That's . . . brutally honest."

"After a couple of years, I decided I wanted more. Or maybe less. I want 9 to 5, not 7 to 7 or worse. A normal forty-hour week instead of sixty. I want to know my weekends are mine. I want a hobby. I want real friends, and I want to be able to wear flats to work. Heels are a plot against women."

"What are you going to do?"

"I have an interview with a small investment firm, working with individual, human, middle-class clients. Real people. I think I'll like it. I'll need to jump through some licensing hoops. It will work out. But it's a hefty cut in pay, of course, at least for now before I build up a client base."

"That's quite a surprise."

"Yes. A good one, I hope."

"I think it's good for you. No one should be a slave to their job."

The server came, a petite young woman with a British accent. They ordered high tea, which Felicity promised included a lot of food and he wouldn't go hungry.

"Sure, I'm game. Is that the thing here, a *Downton Abbey* vibe?"

"Yes, it's very authentic."

"Even the server, unless she's acting."

"No, she's for real. I asked her once. She's from Manchester. More working class than posh, but definitely English."

"So you're a regular."

"Yes. It reminds me of my study abroad in London as a junior."

He scanned the feminine surroundings. "I'm the only guy in the place."

"No, I saw an elderly man with his wife earlier."

He laughed. "So I'm the only 'guy' guy."

"Anyway, what about you? Career-wise, I mean."

"I'm still at the gallery."

"Is your job going all right? I thought you were going to move to New York."

"Funny thing about that. I did go for another interview in January. But I was a different person by then, and they wanted someone who could travel two times a month, and, in the end, I didn't like their attitude and, let's just say, turned them down."

"That's gutsy."

"Not really. I was probably out of my league. Thinking back, I was probably the 'we've got another person in the wings' guy if someone tried to hardball a salary negotiation. Who knows? But I'd refigured my priorities by then."

"I was wondering about that."

"Yeah, I bet you were. You looked pretty surprised when you saw us at the mall."

"Uh, yeah. About the mall meeting . . ."

"We don't have to talk about it, Felicity. You know the short version. I stayed in Charlotte. I adopted Mei instead of trying to get someone else to take her off my hands. And she's doing well. We can leave it there."

The first pot of tea came. "You can let this steep for about five more minutes," the server directed. Kevin asked for a glass of water. Hot tea was for times when you had stomach bugs and couldn't keep anything down. But he played along and took a cup when Felicity poured it.

Felicity made some small talk about tea and English tearooms for a little bit. But when he dated her, she was never much for inconsequential topics. There was a long silence between sips.

"Could you tell me the long version? Sometime?"

The food came. The little sandwiches with cucumber, tuna, and egg salad sufficed, and the three-tiered plate held a variety of sweet tidbits to enjoy. He had cleaned most of the sugar out of the apartment because of Mei's dietary needs, so he ate less of it himself now. "High tea," appeared to translate to "high carbs." Six months before he wouldn't have noticed the dietary components and would only have wished for a burger and fries.

"It's not what you'll expect. Not that I know what you'd expect. It doesn't have anything to do with someone I'm dating or that I got hit with a bolt of lightning. But it is life-changing, I guess. And long."

"Kevin, I was part of Mei's life. I want to know about her."

Kevin began to recount the trip to Memphis, remembering more and telling more than he would have expected. Finding Mei unconscious, the days in the ICU, his change of heart. He had to stop at times and wipe his eyes. He paused after telling about Mei coming back to consciousness. He was talking too much. But Felicity listened, wordless. He knew her well enough to know she was trying hard to keep a passive expression, but her eyes brimmed with tears.

"I grew up. Something snapped. I started, or was able to, love her. I cared about her. Up to then, deep down, I felt nothing for her, except that she was occasionally entertaining and generally a lot of work."

Felicity hid her face and resorted to using her cloth napkin for her tears. "Oh, my," she finally said. "Why didn't you tell me this already?"

"You'd made your feelings pretty clear."

She closed her eyes and tried to calm herself again, but unsuccessfully. Her slender shoulders shook. He regretted what he said. Felicity had loved Mei long before he had. He reached out instinctively and touched her forearm.

"Don't worry. It's all right. She's living with the diabetes, now. It's been tough. I've even lost weight because she has to follow such a strict diet. I wish I'd had the brains to see the symptoms—she had them all, the thirst and hunger, the mood swings, and worse, but I was clueless, of course."

"I'm so sorry." She wiped her eyes.

"Don't be. You were the one who told me to get a pediatrician and I ignored you. I was a heartless turd. But something switched. It was weird. My feelings, my think-ing, everything changed once I saw how weak and sick she was, and that she might die. She was that close. We caught it just in time. Before, I liked her, sort of, mostly we just tolerated each other, but she was a kid I could take or leave, when it came down to it. She was a responsibility that got dumped on me out of nowhere, and I was scared to death of her in some ways. And sometimes it was just overwhelming. Kids are such a full-time job."

"No kidding," she laughed lightly through her tears.

"But I don't look at it that way anymore. We have a good time."

They sat silently for a minute. Eating didn't seem right when Felicity was falling apart in front of him. Slowly her breathing came back to normal and she was able to sip some tea. "I'm sorry. I don't like to cry in public."

"I'm not sure there is a need to apologize, Felicity. You were in Mei's life, and then, because of me, you weren't."

"I do need to apologize. And explain, a little, I think."

"If you don't mind, can we postpone that? I'd like to hear it, sometime, but maybe we've had enough emotion for one high tea?"

"Okay. I'll take a rain check on cleaning out my conscience."

"I appreciate it."

Habitually, she checked her watch. She said nothing but signaled her consciousness of their schedules by resuming her meal.

"Try this," she offered him a scone.

"What is that called?"

"A scone."

"It looks like a biscuit."

"It sort of is, but it has fruit bits in it."

"Interesting," he said, trying to chew and swallow the scone. He kept his opinion of the dry, sweet, bready pastry to himself. "Thanks for the cross-cultural experience."

For the rest of their time together, he played the doting dad and mostly talked about Mei, her schooling, her Chinese, her piano lessons. Felicity listened acceptingly.

"Can I take you to lunch again sometime?" he asked as they finished.

"I would like that," she answered. He wanted to ask her deeper questions. He wanted to know if she was dating anyone. He wanted her to know he had no hard feelings, that maybe, now, they could try it again. But he had already planned not to do that. She had been the one to draw lines and build walls. If she wanted to knock them down, he would let her.

Chapter 50

T heir next lunch took place the following week after exchanging several texts. The food was more his style this time. Felicity had interviewed and been offered the new position. She had said she needed to apologize. Perhaps she would. He was more interested in seeing her and asking honest questions about their future. If she signaled a desire for something platonic only, he would start to consider other women.

After a few minutes of catching up, she began.

"Okay, Kevin, let me get it out. I apologize. Really. I was a, well, you know, but when you called me on Christmas night. I got so upset. I said some stuff that came out of my mouth before I thought. All I saw was Mei being put in the system, tossed around, and you not caring. And me never seeing her again. Obviously, none of that happened. Now I know why. I should never have said those things, and I hope you'll accept my apology."

"I absolutely accept your apology, but only because you offered it. I was all the things you said then. And my timing sucked. I should have told you earlier I was planning to end custody. Maybe you would have knocked some sense into me. I was taking advantage of your entertaining Mei when I didn't want to."

"Still, I had no right to tell you how to live. I wasn't in your place. You were in a difficult spot. I could have made a better case for her instead of attacking you."

"I'm not sure that's true. I mean, you did have a right to give me advice. You of all people had a right to intervene, or at least try to talk some sense into me. But. It's over now."

"Is it really?"

"What do you mean?"

"Kevin," she said after a long sip of ice water and a deep breath. "I want to start over."

"At what?"

"At us."

"Okay." He looked at her deep hazel eyes. "Are you sure?"

"Yes. I feel like, well, we've had a long break, and we're different people now. My job isn't my world any longer. I've gone back to therapy about—you know. I'm not hiding myself behind a business suit. You are a full-time dad of a child with some challenges. You've lost your mom in an awful, sudden way. What was good about us is still here, but there's more."

"Keep talking. You are very persuasive."

"We know now what we're getting into. You know my past. Back in October, I liked you, a lot, and I was considering the next step with you if it happened and if you asked. But then Mei came along. You talk about being scared. I was terrified. As much as I liked her, I couldn't bear the thought of motherhood or even having a child close to me on an everyday basis. Then I thought you weren't ready for it either and I didn't know whether I could be along for that ride."

"I wasn't ready for something that huge being thrown at me. And there was no way then I could have had the empathy I needed to be with you and be a decent husband. So it was best we went our separate ways, sort of."

"Oh."

"*Then* it was best, Felicity. I don't think it is *now*. I know it's not."

She smiled in response. It wasn't just relief; it was pleasure and maybe a little flirtatious.

"Yes, I think we should start over," he said. " But maybe not let Mei in on it, for now. She'll know soon enough. I need some things she isn't involved in."

"I do get the impression she gets her way," Felicity smiled. "But she's so cute, it's hard not to let her run the show."

"Didn't she always? Yeah, to be honest, now that the health crisis is over, she's getting therapy from a counselor who can even speak Chinese with her when it's needed. She's adjusting better. I need to start having a social life again. Something more than G-rated movies on the weekends."

"Maybe I can slowly come back into her life. I actually like kids' movies anyway."

"That would be helpful. Going out for a beer with friends would be a nice change for me. I only watched three games in the whole March Madness Tournament, the semis, and finals, which is unheard of for me."

"Can I ask you the hard question?" she said.

"You might as well."

"Any regrets?"

"Sure, lots. I don't believe in the 'you shouldn't have regrets' advice. It means you aren't admitting to your mistakes. I made a bunch."

"I think not having regrets also means a person hasn't lived." Felicity sighed and looked away.

"If living means being a selfish jerk most of the time looking out for me only, I guess I've lived. I hope I'm making up for it, a little."

Chapter 51

Finding time with Felicity that didn't include Mei proved hard to manage. They fell to sharing lunches three, then four times a week, since their workplaces were nearer each other now that Felicity worked for a private investment firm. The temptation to linger over the table and not get back to work became stronger and stronger. Kevin confided in the empathetic April that he had resumed his relationship with Felicity, telling the whole story.

"I'm going to need you to stay late more often so I can see Felicity after hours. I'll pay overtime off the Nannies' Inc. books if you like," he told April.

April, who was now engaged to Claudio, an electrical engineer she'd known since high school, responded like a true romantic and an ethical social worker. "I'm so happy. Felicity is so sweet. But, no, I can't do that, I mean, the off-the-books thing. Even though I'll be leaving them when I get married and finish my MSW program, it wouldn't be right."

"But it's not fair to you. I'll talk to your company and get you a raise or something."

"That might work. I will be giving you notice in July, though. We're getting married in early August. I'll be looking for jobs after that."

"Oh. That does throw a wrench in it, so I guess we'll have to find another nanny. What will we do without you?"

"I'll prepare Mei for it. She's in a better place now. Four months ago I would have been anxious about transitions for her. Although . . ." April paused. "When are you going to tell her about you and Felicity?"

"Soon. As far as I'm concerned, we'll be getting married, eventually. I think Felicity agrees, or she wouldn't stick around. But not any time soon. And don't worry," he said, reminding himself of April's strict church. "She won't be moving in here before that, or vice versa. That would be confusing to Mei, and complicated. And awkward for you."

"True, even though it's your place. I'm not the morality police or anything. But it wouldn't be best for Mei, especially if it doesn't . . . work out."

"Oh, be hopeful for us. I feel hopeful for the first time in a long while."

"If you propose, just don't plan on August 4," April said. "That's our date, and I want you and Mei there."

"Wouldn't dream of it. She's in love with Claudio, you know."

"Yes, I think she has a crush on him. Who wouldn't? He's the most beautiful man on the planet."

The Cornerstone Primary School Choir's end-of-year program on May 26 featured an around-the world theme, "Friends from Other Lands." Each grade sang songs of African, Asian, Islander, European, or South American origin. Nothing American, until the big finale, with "America the Beautiful." The song included choreography and the showing of colors, to make sure everyone in the audience knew the choir director's loyalties were in the right place. Mei stood in the front row with her fellow pre-kindergarteners, sporting the first gap in her smile to show that the Tooth Fairy had visited her. She sang loudly and more or less on pitch. This time, Kevin didn't need a nudge to take pictures. Instead, he used his phone for video and had a small bouquet of flowers for the singer.

Her guests, Kevin, Felicity, April, and Claudio applauded with the others in appreciation. When dismissed, Mei ran up to Felicity first. "CeeCee, you came. Thank you. April, I bring you something. I made this in class." It was a basket made of construction paper holding small pieces of paper. "These are things I promise to do to help you."

"How very kind, Mei. I'll be sure to use them." She opened the first one and read it. "I will carry out the trash." That will be helpful, Mei."

Kevin stood back and observed, glad to see that his formerly impolite daughter now used her "kind words," as her therapist called them.

"CeeCee, I'm sorry I not have something for you."

"But you did. You gave me a wonderful concert."

Kevin knelt down to Mei's height. "Mei, we do sort of have a present for you. This is a surprise, so don't faint."

"What is faint?"

"Get so excited you fall down."

"Okay, I won't faint."

"CeeCee and I are friends again."

Mei's eyes widened, then she squinted, a bit suspiciously. "When you not friends? CeeCee always is my friend. I just not see her much."

Kevin chuckled. "Well, yes, that's true. I mean we are friends who see each other a lot."

Mei still signaled confusion. "Why do you not take me to see her?"

"Mei," Felicity began. "We are friends like boyfriend and girlfriend. Do you understand?"

Mei looked at April. "You mean like April and Claudio?"

"Yes, like April and Claudio."

"Oh." Mei made a face, processing. "You get married, too?"

"Maybe," said Kevin. "Don't worry about that. Aren't you happy for us?"

"I'm not sure." She tried to speak more slowly and correctly. "I want to be with CeeCee like friends, too. You should let me."

"All right. Fair enough," agreed Kevin. "Now are you happy?"

"April, did you hear?"

"Yes, I did. Aren't you happy for them?"

"I'm so happy."

They prepared to leave the auditorium. Mei walked ahead to the parking lot with April and her fiancé and held both their hands, showing her fondness for the handsome Claudio with his wide dimpled smile.

"That went well," Felicity remarked as she and Kevin followed.

"Sure. Maybe we'll have another announcement soon?"

Chapter 52

Mei's summer included a day camp sponsored by the school system. It cost heavily, and the hours were inconvenient, but she was kept active and around children most of the day. There was also a nurse on duty to give Mei her shots. Her English improved in general, although sometimes not her grammar, and Southernisms crept in. Kevin and April patiently asked her to explain what "fixin' to" meant and she shrugged. "I heard it at camp."

"It means 'getting ready to do something.' It's better to use those words."

"Why?"

"So everyone understands you. You will be able to talk to a lot of people, especially if you keep speaking Chinese."

"Why?"

"Because over 1 billion people speak Chinese."

"I don't know that number."

"It's a whole lot. Just trust me. Maybe one day we can go back to China."

"Maybe. I don't care." That was another phrase she'd picked up, probably from older kids at the camp.

"Someday you will. Trust me on that, too."

Yet he wondered if deep down her childish, dismissive response meant something much deeper, a shielding, a purposeful forgetting.

Kevin planned to propose on July 20, in Felicity's apartment. April agreed to spend the night with Mei, happy to be in on it. After a dinner of delivery from her favorite restaurant, he pulled the ring from his pocket.

"Will you marry me, Felicity?"

Instead of the ecstatic "yes" he hoped for, and expected, she wiped away tears. She reached over to hug him, then took the box from him. She admired the glimmer of the ring for a few seconds before she set the box down.

He began to fear she might actually refuse.

"This is the first time I've done this. I don't think it's supposed to go this way."

She smiled, weakly, and sighed.

"Please don't feel that way. It's just . . . We need help, Kevin."

"Help?"

"Pre-marital counseling, at the very least, if we are going to do this."

"Is that a yes?"

"Not yet."

"Not yet? What does 'not yet' mean? Do we have to negotiate this or something? I'm not into prenups, you know. I don't make enough money. You might, but not me."

"No, that's not what I mean. I need more time, I think. And a premarital counselor will help us work through some things."

"Felicity, I don't think you are surprised I'm asking you. We've talked about it. A lot."

"I know, I know. We just need some boundaries and understanding. We are not two twenty-year-olds with stars in our eyes. Like, it might start bothering you I was married before."

"You know your first marriage is not a problem for me. Have I ever said anything about it to you?"

"No, and I don't know why."

"I know you were, and his name was Todd Jenkins—see, I remembered. Not that I have much of an opinion about him and how he treated you. He's not in your life, is he?"

"Of course not. I send him a Christmas card every year. That's all. He remarried a long time ago."

"So, what? Sure, premarital counseling is a good idea. I'm all for it. But we've talked about kids, yes or no and how many, and what might happen, and if we have our own you won't want to work full time, and we've talked money, and in-laws, and politics, and Mei, and vacations and I think everything else, and I even overlook that you're a Duke fan."

"Very funny."

He pulled her in tight and kissed her.

She pushed away, gently. "Remember when I asked you whether you had any regrets?"

"Yeah. And I do. A lot. I should have tried harder with my mom, and now she's gone. I wouldn't have been in the dark about her life and her choices and Mei. I should have done better with Mei at the beginning, seen her side of it, and had some compassion. I should never have even considered reversing the adoption, and I hope she never, ever knows about it. I should have tried to contact you sooner and not waited until we had a lucky break seeing each other at the mall, and only because Mei has better eyesight than I do."

"I didn't ask to make you feel bad, Kevin. I asked because I have so many, too, and yet, they don't seem to matter now."

"So we have regrets. We can't let them come between us. I get you're afraid. When I'm standing at the altar, I'll be afraid. There's a lot to be afraid of. I'm asking you to marry me when I already have a six-year-old daughter with her own complications. You've been through so much, and I never want to hurt you, or let you be hurt again."

"There are no guarantees, Kevin," she said. "We go into this marriage aware of that."

"I know. But say yes, and I'll do whatever you ask. I want you. Now. Forever."

"Really? Forever? No matter what, no matter if we don't have our own children, if . . . it happens   again. . . "

"I hope you believe me. I'll be there, whatever happens."

"I do. Yes, I'll marry you."

Epilogue

"**M**ei, are you ready?"

Mei Elcott answered in a string of sounds that made Kevin smile. "I don't have a clue what you just said, but I'll take it as a yes."

"It was, Dad."

He reached over to tap Felicity on the leg. "What about you?"

"I'm good. Tanner is still asleep," she said, peering down at her fourteen-month-old sleeping against his mother in a sling. "He's going to be kind of confused with his sleeping, and he's not the only one."

"You do look tired. Jet lag going this way is a whole different ball game."

Kevin sized up the last member of the family. "Jackson, welcome to China."

"Wow." The six-year-old craned his neck to see if the plane had magically transformed now that they were on the ground in a new country. He squinted out his window. "It looks different."

"We didn't come all this way to see same," Kevin said as the Airbus 330 taxied to the gate. He mused that taking a family of five, including a toddler, on an 8,000 miles plane ride seemed like a good idea at the time they began to plan it. And now, as the Elcotts landed in the city of Changde in the Hunan province of the People's Republic of China, Kevin knew it was the best decision they could have made. All the expense, preparation, trepidation, and drama were worth it.

Not that they started planning the previous month. It was a trip four years in the making. Ever since Mei Louise Elcott began to question who she really was and where she really came from, he and Felicity faced the reality Mei would have to meet her biological parents, if possible, and revisit her orphanage home, and see the country where she was born. It was only fair and right, although difficult and costly.

Kevin and Felicity knew eventually her questions would become more searching and demanding. Any dismissal or postponing of answers would only deepen her confusion. Fate, or providence, or Sabra Timothy's wild decision seven years before had snatched Mei from her home, her disadvantages, her culture, her aloneness. Being taken from China meant a new life, privileges, two parents who put the pieces of their lives together in place, siblings, friends, medical care for a chronic disease, education. All that, and a sense of loss, of something missing.

Kevin did not tell her at first her parents were alive and well. He and Felicity had to make sure they could reach Mei's family, her parents were willing to correspond through a translator, and they wanted to see their daughter. He doubted they would. It took three years, from the time Mei was eight until she was eleven, to complete this delicate mediation. Then they told her the truth and promised if she wished to, she could video chat with her biological parents for the first time.

Felicity, especially, had ensured Mei kept and improved her first language through weekly meetings with other children and classes at the Chinese Cultural Center in Charlotte. Kevin repeated the mantra, "She'll always be in demand and employable if she speaks and writes a Chinese dialect." But he knew her native dialect meant more than career opportunities. On the memorable day when she first saw her birth mother as an indistinct image on a computer screen, her mother Bao Cheng tried to say "good morning," in English. Mei replied at length in Xiang, to prove her proficiency, and perhaps to assure her mother that being Chinese still mattered to her. Bao dissolved into tears. Their conversation was a private matter and neither Felicity nor Kevin pried into what the reunited mother and daughter shared.

The chats continued about once a month. Eventually, her father Delun joined the video chats for brief moments of hello, but Mei had never seen her much-favored brother. That was probably for the best at first. Mei lived in North Carolina rather than Changde because an authoritarian policy forced her parents to choose between her and her brother. A preteen could not fathom the oppression and centuries of cultural demands that went into such a choice.

Allowing Mei her privacy about her feelings towards her parents and brother in China was their unspoken policy. If she wanted to talk about it, she would. They encouraged her to discuss it with her counselor, whom Mei saw off and on throughout her childhood. Mei by nature was neither shy, nor quiet, nor slow to state her opinions or advocate for herself. She would need that inner fire, especially to help her live with diabetes and to negotiate life as a member of a minority. Too many would take advantage of her, discriminate against her, or overlook her. Being ignored when she needed a meal, a break, a shot, or a different snack would mean grave illness. Being discriminated against would hold her back. Kevin and Mei had been through too much to let that happen.

Kevin looked over at Felicity, whose eyes betrayed a lack of sleep. He whispered "thank you" and kissed her cheek. He knew what other men meant when they said they didn't deserve their wives and their wives were out of their league. Seven years before the trip Kevin and Felicity had married in an early November ceremony at a mountain chapel near Asheville, attended by Nancy, Tom, Dustin, Hunter, Felicity's parents and siblings, Mei, April, Claudio, and a few friends. Jackson Thomas, strong and solid and stubborn, "a little Viking baby," as Kevin called him, came along in a little over a year. Felicity slowed her life to survive a high-risk pregnancy. By then, Mei took to calling them "Mom" and "Dad." Legally, they were both her parents now, and she felt the peer pressure of her classmates who made faces when she spoke of Kevin and CeeCee. Her parents were glad; it was going to be hard to discipline Jackson for using their first names when his sister didn't.

When Jackson was almost five, Felicity surprised Kevin with a positive pregnancy test announcing a new member would be arriving in seven and a half months. Tanner McCoy Elcott came, on time, and proved the opposite of his older brother; calm, gentle, and full of smiles. Felicity breathed a prayer of thanks, believing in her heart her two little boys were both a source of healing and indescribable gifts in themselves. And she was grateful at forty to have a calm child after the never-still Jackson.

Kevin's musings about his family ended as the flight attendants appeared to assist passengers on their deplaning. The pilot, speaking in English translated into a Chinese dialect, thanked them for their presence on the flight and welcomed them to Changde.

Mei put her hand in Kevin's. "Thanks, Dad."

"I should thank you, Mei. You made all this possible."

And he meant it as much as he had ever meant anything before.

Afterword

Every fiction writer is asked, "Where do you get your ideas?" *Sudden Future*, like most of my fiction, comes from a confluence of three factors: character, context (setting), and problem (or problems).

Character has to come first. I confess some readers may not like Kevin at first. He may seem like a typical career-focused millennial, privileged and self-absorbed. He should seem that way because at the beginning and throughout most of the story, he is. Character must change in fiction; character should be redeemed in some way if the writer chooses to write in hope rather than despair.

Kevin is not the only character; specifically, Felicity has her arc, and it is both connected to and yet non-dependent on Kevin's. The other characters speak into Kevin's life and serve almost like mirrors he chooses to ignore until he no longer can do so, until the crisis point.

In *Sudden Future* I have chosen not to write from the adopted child's point of view for two reasons. One, and mainly, that is another book I hope to write, one requiring much research and empathy. This is Kevin's story. Second, Mei is five and six years old in the story and struggling between two linguistic and cultural worlds. I believe it would be a conceit to write coherent prose representing the minds and thoughts of a child in this situation. If doing so is possible, it is beyond my talents.

Context, in this case, is 21st century United States, which includes our affluence, our generosity, and the international adoption movement, specifically from China after the institution of its harsh one-child policy. I have many friends who have adopted children from other countries and this is a field ripe for stories. Their love and devotion to their children inspires me every day.

Finally, **problems**. Or better, barriers, obstructions, interventions, intrusions. A screenwriter friend says that all stories are either about a stranger coming to town or a hero going on a journey. I suppose that is true, although I struggle to apply the principle to my own fiction. Kevin goes on a journey, of sorts, but he is not a hero. Far from it. If a stranger comes to town, it is either Mei, who at five has little agency in her particular situation (but a strong will to respond to it), or it is cancer, an unwelcome stranger to many of us. I prefer not to try to fit a square peg into a round hole and to let Kevin, Mei, Felicity, and

Sabra's stories unfold according to human reality rather than a mythic model.

I would like to thank Karli Land and Colorful Crow Publishing for believing in the value of this novel, for their diligent efforts in bringing it to the public, and their wisdom in helping me with the task about which I confess my failure: marketing. The day I heard Colorful Crow would publish it was a true breakthrough. I had committed to not self-publishing this story but had met with several rejections, including one suggesting Kevin be rewritten as a female in the LGBTQ community. Karli and associates respected my vision and helped make it clearer.

Also, thanks to the Northwest Georgia Writers Group for their input before and during the COVID pandemic, when we met online for over two years. These folks make me believe in the power of community for writers. There were several other beta readers whose aid and time I value. And thank you to the people in my universe whose lives I explored for creating these characters.

Of course, thank you for reading.

Barbara